"Are you a heretic? One to be reported to—"

"To whom, Doctor?" asked Colonel Tek. "To the First Maniple? *We* are the First Maniple; report us!"

And now Dyse saw himself trapped . . . Smiling, reading Dyse's anguish, Colonel Tek relented.

"Doctor, there was during the Ascendancy a prophet bearing the name Dyson. He fortold the exploitation of the matter resources of the surfaces of moons and other large objects. Resources, Doctor, that exceed by many millions of times those of the rocks that are now so carefully hoarded by the princes and matter-brokers. We hope to discover some of his works, in so doing perhaps unlocking the secret of stealing from Gravity the materials humankind needs to survive . . . we have reason to believe that these works survived the purges that destroyed Old Wirtanen two thousand anni ago. Yes, we seek access to large body matter!"

"But no man, no syne, could survive the twisting of Gravity on such a body!"

In the far distant future, much has been lost . . . but so much more has been gained!

The Helix and the Sword

The Helix And The Sword

John C. McLoughlin

TOR

A TOM DOHERTY ASSOCIATES BOOK

This is a work of fiction. All the characters and events portrayed in this book are fictional, and any resemblance to real people or incidents is purely coincidental.

THE HELIX AND THE SWORD

Reprinted by arrangement with
Doubleday & Company, Inc.

A TOR Book

Published by
Tom Doherty Associates,
8-10 West 36 Street,
New York, N.Y. 10018

Cover art by Alan Guiterrez

First TOR printing: July 1984

ISBN: 0-812-54556-7
CAN. ED.: 0-812-54557-5

Printed in the United States of America

This book is for Ariana Merrill McLoughlin.
*Sera nimis vita est crastina: vive hodie.**
—Martial, *Epigrammata*

* "Tomorrow's too late; live today."

To Dyson III, Chancellor of the Home of Life, my humblest greeting:

I, Chidarine the Peregrine, grandson of the Whip Saker the Swift and Sandpiper Flautist of the Islands of Wirtanen II, dedicate this small work to the memory of our illustrious forebears and to the future diversity of living beings throughout the Systemic Sphere.

Although I have spent most of my life searching the memory of the Mind of the Islands of Wirtanen II, I hope soon to deliver this manuscript to you in person, in so doing committing myself to your presence and service for the remainder of my days. I am but a historian, this work but a history of the short War of Rocks; should it seem a work of fiction or a myth, it is only because history is the stuff of which both myth and fiction are woven, and is itself purer than—and thus often stranger than—either fiction or myth. In this light, I hope I will be forgiven for my attempts to reconstruct the minutiae of conversations and emotions that transpired before our own births.

In composing this record, honored Chancellor, I recall

again and again the time of the European Ascendancy some six millennia past, during which the Filtration was initiated and life evolved into the Deep. It seems sometimes eerie, this echo of the long-gone Earthly past that was so often heard during the terrible time of the War of Rocks; even during my own lifetime, as the lethal creatures of war continue to sail undirected among the Rocks, I am reminded of the deadly yellow clouds that enshrouded Earth during the centuries following the end of the Ascendancy. But history is full of such echoes, my Lord, and their whispering bears the lending of our ears that we may avoid repeating the errors of the past.

My primary hope in compiling this history has been to keep it accessible to the young men and women of Life's Home, in so doing perhaps enhancing their interest in our origins and evolution; for without that interest, of course, our kind is lost. I have paid special attention to the interesting mirror-image inversion one finds in comparing the ecosystems of two great civilizations, the Earth-bound Ascendancy and our own in the Deep: the European Ascendancy possessed abundant matter and limited energy in a Machine-based economy, while the Peoples of the Deep are blessed with essentially unlimited energy and precious little matter, both disseminated within our intimate symbiosis with living synes. Again, I hope that future generations will ever bear in mind the Four Faces of the Living Tetrahedron, and to this end my little work may seem but a meditation on Ecology itself. And so it must, my Lord Chancellor, for Ecology and Evolution are the melody and rhythm to which is danced the Fourfold Saraband.

With me I bring for distribution to their proper biomes thirty blue whales *Balaenoptera musculus*, thirty clouded leopards *Neofelis nebulosa*, thirty mountain gorillas *Gorilla gorilla*, two hundred and fifty musk oxen *Ovibos moschatus*, forty golden eagles *Aquila chrysaëtos*, forty martial eagles *Polemaetus bellicosus*, and one hundred Andean condors *Vultur gryphus*, all young, healthy, inoculated, with each species' sexes equally divided in number, as a gift from Chancellor Rosia V of the Islands of Wirtanen II to Life's Home.

From Darwin Melliden of that noble house I bring one hundred Bengal tigers *Panthera tigris* var. *bengalis*, sexes equally divided in number; from my own humble house I bring one hundred peregrine falcons *Falco peregrinus*, one hundred Nearctic kestrels *Falco sparverius*, and two hundred saker falcons *Falco cherrug*, sexes equally divided in number. We are indeed beholden to our ancestors that so much of the diversity of Life's Home has been preserved in the Deep.

Also with me come the loving greetings of the Mind of the Islands of Wirtanen II, the sweep Catuvel, and all of the Peoples of the Deep, for whom the image of Life's Home is the holiest of icons. But forgive my brevity, honored Chancellor; I am unwell for the moment, having received the first inoculations preparing me for my arrival at the Court of Life's Home. However, shortly I shall have the pleasure of taking my Lord Chancellor's hand in my own.

> At the Fane of the Blessed Gerard,
> Your humble servant,
> Chidarine, Peregrine, late of the
> Islands of Wirtanen II

Contents

The Systemic Sphere, I: the two Hemispheres, bisected by the Plate. In this drawing, the scale is too small to depict orbits (Earth, Venus, Mercury) lesser in diameter than that of Mars. The Plate, or plane of the ecliptic, is presented obliquely; within the Plate is concentrated most of the matter in orbit about the Sun. The diameter of the Plate and Sphere, approximately 14,654 million kilometers, is so great that light takes almost fourteen hours to cross it.

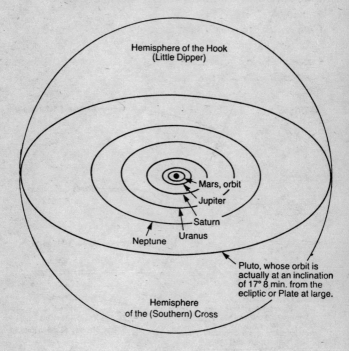

Hemisphere of the Hook
(Little Dipper)

Mars, orbit

Jupiter

Saturn

Uranus

Neptune

Pluto, whose orbit is actually at an inclination of 17° 8 min. from the ecliptic or Plate at large.

Hemisphere
of the (Southern) Cross

The Systemic Sphere, II: a pie-shaped section of the Plate, showing the orbits of the nine major planets in scale. Distances from the Sun are given in mikas (megakilometers, one million kilometers or about 621,370 miles apiece).

← Pluto 7,327 mikas from Sun

← Neptune 4,542 mikas

← Uranus 2,993 mikas

← Saturn 1,449 mikas

← Jupiter 773 mikas

← Mars 227 mikas
← Earth 150 mikas
← Venus 108 mikas
← Mercury 58 mikas from the Sun

The Rocks, the asteroid belts between the orbits of Mars and Jupiter, are humankind's major material resource. Very little human life occurs beyond the orbit of Jupiter because of the scarcity of matter there.

the Sun, Old Brazenface himself

Chronology

A SHORT HISTORY, much simplified and condensed from the Annals of the Hand of Man, of the Peoples of the Deep. Although many historians differ with the Hand's interpretation of the flow of events long past, the Annals remain the best-known historical record.

Because the Annals of the Hand begin their reckoning with the time of their estimate of Closing, this Chronology is divided into AC (Ante-Closing) and PC (Post-Closing).

AC 2000: Birth of the prophet Christ, founder of the European Ascendancy; Christ is said to have convinced the Europeans of a supposed European destiny of world conquest if they would but follow his teachings. Earthly human population about 300 million.

AC 200–100: Awareness, the discovery by the prophet Saint Charles Darwin and others, at the peak of the European Ascendancy, of the fact of evolutionary continuity within the living system; these prophets are dipped in hydrocarbon fuels and burned alive by the rulers of the Ascendancy, but their analysis of Earthly evolution is nonetheless ultimately accepted by most academics. Earthly population about 1,500 million.

AC 50: Filtration, the invasion of the Deep by living forms, said by commoners to have been initiated by the mythological Trickster, Gagarin. Foreseeing the impending limit to availability of protein and the fossil hydrocarbon fuels supporting the Ascendancy, the rich and powerful of all Earthly nations purchase places for their offspring on the new Cities of O'Neill (named after their chief European advocate, Saint Gerard O'Neill of the Cylinders); these offspring are sent to the Cities in the form of fertile human eggs. Along with these incipient human beings are sent the fertile eggs of many other species judged by their senders to be potentially beneficial to human life; all species judged troublesome (such as viruses, disease bacteria and other parasites, bothersome insects and mammalian vermin such as rats), with the notable exception, of course, of human beings, are left behind. Earthly population about 5,000 million.

AC Zero: The Closing: reaching its limits of protein and hydrocarbon fuel availability, the Earthbound European Ascendancy bows out in an enormous puff of poison; in the process, Earth, ashamed of Herself, wraps Her scarred person in an impenetrable cloak of dirty yellow cloud from which She will not emerge for centuries. At Closing the dynasty of higher mammals, including human beings, on Earth is ended. Earthly population extinct; about 750,000 fertile human eggs from all major cultures ride sleeping on five glass and metal Cities of O'Neill. Descended from the people born of these eggs will be all the Peoples of the Deep of future ages.

PC (about) 150: Synthesis, the interfacing of the sciences of cybernetics and molecular biology permitting the growth of useful organisms (synes) from purposefully sequenced nucleic acids. At this time there may have been twenty-five to thirty Cities of O'Neill in orbit within the Earth-Moon System, together housing a population of about 2.5 million human beings.

PC 200–500: The Synthetic Wars, vast social upheavals resulting from the rapid evolution of syne technology. These Wars see the spread of life toward the matter-rich asteroid belts as competition increases for the sparse asteroidal matter nearer Earth (mostly in the form of Apollo Objects). The Synthetic Wars may be regarded as the inevitably violent process by which the simpler syne-growing technology replaced the older and more complex European industrial one, in which human beings had been forced to devise and build their tools and dwellings from inanimate matter. The old inanimate Cities of O'Neill were pierced and destroyed during this period; 271 living (syne) Islands, supporting about 45 million human beings, survived the Wars.

PC 647: Concordat of Wirtanen, the establishment (by Pollex Damaren II) of the Apostolic Vicarage of the Hand of Man at Point-of-Earth in response to the acceptance of the Hand as the true faith by Tryder Redbeard of Wirtanen. The support of Wirtanen provided the infant Hand with sufficient military and economic clout to enforce its new One-True-Faith status.

PC 782: Legendary founding of Aresia Alpha in the orbit and proximity of Mars by the Brothers Newgard of Wirtanen; human population of Aresia grows quickly as Mars-proximal asteroids are utilized.

PC 1124: Legendary founding of Old Troy Prime at the leading Trojan Point of Jupiter by the Trucidate Stirps Holt. Stirps Holt and its retainers purchased a Seed and left Aresia after having avenged a blood feud with the ruling Stirps Newgard; with this act the Newgards became extinct and the new nation of Troy earned the unending suspicion of its Aresian cultural progenitor. The Peoples of the Deep number about 100 million in 582 Islands.

PC 1221 and on: Rise of the Batesian Heresy; its leader, Har Bates, disemboweled in public ceremony at Point-of-Earth. About 250,000 Batesians take to the wilderness of the Hemispheres to avoid a similar fate. Eternal Interdict of the Hand of Man forbids travel in the vicinity of Earth forever.

PC 1400 and on: Rise of the Hamtsan Brokerage, the Tetravalency, the Riders of Oort (brokers respectively in oxygen, carbon and cometary volatiles) and other syndicates of matter-brokers, each of which ultimately monopolizes some specialized resource not previously claimed by other powers.

PC 2120–2131: The Chimaeric Wars, in which Aresia and the Apollonic Islands led by Wirtanen assault one another with humanoid synes (Chimaeras) in the form of warriors of many specialized types; after the deaths of untold millions, the Chimaeric Wars are ended by a bulla pollicis (of Pollex Darwin Shibuya III) prohibiting the incorporation of human nucleotide sequences in syne growth.

PC 2471: Destruction of Old Troy Prime by Oakleaf Carraghan and his allies, all using the name Carraghan. Founding of the Trojan Regency under the Trucidate Stirps Carraghan; growth of New Troy Prime from asteroid Achilles, which is first moved to polar orbit around Jupiter to centralize it as capital of the civilizations growing at the two Jovian Trojan Points. The Peoples of the Deep number about 400 million in 1,500 Islands.

PC 3000 to (about) 4000: The Great Black. Several centuries' revival of Batesianism results in systematic persecution of the sect by the forces of the Hand. In response, Batesians attack Point-of-Earth, are repulsed after destroying seven of the Holy Isles and almost two million people. Batesians clash with forces loyal to the Hand throughout the inhabited Plate, resulting in some 45 million deaths before Batesians withdraw yet again to the Hemispheres. Period of social upheavals, rebuilding lasts almost seven centuries; many Islands lose all inter-Island communication for centuries.

PC 3276: Founding of the Apollonic League, trade pact among the old Apollonic Islands (Wirtanen Federation) located between the orbits of Earth and Mars. Parties to the League dub themselves ''Apollonia.''

PC 3444: Staton V of Apollonia accepts the Batesian Way, declaring it to be the One True Faith of all the League.

PC 3445–3519: Combined forces of the Holy Fist of the Hand of Man attack and destroy Apollonia; Batesians abscond to their compatriots in the Hemispheres, taking with them many ancient Earthly records from the universities of the old Wirtanen civilizations and other (now extinct) Islands of the League.

PC 4000 on: Beginnings of trouble with organized forces of piracy from the Hemispheres; initially preying on matter-brokers, these pirates gradually extend their depredation to various unprotected Islands. Question arises as to true population of Hemisphere peoples; question never resolved. Population of the Plate about 1,500 million in 7,500 Islands.

PC 4920: Phelps IV of the Tetravalency accepts Batesianism as his faith; other three Bonds of the Tetravalency follow suit, so that the carbon-brokerage becomes the prime institution of Batesianism in the Plate within less than a century. Hand of Man issues writ of excommunication against Tetravalency, originating lasting enmity between these groups even though they continue ecologically and economically interdependent.

PC 5211: Margrave (the Disturbed) Semerling and followers destroy Stirps Carraghan's Trojan Regency; surviving Carraghans flee to Aresia for asylum. Founding of the Trucidate Stirps Semerling as Trojan Regency.

PC 5345: Imperium of Aresia "lays claim" to the Inner Belts of asteroids, those closest to the orbit of Mars; in response, Trojan Regency "lays claim" to Outer Belts. No concrete action taken by either nation until:

PC 5721: First Trojan retiaries swing across the Outer Belts to sense movement among them, closely followed by a mighty flotilla of Trojan raptores; thus in

PC 5747: A summit is declared, to take place at Troy Prime, in order peaceably to decide the fate of the asteroids. Perhaps riding in the balance are the lives of more than 11,000 million human beings in 74,922 Islands, all of them more or less dependent on the distribution of matter in the asteroid belts.

Here, as in all time since the origin of life, the expansive world of living matter is faced with a limit in the static nonliving matter on which it subsists; here the living must change its ways in response, or cease to exist. Here, then, is Evolution.

Introduction

IN THE YEAR 5720 Post-Closing, Hirayama Teague, twenty-fourth Lord Director of Island Teague of the trailing Trojan Point of Jove, distaff cousin to Stirps Semerling and banneret of the Regency of Troy, was saved by his steward Watson Tessier from almost certain death by pirate attack during the Ursid Harvest. Owing his steward life for life, and empowered by his noble birth to grant (or take) same, Lord Teague issued in that same year one Writ of Generation to the distinguished Clan Tessier of the Trojan seneschalate sept, said Writ to be discharged specifically by Watson Tessier. In the same year, Tessier married Anastasa Spica, also of the seneschalate sept; these worthies discharged their Writ of Generation in the year 5722 with the birth of a son, Dyson, born into the Directorate of Teague and attended at his birth-recording by his grateful master, Lord Teague himself.

For his first three years the boy Dyson Tessier enjoyed the companionship of his lovely young mother; then, being favored of the Forces of Selection and of the Lord Director, he was sent, as were all his male forebears for five centuries past, to spend the next two decades of his life at the

Academy of Stewards at Priam. Here he was trained under the direction of his cousins of the sept of seneschals, always aware of his Tessier ancestry, to lofty position within the House of Teague. Here he read the classical literature of Troy and learned the languages of Aresia and of the matter-brokers, and mastered Lubret, the lingua franca of civilized persons empowered to travel off-Island.

Here, too, Dyson Tessier read the Annals of the Hand, studying under the Teaching Friars the splendid and sorrowful histories of peoples long since eliminated by the Forces of Selection. He learned of lost Wirtanen and the Apollonic League, of the founding of the Hand, and of life in the dimmest past, of Saint Gerard of the Cylinders, who foresaw the Filtration from his hole on wretched Earth, of Saint James of the Helix, prophet of Synthesis, and quiet Saint Charles, first apostle to the Europeans of the Forces of Selection, who with others of their gentle kind had saved the Seed of humanity from the Earthly extinction.

On a more mundane level, Tessier was taught the Forms of Address, the modes of dealing with the dominant classes of the myriad Peoples of the Deep among whom he would spend the rest of his days. He learned of the prejudices separating classes and races and cultures, and of methods of transcending these prejudices, of smoothing the paths and soothing the palates of those for whose security and well-being he would one day be responsible.

But not all the arts of Priam were the arts of peace; a steward, after all, is responsible for the life of his master and his master's family. Therefore on each day of his life for twenty-one years Dyson Tessier practiced under the proctors of dance, learning the Arts of Fist and Foot, so that by the time of his majority he had slain with his bare hands seven superbly trained prisoners against whom he was pitted in the examination ring. Else they'd have slain him, for the prisoners were sent to the ring with promises of freedom should they kill this boy—and at Priam the Arts of Fist and Foot are graded simply and inexorably by the Forces of Selection.

Similarly the Piercing Arts, those of the Vertical and Horizontal, in the study of which Tessier learned the use of long knives in striking at the central nervous system (the Vertical) and the many short knives in striking at the viscera (the Horizontal). By men and synes he was taught the use of bolt and spring and the ordering of raptores and other synes against attackers. In all these arts he was examined in the ring and in the Deep by the Forces of Selection and not found wanting. Indeed, by all counts Tessier was judged an extraordinary student, so much so that he was enrolled in the College of the Mistresses of Synes at age sixteen.

During his first year under the Mistresses, Tessier was nominated for Okumura surgery by the Provost of the College herself. The nomination approved, an Okumura mycelium was grown into the hearing and linguistic centers of Tessier's brain, thus changing his awareness forever. Henceforth, Tessier would be very closely dossed indeed by the Regency security apparatus, for with implantation of the Okumura mycelium comes understanding of the silent communication of those higher synes who speak over the radio spectrum—and such understanding might, by the wrong person, be very inappropriately used!

But the young Dyson Tessier was early judged to be very much the right sort of person, and under the syne-encyclopedias of the Regency and a dozen other nations he learned more of the ways of humanity and its works than most men might imagine existed. Graduating from the Priamic Academy, a Doctor of Synes at twice twelve, he might ordinarily have returned to Island Teague to work under his father Watson Tessier in the service of the Directorate. However it happened that in that year the Regent Lothar Semerling IV called on Lord Teague for favors past due; when the Regent's procurators came to Priam in search of a young subseneschal to serve on the Regent's own sweep Catuvel, young Tessier was called forth for review with the rest of his class.

The purchasing agents, three sharp-eyed men and two pheromone-sensitive synes possessing language, sensed in Tessier a strength belied by his comparatively light build. Tall and olive-skinned as were all of the Trojan seneschalate sept, Tessier reflected in dress and demeanor all the years of his Priamic training superimposed becomingly on the near perfection of his genetic inheritance as a Tessier of the sept. The record of Clan Tessier, being one of unbroken fealty to its masters through centuries of changing fortunes, spoke as well for the graduate as did his own scholastic record.

So it was that Dyson Tessier passed from ownership by the Directorate of Teague to ownership by the Regency Stirps Semerling, a gift of the Lord Director in recognition of certain covert services rendered his family by Regency troops in recent years. Dossed and redossed by the Regency, he was granted a Regency tattoo—three lupine leaves above his navel—and might have expected a long and comfortable life aboard the great sweep Catuvel as a favored possession of Stirps Semerling.

However, as is so often the case in the affairs of men, the principle of Uncertainty—in the guise, some say, of the Trickster Gagarin himself—intervened, changing the course of human evolution.

Now follows the tale of the astonishing fortunes of Dyson Tessier, who sidestepped his social niche to touch and divert the very Forces of Selection.

The Helix and the Sword

Chapter 1: **In which a civilized man must prepare dinner for beasts**

> Behold the Hand of Man, that spanned
> The silent halls of Space with song!
>
> —From hymn att. to Lavenbrook of Aten

SONG INDEED—and is it not said to soothe the savage breast? Or was it "beast"? And so, for the last evening before arrival at Troy Prime, as the Regent's sweep Catuvel began the slow contraction of her radial muscles, the steward Dyson Tessier offered a concert and dinner for the pleasure of the influential company in his care. Six months' sleeping passage, all the way across the Rocks from V Aresia just outside the orbit of Mars to Jove System with stops only at four somber ports of the Hamtsan Syndicate, had left his passengers more restless, perhaps, than was appropriate for their forthcoming debarkation.

As a recent graduate of the Academy of Stewards at Priam, Dyse might have been expected to approach this last task of the voyage with greater confidence; but the superstition and xenobiophobia of his wards had left him nearly drained of the sense of hospitality for which graduates of the Academy were renowned. In fact, the young Regency seneschal found himself almost despising the assorted ambassadorial parties for whose comfort he was responsible.

Even Catuvel, full two-minute sweep and the traveling residence of twelve generations of Trojan Regency, even she had not effectively dispersed within her spacious shell the hereditary mistrust and jealousy of her diplomat passengers. Her great bathing pools, her gymnasia, her ponds and gardens and wonderful forest of fruitwoods, all had been subtly calculated by her Sisterhood growers to erase care and promote concord among Regency and guests alike. However, thought Dyse, even the finest work of the Sisterhood could not stay the everlasting apelike posturing of men of importance!

The security men, the strong-arm thugs, the bodyguards clamored incessantly for the steward's attention. Brute watchdogs they seemed, yapping at him throughout the entire passage. Professionally paranoid, each such creature seemed to perceive his master threatened by some security breach at all times. It annoyed Dyse that for but six diplomatic envoys more than a hundred of these ferocious louts had boarded Catuvel and now defiled her elegance with their snooping and snarling. All of them—from the berserk black-bearded giants accompanying the Hamtsan Syndic to the identical hairless triplets rooming with the nameless pirate Whip from the Hemispheric tribes—spent their time yowling and whining at Dyson Tessier on behalf of their various masters.

To complete Tessier's discomfiture, the Regent's fool son Homar *princeps* was aboard as representative of the Regency house, Stirps Semerling. This unfortunate specimen had responded to the unaccustomed responsibility by taking to vituperation, solitude and, with far more than his usual enthusiasm, brandy from his no-Charentan vineyards. It would do no good to have Homar appear before his father like this after a voyage under the care of Dyson Tessier and his staff—no good, that is, for Dyse, who thought with a chill that Catuvel had lost much of her Regency grandeur and become something of a zoo.

Sequestered in his apartment with his encyclopedia, Pantolog Five, Dyse pondered his plans for the evening. The menu was calculated to satiate, to dull the passions and ease the tensions of statecraft. Composed partly of gifts from the guests themselves, the meal would begin with caviar from sturgeon of Isle Bakchar, a princely offering of the Aresian Imperium, followed by fat and well-hung ruffed grouse from Catuvel's antique stand of fruitwood. These birds, stuffed with wild rice, chopped water chestnuts and currants, and glazed with a maple-based sugar (a gift of the envoy of the Tetravalency), were to be accompanied by a cold Lapalissoise creamed-herb soup uniquely suited to resonate with the flavor of the grouse. Arriving at table with the birds would be a choice of dry sherry or Felan wine, both gifts of the junior Nuncio of the Hand on this mad voyage.

Dyse centered the main course around a prized provision from his personal stores. He had selected a wild boar from his ancestral Teaguan forest, a boar slain after a long chase to achieve the "hunted glow," the unique flavor of stressed gameflesh. This boar had fed throughout its life on acorns, beechnuts, apples and other foods edifying to swine; roasted, it was to bask in a red sauce subtly echoing the red no-Rhone wine brought from his ancient family holdings by Cardinal Tamilaria, the senior Nuncio of the Hand. An assortment of fresh vegetables grown by Catuvel herself should serve elegantly to complement both wine and swine, and in anticipation of the event she had filled her Great Hall with air reminiscent of the gentle Teaguan autumn so beloved by the steward.

With a dessert of weighty pastries created by the master chef Levon, such a meal might be expected to be foolproof; but Dyse desired to leave nothing to chance and had prepared for the occasion a program of chamber music to be played by the members of the Pro Musica Antiqua Troia who were present as troopers-musician on the voyage. His choice of pieces spanned the history of composition from early European Ascendancy, through the lunatic wailing of the t'sai hsiao flute and the *shê* and *chung* in a song of the Hemispheric tribes, to a piano-flute duet by Esance of Vanadest and a traditional ballade for two female voices arranged by the encyclopedia, Pantolog Five.

There was also to be a short chamber concert for banj by Lavenbrook, in which Dyse had asked one of the guests to join. The Aresian Senator, most dangerous and unpredictable (and, for a variety of reasons, potentially the most powerful) of the diplomatic assemblage aboard Catuvel, happened also to be an accomplished scholar of classical banj and mandolin. He was also an accomplished raconteur of spicy stories from the lives of well-known composers. His presence among the talented Regency castellans should aid in leavening the atmosphere of the gathering while diverting the Senator's attention from his own uniquely sensitive position among the voyagers.

To complete the planned effect, Dyse had arranged with Catuvel to expose, through the three-meter-wide mullioned leeward windows of her Great Hall, the spectacle of approaching Troy Prime against the stupendous Jovian crescent and rings. The Hall itself, hand-carved from a gigantic burl of walnut grown in freefall and intricately embellished with allegorical figures from the Ascendancy and Synthesis, sported six of these windows on each side of its thirty-meter length; through them, sight of the immensity of the Regency seat should sufficiently impress the Regent's sated guests with the powerful role he hoped to play in the future distribution of the Rocks.

Dyse reflected that, for all his disgust with these people, he was himself at bottom a politician. His service would prepare these people so that his master, the Regent, might more easily work his will with them. Lothar IV would certainly weigh Dyse's performance against their moods when he met them; Dyson Tessier must not be found wanting!

All too true, for this voyage was Dyse's first major assignment since his purchase by the Regency from the last graduating class of the Academy—a choice finalized on the basis of Catuvel's immediate liking for him. She was old and wise and idiosyncratic, and the Regent's procurators had seen fit to let the sweep have her way. Now it remained for Dyse to prove the value of her choice.

Having worked with Catuvel for less than an annus, he concentrated on acquainting himself with her profound understanding of Stirps Semerling, the Regency house by whom she had been loved for three hundred and ninety-two anni. Catuvel had observed Semerlings in infancy, youth, adulthood and old age, in love, in war, in peace. Her mirrors had netted sunlight for Semerlings throughout those centuries, her gardens had converted that sunlight to food, her staff had stuffed that food into Semerlings, ever since she was given life by the Sisterhood of the Nucleotides and sold to the Regency for training. For nearly four centuries she had created night and day from the endless Sunsea, and who could tell for how many tons of Regency and their people the two-minute swing of her long radial musculature had provided the sense of mass so beloved of human beings?

Catuvel had outlived ten Regency stewards. Her intuition spoke best of the eleventh, Dyson Tessier. The sweep and her young steward seemed already to work as one in the service of the Regency, and on this their first long voyage together she sensed more than ever the importance of delicacy in the management of passengers. Like Dyse, she was uncomfortable with her diplomatic wards. Like him, she strained to cushion this explosive cargo against any unforeseen blows.

Things had gone relatively well so far—too well, perhaps, such that there grew a sense of portent, a feeling that the calm aboard Catuvel was imminently threatened. Pantolog Five, Dyse's recently assigned Regency encyclopedia, expressed the general tension most succinctly by announcing the loss of his appetite; this syne, a superciliously near-perfect information-retrieval system ornamentally grown within the genetic matrix of a cheetah, was perhaps best known among Catuvel's personnel for his stupendous appetite. Now Pantolog's legendary gourmandizing had faded to an anemic ghost of its former self, the big cat showing little interest in food beyond a meager few liters of milk and a half dozen or so chops each day.

Pantolog's anxiety was justified. The entire future of the Rocks, the enormous belts of asteroids spanning some five hundred and fifty mikas of the Radius between the orbits of Mars and Jupiter, might depend at least in part on how he, Catuvel and Tessier handled their guests on this journey to the summit at Troy. Not only the states represented by the delegates aboard Catuvel, but hundreds of smaller nations throughout the Systemic Sphere, all had watched for more than a decade the preparation for this summit. In the past two anni alone, Aresia Alpha had hosted some thirty preparatory debates, at which immense blocks of matter had changed hands in the purchase of influence for the ultimate wrangling at Troy Prime. Now, having declared a summit, the Regency promised safe passage across the Rocks for certain legators attending the damned thing. Of these, the five aboard Catuvel just happened to be hereditary enemies of one another.

Odd, Dyse thought, how summits have always occurred immediately before the mutual retreats and armings they are supposed to prevent. The ancient word "summit" itself, dredged (according to Pantolog) from somewhere far back in the European Ascendancy, smacked of death and of the poisoned smoke in which the Ascendancy was snuffed out. Throughout history, summits have appeared like fungi wherever a limiting factor is reached in the expansion of civilizations; this summit at Troy Prime marked

the limiting of the freedom to glean the precious matter of
the Rocks.

As had not happened on such a scale since the miserable
end of the European Ascendancy almost six millennia
before, the age of "free" or unowned resources was coming to an end. The Law of Limits was rising like a bloated
corpse to trouble the minds of men. Thus arose the summit,
primarily a diplomatic confrontation between Troy and
Aresia but threatening to drag in every civilized people of
the Systemic Sphere. Riding the orbit of Jupiter and originally founded in the matter-wealth of His two Trojan
Points, the Regency of Troy was now preparing to enforce
its traditional claim to the Outer Belt of Rocks, while for
some five generations Imperial Aresia had functionally
controlled the distribution and sale of the Inner Rocks near
her location in the orbit of Mars. The Middle Rocks yet
remained a wilderness crisscrossed by the trade routes of
the matter-brokers, the Hamtsan, the Tetravalency, the
Riders of Oort and their ilk, and sailed and plundered at
will by the blackbody chebeks and badans of the wild
people of the Hemispheres—but the rulers of Troy and
Aresia were now considering an alliance that could permit
them to effect the extinction of those savage folk.

Humanity had harvested Rocks for thousands of anni,
for the most part peacefully distributing the more easily
moved specimens smaller than fifty kilometers or so in
diameter. Larger Rocks were broken to facilitate their
moving and distillation, and the Syndicates had long ago
arisen to specialize in the capture and transport of various
pure elements and compounds necessary to the growth of
life in the kindly Deep. Until now, a man and a woman
with a Rock and a Seed might theoretically have founded a

civilization. While the purchase of Rock and Seed actually required enomnous wealth, the hundreds of nations of humanity had almost all been founded by such enterprising pairs, their children and whomever else they chose to share the new lands they grew. He who controlled Rocks, in short, might create worlds and found civilizations. He who had no Rocks, however, must purchase—or steal—matter for his people's future; he must do this or restrain his kind to a gruesomely static society in which creativity was stifled and cultural evolution ceased.

But there was another possible alternative, heretofore unthinkable, to him who was cut off from the resources of the Rocks. Such a one could look to the incalculable wealth of matter locked in the planets themselves, and in their larger satellites. In so doing, however, he would have to face the horrors of Gravity, the frightening bending of the Deep that occurred around all matter but whose power reached destructive proportions around any object greater than a thousand kilometers in diameter. Near such dangerous bodies, this malevolent twisting of space could tear the life from the vast and delicate organisms within which humanity lived; thus planets and large moons were always studiously avoided by the Peoples of the Deep, their immense matter-riches remaining untouched by the influence of life. Who can say, though, to what extremes of risk taking the threat of starvation would lead the People?

Observing Dyse's thought-furrowed brow, Pantolog purred sarcastically through their Okumura link, " 'Gravity! Gravity, the Mouth of Earth, through which evildoers are sucked back to the hell of Earth Herself! Oh, woeful Earth, from whose diseased womb the Seed of life escaped to bathe, free at last, in the sweet singing Sunsea!' "

Dyse sighed, said wearily, "Would you mind starving in silence?"

The spotted cat bared his teeth, allowing a sliver of pink tongue to protrude for an instant. "Why, sir, I'm just quoting from the Annals of the Hand—have you some aversion to Holy Writ? Or do you merely wish to prick the tender sensibilities of your devoted encyclopedia, mmmm?" He laid his black-edged ears back in mock humility, rolling his golden eyes in his round feline head and purring from somewhere deep in that strange Okumura voicebox of his. "Or, if I might make an attempt at diagnosis, might it be the impending marriage that troubles my Honored Master so?"

Indeed, this impending marriage was not least of the discomfiting subjects battling for Dyse's attention. Such a marriage seemed doomed from the start, but of course it is not the place of stewards to comment on the affairs of their betters. Still, the idea of attempting to resolve the hereditary conflict between Troy and Aresia by marrying off the Regent's eighteen-year-old Princess-daughter to the forty-two-year-old Senator from Aresia, himself twice married before, seemed shaky. Surely, the intent was good: to create between Aresia and Troy a familial alliance that would promote a mutual ordering of the resources of the asteroid belt whilst evading the war which their long-standing rivalry threatened.

Alas! As Dyse, recent student of history, knew all too well, the trajectory to Earth is paved with good intentions. Such marriages of convenience and alliance, especially between parties who have never met, have a way of going quite awry. The Princess Linsang was reputed to be of a fiery and independent temperament. In a foreign and con-

servatively hostile society like that of the wellborn of
Aresia, she might find herself beyond her depth. Tessier
had never met the Princess, of course, but he'd had more
than enough during this voyage of the Senator to whom
she was affianced. The man forever relived his family's
humiliation by Stirps Semerling some five centuries before.
Such a marriage could propel them all into the very war
they hoped to avoid!

Dyse sighed, and the encyclopedia imitated him precisely.
Over the Okumura link between them, Pantolog no doubt
felt his master's thoughts; he hummed a few bars of an old
wedding march. Slipping for an instant from his poker-
faced seneschal's calm, Dyse lunged at the wordy syne in
an attempt to tweak an ear or two; but the encyclopedia
dodged with the agility of a real cheetah. "Oh, you're a
cruel one, you are, crowning your loving servant with
thorn! I'll retire now, hoping that your reason (such as it
is) will return before you, ah, 'entertain' our guests this
evening," and, lifting his tail in an indignant question
mark, the creature swaggered from the room.

So it came to be that Dyson Tessier and his friend the
sweep Catuvel were that evening to compete for the attention of their guests with the likes of Gravity, War and
Marriage—and not only with this formidable trio but with
the monkey striving for dominance that is the goad and joy
of politicans in every time and place. No small task, this,
thought the steward, and a tight smile flashed across his
face as he recalled a gent called Hercules from far back in
the European mythos, and of some stables old Hercules
once had to clean.

Chapter 2: **In which eight men dine at the board of Catuvel, and seven survive the meal**

> From the cloudy web
> On the broadloom of slaughter,
> The cloth of Man, grey as armor,
> Is woven now.
>
> —From the Edda of Njal the Icelander
>   (of the Europeans)

LOOK NOW, through your mind's eye, and try to see the homecoming of Catuvel, ancient of days! Across the star-bejeweled Deep to Troy Prime she sails, herself a jewel reflected lovingly in her three vast lupine-leaf mirrors.

Jewel of Troy, she calls in her retiaries, her drifting legions of eyes and ears, as she penetrates the Trojan sensory net; fifty thousand of the creatures, most less than ten centimeters long, converge in a sweetly glowing vortex from their traveling stations hundreds of thousands of kilometers away.

Across the wilderness of the Rocks the retiaries had formed an onion-layered lightlinked sensory sphere centered on the sweep and her precious cargo, each tiny retiary alert to the bending of space around any bit of matter greater in mass than a milligram. Encountering such, the outer retiaries instantly flashed word of its mass and trajectory to their raptorial brethren closer to Catuvel; these in turn intercepted and captured the flotsam, such that on this voyage nearly a half megaton of precious micrometeoric dust had been netted to enrich the coffers of the Regency.

Had the approaching matter been animate, a pirate Vessel perhaps, hundreds of raptores would have arrayed themselves in a deadly lattice across its trajectory hours or days before it reached striking distance of the sweep herself. Nothing of the kind had happened on this voyage, however. The many enemies observing the transit of Catuvel had rightly judged the sweep more than capable of defending herself, and contented themselves with less formidable prey.

As Catuvel comes home her three lupine-leaf mirrors furl, seeming slowly to distintegrate into the Deep as their thousands of reflective hoplites disperse on command from the sweep. At each such dissipation of this gigantic representation of the Trojan crest, the mirrors seem to portend something—But what? No one dares even think on such an

idea, and in the heavily traveled environs of Troy Prime
such glossy heraldic conceits, eleven kilometers in diameter apiece, become at best unwieldly obstacles to commerce.
For Catuvel, the enormous menagerie of retiaries, raptors,
hoplites and other synes among which she traveled were as
much a part of her physiology as, in a man, are his cells;
so smoothly did she and her symbiotes function together
that no man aboard need bother himself with thought of
the Argus-eyed immunosensory system that surrounded
them all.

Within, at the leeward wall of the Great Hall, Dyson
Tessier completed a last inspection of his settings and
turned his wearying attention to the carpet, a grandiose
affair on which was wrought a bombastic history of Stirps
Semerling. The thing measured four by ten meters and had
been designed to fit precisely beneath this great oaken
table over which so many political melodramas had been
enacted through the centuries. The violent and inflated
scenes were so arranged about the rug that as each guest
walked to his chair he would cross one or two, all in
accordance with the design of some long-gone steward
with a hefty bent for the sanguinary. The idea had immediately taken the fancy of the Regents, and the carpet remained to trouble the guests of Dyson Tessier across some
two and a half centuries.

The steward wore the formal vestments of his position,
a Regency orange tunic and trousers over which hung,
pinned at the neck with a silver subseneschal's brooch, the
short black and red pallium of the Doctorate of Synes. It
was 1755 hours Trojan, and he felt desiccated in the
warmth of the two hundred and thirty-seven candles bathing walnut and damask and plate with amber light, aided

in their work by a fire gnawing eagerly at a two-meter log
in the Sunward fireplace.

In the antechamber without, Homar *princeps* and the six
summit delegates awaited 1800 hours and the call for
dinner. Here they met together in one room for the first
time since embarkation, and here they sampled spirits or
chewed betel or smoked ganja or abstained according to
their likes and dislikes. The murmur from beyond the
heavy doors suggested to Tessier the strained familiarity of
men who have rarely met but who have perused extensive
dossiers on one another. They were getting a good deal of
talking done. This, at least, was a step in the right direction.

A small door within one of the large ones opened and
quickly closed, the murmur rising for an instant and then
falling as the alcoholic Homar Semerling let himself in.
"Ah, Doctor Tessier," murmured the Rising Regent, "you
are a genius. The scent alone is worth the whole bloody
voyage!"

"Sire, you're much too kind," said the steward. "Still,
if you believe we can distract our little company enough to
permit us all a digestible meal together, I'm satisfied for
the moment."

Homar Semerling pulled thoughtfully at his rounded
chops and chin. The Prince ate and drank more than was
good for him. His bulk was distributed, Tessier thought, in
a form rather similar to that of the silver water pitchers
spaced at regular intervals along the table. With his royal
right hand, Homar steadied his ever present brandy snifter,
with his royal left he scratched absently at his sparse
yellow hair. The Rising Regent wore the Regency orange,
the lupine leaves of Troy embroidered green at his left

breast, an anlace ridiculously protruding from the top of his high-laced right boot.

He wore a baldric, too, at mid-breast on which was mounted a diamond the size and shape of half a hen's egg, grown centuries ago by the Tetravalency as a gift to House Carraghan, the Trojan Regency Stirps-ci-devant. Homar no doubt wore the thing to irk his future brother-in-law, the irascible Senator from Aresia. There's trouble here, Dyse thought. We'll have blood on this ghastly rug tonight if I can't control this fool. So unlike his father, this one, and so unlike his mother, the Regenta, also. And so unlike herself old Troy will be if Homar lives to assume the Regency!

At 1755 the security details busying themselves about the Hall began to station themselves along the walls and behind their various masters' seats. Dyse had specified in advance that only two bodyguards per delegate might attend the meal in order that the Hall might not seem too much like a market place. Six delegates, twelve watchdogs, each deploying a toxor and a few venator flies genetically imprinted on the scent and appearance of his master-legator. Expecting assassination attempts, each guard carried the insects to spot and capture any of the midges traditionally employed by murderers; such midges, imprinted with the unique pheromones of their intended victims, always sped unerringly and invisibly to target, and only with the aid of the fine-tuned senses of predatory insects might one hope to deter such an attack.

Six delegates, 1800 hours. Two Trojan castellans seized the bronze handles of the massive walnut doors, Dyse and Homar stationed themselves behind their chairs at opposite ends of the table, and the Hall Chamberlain took his place by the entryway. Homar *princeps* placed his brandy on the table and nodded final approval, the Chamberlain snapped to attention, the doors swung aside, and the envoys filed in as the Chamberlain spoke:

"His Eminence Canopus Cardinal Tamilaria, Archbishop of Caltanis, and the Right Reverend Father Huxley Vereker, Lord Bishop and President of the Collegium Pollicis, together the Nunciature Pollicis of the Hand of Man to the Summit at Troy!" The two clerics nodded to Homar and Dyse and moved to their places with a swishing of robes. Oh, protect us from the religious, thought Dyse, scanning the Cardinal's long black cassock with its red piping and buttons. Wherever affairs of state must be decided, there, too, must appear priests—the spies of the Hand. And this Father Vereker, the academic—what must the Hand intend, sending him? The Bishop's cassock was seized at the waist with a violet sash from which descended the bright cordons of his scholarly orders. Like his Cardinal, the man wore a gold Sword-and-Helix on a silver chain about his neck. Both Nuncios stood behind their chairs and turned as one to face the doors as the Chamberlain shouted:

"The Honorable Ammihud Lewic, twelfth Vice-Syndic of the Hamtsan Brokerage," and the pale Syndic, black-bearded, blueclad and wearing the blue collar of the oxygen-brokers, silently took his place to the left of Homar. The Chamberlain, orange-clad and red-faced, roared:

"The Honorable Albemarle, Lord Durrell, Envoy and third Bond of the Tetravalency," and, dressed in the somber black of the carbon-brokers, a short bowlegged man strode to the seat to Homar's right and opposite his colleague the blue-clad oxygen-broker. Durrell wore two things that were not black: about his neck a long white tie, and, in the buckle of his belt, a diamond larger by half than that worn by Homar Semerling. He nodded at the Prince, at Lewic and at Dyse, and faced the door as the Chamberlain announced:

"A Whip, representing the interests of the Peoples of the Free Deep," and that delegate, but a hundred and sixty centimeters tall, with skull shaven except for a narrow brush of black hair from crown to nape, glided to his seat. The Whip's skin was dyed orange (in honor, Tessier understood, of his Trojan hosts), and his clothing was woven of green silk over which his living syne-armor jerkin, belt and boots of well-used ivory white emphasized his air of martial preparedness. In flagrant violation of Plate meal-time tradition, the little man wore at his waist a springbolt intricately carved and mounted on a narrow leather belt from which also hung its thirteen tiny broadhead darts. The Whip's warlike appearance was startlingly enhanced by his smile; his teeth, dyed red from chewing of the betel nut, were filed to points. Dyse seated the tiny warrior, by nature suspicious of his neighbors of the Plate, to his own right in hopes of controlling his unpredictable manners.

"His Excellency Carraghan Angetenar Detering Fairleigh, Senator from Abarricanna Blee to the Court at I Aresia, Legator from Aresia to the Summit at Troy!" Dyse's glance was drawn to the face of Homar *princeps* as this powerful adversary to the Regency crossed the room to his chair. "In honor of my host," as he'd said before, the Senator wore the orange and white of Troy. He had been feeling irascible this evening, and during the hour before dinner had spoken to Homar in reference to the latter's great diamond, saying, "Aha, m'Lord, still wearing my stone?" His elegant syne-armor, embossed with his family arms (quartered as these were with the three lupine leaves of Troy), suggested that the Senator hoped this night to indulge himself in a bit of verbal sparring with the weak Homar. Dyse gritted his teeth in anticipation of a rough meal.

Homar himself looked uneasily about the assembled party. Placing his chubby fingertips together beneath his chin, he piped: ''Well, gentlemen, welcome at last to my father's board. It's a pity that we haven't all dined together before, but by the same token we're all deeply indebted to the artistry of Doctor Tessier in having brought us here tonight.'' The Prince nodded toward the steward, again allowed his watery blue eyes to dart across the guests, and concluded: ''We are doubly favored tonight, not only with the unparalleled work of Doctor Tessier but also with the presence of the Nuncio Pollicis, Cardinal Tamilaria. From him I now beg intercession with the Forces of Selection, who, as ever, share this meal with us.''

Homar nodded to the black-clad Cardinal, who stood and in his own turn placed his fingertips together, looking about the company with lively black eyes. He was an aged man, this Nuncio from Point-of-Earth. His face was crevassed with the cares of a lifelong climb through the hierarchy of the Hand, but as he examined his audience his eyes were bright and probing, his hands rock-steady.

''My thanks, m'Lord Homar, for this deep board, and to you, Doctor Tessier, and you, too, Catuvel.'' (Here he nodded at the Sunward fireplace, for lack of a better place at which to nod.) Then the Cardinal bowed his head (with all present save the Tetravalency envoy and Whip doing likewise), saying:

''This night we are met in preparation for a great task.

Together we are a branch of the Tree of Life; smile on this company, Horsemen, eat with us in peace and hew not with Thy blades this limb of Thy growing. Amen.''

A flurry of movement as retainers stepped from the walls to seat the eight at table. Servants-yeomen wearing Levon's blue hatchmarks on their sleeves entered with grouse, caviar and tiny pastries stuffed with sweetmeats, chopped fruits, smoked fish and other niceties. The chamber orchestra opened with a composition by the ancient European Fleming, Brumel, an instrumental song called the "Mater Patris" that embodied in its light melody the mood with which Tessier hoped to infuse the occasion.

Setting to this first course with delight, the Whip spoke in the slow, heavily accented manner of one unaccustomed to use of diplomatic Lubret as a dinner language. "My Lord Homar, this meal is to me an experience of a perfection. Never in the Free Deep do we so eat, sir, and it is with astonishment that my kin will share through my words this night with you!"

Dyse could not suppress an inward shudder at that crimson-toothed smile and at the epicantheal folds slanting the Whip's eyes. There was an iciness about the little man in green silks and pale fighting wear, an iciness born of long ancestry in the starveling wastes of the Hemispheres.

"Why, thank you, Master Whip," said Homar, "for your kind words; but as I said before"—he sipped at his brandy—"it's Doctor Tessier's work that makes all this possible. Indeed, it's probably due to the efforts of such as he that we of the Plate are perhaps, ah, less finely conditioned than are you for the exigencies of, ah, trading among the Rocks." The Prince patted his ample gut in an obvious attempt at jest at his own expense.

"Eh," agreed the Whip, "we keep in trim, for a man must be as a badan, agile and quick to change trajectory, is not so?" He bared his pointed teeth and took with his fingers a tiny bone from his plate. "At this summit, I foresee a certain necessity for the adaptability of the Peoples of the Free Deep and perhaps an abandoning of some of the more settled ways of the Plate, is not so? I live, while this excellent bird does not. By the rigidity of its ways it gave itself that I might be enlarged tonight. So I perceive it to be that some among those present are not yet prepared to adjust their ways. And yet we eat with one another in peace; such is the wonder of Man, is not so?" He raised his glass in a salute to the company at large.

"Surely so," responded Lewic of the Hamtsan. He examined the Whip thoughtfully, noting well the lovely patterning of the syne-breastplate, how it had been grown as one with the armor protecting the Whip's thighs and groin. "Many of us," continued the Syndic speculatively, "are actually *accustomed* to sharing meals with those of differing cultures, rather than carving one another to pieces as we have done with these little birds. We restrain our competitive instincts, relegating them to the arena of peaceful trade. Our restraint is the handle by which we hope to grasp, through our summit, a reasonable future for our peoples."

The Whip turned, leaned toward the Syndic. In that liquid movement, Dyse marked the boiling of the ancient rivalry between matter-brokers and the peoples of the Hemispheres; the brokers lay claim to certain elements and compounds, and the Hemispherics (calling their desolate space the "Free Deep"), having little concept of "ownership" of natural resources, often "liberated" these same elements and compounds by use of chebek and projectile. Lest Lewic and the Whip begin to enact this competition at table, Dyse planned a diversion. He moved his hand beneath the table in a signal to the Chamberlain, who in turn signaled the musicians. The Pro Musica deftly closed their "Mater Patris" and began a piece whose instrumentation and tonal structure were so different as to successfully derail the conversation.

"Doctor Tessier, your attention to the welfare of your guests is without compare," said the Reverend Father Vereker with visible pride. "This, gentlemen, is an evening piece of my people; one of my favorites, in fact, the 'Amazing Grace,' very, very ancient. My father played it in my youth, almost as well as does this scholarly Trojan musician." The Bishop winked at Dyse, knowing full well the object of the musical shift.

Homar *princeps* leaned toward Vereker, said: "Your Excellency, many Trojans avail themselves of the facilities at the Collegium Pollicis. I myself was lucky enough to have spent several months there researching the Food and Oil Wars as part of my preparation for the Ars Diplomatica—my studies there permitted my position on this voyage, in fact."

"It's well, m'Lord Homar, that the Regency has prepared itself with such cosmopolitan attention to detail. We would all avoid another such event as the Food and Oil Wars." Vereker smiled a thin smile at his fellow guests.

"Food and Oil Wars? What is that?" The Whip leaned over his plate, a bite poised on his fork (to whose use he was unaccustomed) midway to his mouth.

"It is an event of the time of the Closing, perhaps better known as the Protein Wars," said Vereker. " 'Twas the incarnation of the Fourth Horseman, the god or lord of the pantheon of my Earthly predecessors. In this form he is said to have wiped his slate, if you will, and begun anew. The Filtration occurred at about the same time, and is said to have begun the second cycle of the human incarnation. We tend to view the entire human experience as one of repeating cycles, but we share in the hope that one day such cycles will pass under our own control,'' and Vereker lifted his glass to the other guests as the venerable hymn droned on.

Senator Carraghan Fairleigh smiled beneath his broad black mustache. ''I'm honored to toast this aspiration of ours, and to add to it the hopes of the peoples of Aresia that the nations of the Plate will share justly and equally in the bounty of the Rocks.''

''As, it's hoped, will the peoples of the Hemispheres,'' added Dyse hastily, glancing sideways at the little Whip.

'' 'Twill be useful to all of us when the peoples of the Hemispheres begin to share their *names* with others in the manner of most human beings,'' began Lewic, again leaning forward to observe the Whip at Dyse's side. That worthy, however, merely widened his slanted eyes a bit in polite attention, and the Syndic felt free to enlarge on his theme.

''Surely, once they are freed of this tendency of theirs to *pirate,* the folk of the Hemispheres will delight in operating within the traditional pale of trading peoples, rather than insisting on violence as a tool of mercantile intercourse . . . eh?''

Can this man not control himself? Dyse thought. He stiffened, prepared to speak, but was cut off by the soft voice of the Whip.

" 'Pirate,' m'Lord Syndic? Why, I believe that you would so regard *any* competition in your role as oxygen-broker. But I am afflicted with a similar prejudice, for *I* regard most inhabitants of the Plate as pirates—*rich* pirates, yes, but pirates—who by dint of their uniquely superior brand of rapacity have so sacked the holy Rocks.''

" 'Pirates!' '' The Syndic sniffed, looking about the table and licking his lips. "Why, for centuries we of the Hamtsan have peacefully distributed oxygen among the peoples of the Plate; surely, no one questions the necessity for an orderly apportionment of the elements!''

"*Orderly.* Very much so.'' The Whip pleasantly exposed his red pointed teeth. "Nonetheless, I cannot help myself. As you will be quick to agree, we of the Free Deep are, ah, primitive souls who are perpetually victims of ignorance and superstition. In my own ignorance, m'Lord Syndic, I would not hesitate to take your entrails to string my daughter's lute, were it not for the presence of m'Lord Homar and the munificence of Doctor Tessier and Catuvel, may the Forces of Selection ever smile on their trajectories. And as for *names,* m'Lord Syndic, you may call me Hook.'' The Whip smiled again, a small polite smile.

"Hook. An interesting name.'' Cardinal Tamilaria nodded appreciatively at the Whip, added, "We of the Hand must also pay the syndics handsomely for our organics. Unfortunately, being a settled people, we are not able to, ah, *bargain* as efficiently as are you of the Hemispheres for the favors of the brokerages. Luckily, of course, our adherents of the great states of Troy and Aresia are always willing to donate to us a bit of their surplus.''

The Whip examined Tamilaria's old face minutely, sensing beneath the motionless exterior a hunter like himself—

but a hunter of minds. "You are vulnerable, as are all sedentary folk. We too are vulnerable to a certain extent, but we are not content in our vulnerability. Your Excellency, you are well versed in the Annals of the Hand. In it we find a principle of the commerce of the Plate: 'Power is the ability to impose a systemic limit; the direction of a living system is best influenced through manipulation of that limiting factor.' "

The Cardinal smiled gently, a priest's smile. "Gentlemen, gentlemen, we are at the Prince's board tonight. I, for one, perceive no limits here. Please, let's permit affairs of state to await our arrival at Troy."

Durrell of the Tetravalency smiled at the Cardinal in turn, said: "We of the Bonds sometimes impose limits on the availability of carbon, and the Hamtsan limit oxygen at times; the Hand, Your Excellency, limits *information,* yes? You are information-brokers who choose, in accordance with any favors you receive, whether the minds of your adherents shall be enlarged or diminished! But I share your desire that we leave our squabbling and continue with this peerless dinner."

The boar arrived, a glistening mahogany in its glaze. The eyes were cherries, and down its back bristled a colorful mane of fruit slices impaled on ivory picks. The long tusks curving above its snout were tipped with ripe figs, and in its mouth it gently cradled a fresh red pomegranate. Steaming on a vast silver platter, the beast grinned smugly at the diners as a castellan began the carving of broad slabs of meat from its flanks.

"Oho, Doctor, you've outdone yourself!" The Rising Regent stood and clapped, the rest of the guests joining in honor of the meter and a half of aromatic pork. Dyse saw his chance to grab the conversational reins, said:

"This boar, like myself, is a native of Teague. He was hunted by men on foot through a forest of oaks a thousand years old. He led a tribe of wild swine whose remotest ancestors are said to have inhabited the Ural Mountains, part of the Empire of the Rose, throughout the European Ascendancy—he's a noble. Perhaps we can divide him with a measure of gratitude for his contribution to our lives."

"Hunted on *foot,* you say?" The Whip stared at the boar, fascinated. "What manner of beast is it? Its teeth, they are so mighty—is it an eater of flesh?"

"It's an artiodactyl, honored Whip, an even-toed herbivore, though it'll sometimes sample flesh." Dyse, knowing that few if any ecosystems capable of supporting large wild mammals existed in the Hemispheres, continued: "These swine are highly social and have a complex community behavior; one might even say that they talk with one another. They move in tribes; the killing of this one left a gap which will be filled by that young boar who best uses his tusks in battle."

Senator Fairleigh, thorn in the Regency side, betrothed to the Princess, brightened at this remark. "There exists, then, a sort of diplomacy among these swine? Are the beasts practitioners of statecraft?"

"Yes, sir, in a sense. The tribes divide available resources into territories, and these they defend through a variety of rituals designed to express hostility without resulting too frequently in bloodshed. We might say that they participate in *summits* at times," concluded the steward with a small smile.

"Aye," said the Senator, "and their succession is determined through warfare." He grinned at Homar Semerling and mockingly saluted the Prince with hand over heart in the manner of Troy.

Homar inhaled deeply and, to his credit, politely saluted back. Heir to the legendary quick Semerling temper, if not the powerful Semerling physique, the Rising Regent was lucky enough at this point to be insulated by a fog of brandy from the full effect of the Senator's taunt.

Senator Fairleigh, however, was a man of perseverance as well as one of exaggerated familial awareness. The defeat of his remote Trojan ancestors at the hands of Stirps Semerling hung heavy on his mind tonight. "M'Lord *Princeps*," said he with a bit of a leer, "is a descendant of true experts in the employment of their tusks. We're all very fortunate to be traveling under the protection of such a skilled clan of—what was it, Doctor Tessier?—artiodactyls. To our hosts, then, the Trucidate Stirps Semerling!"

What'm I going to *do?* thought Dyse. These people can't even *eat* without snarling and spitting!

Feeling less experienced all the time, the steward looked about for the encyclopedia Pantolog, wondering whether the creature might help keep the peace with a show of his sometimes comical erudition. But that canny beast was elsewhere, as was his wont when human affairs slipped back down the evolutionary ladder.

The guests, however, were skilled to a man in the ways of diplomacy. Not a one showed emotion as all raised glasses in response to the Senator's toast, and each tossed back his wine as if the toast were a harmless salute to the Deep itself rather than a dinner-table *casus belli*. Squirming, Dyse signaled the Chamberlain for a musical shift. That

wise castellan opted for a traditional ballade for two female voices, "The Lancer's Maid." Accompanied by an
instrumental sextet of violin, banj, viola, cello and two
horns, the piece was arranged in a rondo, each instrument
to slip into the melody with the passing of a new verse,
two young women beginning the words:

> The ten-hour swing of the Eye of Jove
>   scans many a wondrous sight;
> But the strangest of these was the meeting one night
> Of a shrouded man with a sorrowful girl
>   who mourned a long-lost love.

> "And why your mournful mien," he said,
>   "your pale and cheerless face?"
> "My love is with the Regent's Spears;
> On the Path of Jove for seven years
>   he's sailed the jeweled Deep."

The elegant use of the banj, its bright metallic notes
meshing with the violin in the second verse, attracted the
truculent Senator's attention in precisely the manner intended by Catuvel's worldly Chamberlain. Fairleigh signaled his bodyguards at the wall, and one of these brought
to table an instrument case of fine amber-shaded leather.
From this the Senator drew a new banj, a present, in fact,
from his bride-to-be the Princess Linsang Semerling. It
was an instrument of rose-colored wood and ivory-inlaid
neck; its tattooed parchment head spoke eloquently of its
origin in the Hemispheres, wherein the best such banjs are
made. Withal, the banj was likely loot from the capture of
some pirate caracor by Lothar Semerling's minions.

Clasping the lovely thing lightly across its strings to mute it, the Senator became a new man, a musician, a lover of the beauty that his instrument embodied. His eyes half closed, he seemed to ride with the old ballade on its journey through the centuries. Gone was his vengefulness, gone, for the moment, the threat to the peace of the meal and the reason of Dyson Tessier.

> "He'll have seen many battles then,"
>   the hooded stranger said;
> "He could be in some prison bound—
>   Perhaps he has some new love found;
>   Perhaps he's lost, long dead."

But as the piece swung through its third verse, joined by the warm tones of the viola, it become apparent that the Senator was moved by more than the love of music. The corners of the man's mouth began to twitch, his eyes pinched themselves ever more tightly shut, and he began to tremble as he placed his instrument on the table—precisely in the middle of his plate of food. His limbs jerked, the neck of the banj struck his wineglass and spilled its contents across the linen, and his bodyguards ran to his side.

> "Your faith is but a hollow thing,
>   you'll waste within that cage,
> Gray hairs will come to dull the gold—"
> Said she, "I fear not growing old
>   if my love light my age."

The emotionless troopers-musician of the Pro Musica continued without interruption, the throaty voice of the

cello and the bright feminine harmonizing punctuated by a
muffled hacking sound as Carraghan Fairleigh pushed himself convulsively away from the table to fall, chair and all,
on the floor. Spray issued from the Senator's lungs, a pink
foam beaded his lips and spattered across his clothes. He
kicked, flailing his arms, his eyes now protruding unnatu-
rally from their sockets as his bodyguards and a half dozen
Trojan castellans attempted to restrain him.

> "Lady, I serve the Regent too;
> Am I not good as he?
> Over my treasures you might reign,
> My pillared halls, my ancient name—
> all this I'll give to thee."

Catuvel, sensing the horror and loathing of her passengers,
switched the polarity of the Great Hall's windows, accent-
ing with the sudden vision of the sparkling Deep the
entrance of the first horn into the ballade. For a moment
the guests were distracted; but only for a moment, as the
Senator's syne-armor awoke to his agony and spoke for the
first time: "Who slays my master, so slays he me! Who
slays my master, so slays he me!"

The creature repeated this phrase again and again, its
guttural stony voice seeming to accent the rhythmical twisting of its master. Now the armor's sculpted surface erupted
into a multitude of hooks and talons as it searched for the
Senator's attacker; it contracted its leg muscles with super-
human strength, lifting the dying man to his feet, propelling him jerkily and aimlessly across the floor.

Even as Carraghan Angetenar Detering Fairleigh, Senator to the Imperium at Aresia in the Path of Mars, even as

this mighty man died, he continued his *danse macabre* across the Great Hall of Catuvel, his living—but now also dying—exoskeletal armor vainly seeking an attacker that worked from within.

> "Kind sir, you move me not," she said,
>   "your name and treasures keep.
> You waste your time in trying to prove
> That mine is idle, hopeless love;
>   'tis boundless as the Deep."

In the sixth verse, the second horn countered its twin and the other instruments in a spacious crescendo. The terrified diners backed from the table, their bodyguards springing to their sides as they looked from the insane paroxysm of the Senator's dying to the stricken face of Homar Semerling, then to the musicians and at last to the vast windows through which the Deep mirrored Catuvel's two-minute rotation, turning, turning, the bright Islands of Troy Prime glimmering like cylindrical pearls against the terminator of the marbled person of Jove.

> He lets the shroud fall from his face,
>   he bids her smile and rise;
> Now to each other's arms they leap,
> And stolen from the bright-black Deep
>   the stars shine in their eyes

The body of Carraghan Fairleigh thudded abruptly against the wall, its head lolling lifelessly about its shoulders as the armor grappled with a life-sized carving of Blessed John the American and his brother Robert. Chunks of walnut clattered across the floor as the armor burrowed for a moment into the wooden abdomens of those obscure European martyrs before crashing, dead at last, to the floor.

Without, aloof in its perpetual scanning of the Deep, the orange Eye of Jove passed beyond the Archipelago of Troy Prime. Jove Himself, Prince of the reign of the Sun, wrapped His radioactive cloak comfortably about His many satellites and looked with satisfaction on His narrow rings.

> The ten-hour swing of the Eye of Jove
>   scans many a wondrous sight;
> But the strangest of these was the meeting one night
> Of a shrouded man with a sorrowful girl
>   who mourned a long-lost love.

For Dyson Tessier, steward of Catuvel and one of many young subseneschals of the Regency of Troy, the multicolored Jovian hemisphere seemed for an instant to exude a comforting fatherliness. That sense of warmth passed quickly, however, leaving the steward feeling very small and very frightened indeed as the first Regency galliots swung to leeward in response to Catuvel's call for assistance.

Chapter 3: In which we visit the home of Stirps Semerling, learning something of the customs of that spectacular dwelling

Semerlinga!
Semerlinga, most exquisite gem to stud the diadem,
    beringed and multimooned, of Jupiter;
Semerlinga, wintersummer twin, home of that dread
    House
Whose power knits the Path of Jove
And chastens far-flung Troy!

—Laudatory anthem of the First Security Maniple, the
    elite unit of bodyguards and other agents surrounding
    the Regent of Troy and his immediate family

IN THE VAST CYLINDRICAL WORLD called Summer Semerlinga the Sunward pole sloped gently, terraced, ever glittering with the myriad tiger lilies favored of the Regency house. The gentle winds, playing among these lilies, bent them so that waves of the light gold of their petals' undersides shifted across the rich Regency orange of the blossom-throats in their millions. Thus from any of the thousand palisades of the ancient House, one looked on a swirling sea of orange and gold stretching kilometer after kilometer down to the "valley" floor. Thence a hundred kilometers to the other end of the Island, disappearing in the atmospheric haze, stretched the forests of the Regent, spangled with lakes, rich with game, redolent with the air of sweetest perpetual summer.

In a room of glass and burnished cherrywood, a library lined with the books of all her young life, the Princess Linsang Semerling of Troy leaped to her feet, her eyes aglow with rage. "You mean to suggest that I could have stood life with that—that PIG? And make a mockery of my Stirps by trying? Father'll cover—you know he will, Merry, and I couldn't just throw everything away!"

Merry—the Princess' secretary America Berecynthia, assigned to her service since the royal daughter's birth eighteen anni before—felt her own forty years today. "Mark my words, girlie, your troubles have just begun. How am I ever going to teach you to muzzle that temper of yours? Your father knows everything, and heads'll roll, I assure you."

Knowing her servant-friend well able to handle the outburst, Linsang shouted, "Oh, Merry, you're such a prig. It happened on Father's sweep, and it happened at dinner. It's a perfect setup for a poisoning attempt. Look, there's a new steward on Catuvel—they'll no doubt shift the blame to him and give him to the Aresians.''

"Give him to the Aresians! A Doctor of Synes at twenty-five, trained at Priam—*give* him to the Aresians! Better they give *you* to the Aresians, you witless slut!" Meaning it, Merry almost feared a blow from the Princess, but drove on. "Do you remember Sarl and Bonnie Spier, the royal hostages held by Aresia to ensure the Senator's safe conduct? You know that the scannings of their treatment in Aresia have arrived? The whole Spier family's dead, Linsang, and at your hands!''

It worked. "I—the scannings? Then they *are* dead! My cousins—Sarl—they couldn't have—not already? I thought there'd be a waiting period! Do you know—did they die cleanly?''

"Filthily. And your father offered 'em as a hostage family only because he knew that he could trust Catuvel and the new steward. But not his daughter, no, not the spoiled royal Linsang.'' Recalling her years of training with the First Security Maniple, Merry sneered. "It was the Twelve Maidens took 'em, dearie, thanks to you. The Aresians learned that method from your own family, the great Semerlings, always good for a slow kill, eh? Yah! Well, *Princess* Linsang, I see now why only men succeed to the throne of Troy—Semerling women are just like the men, but they lack *sense*. Cold, calculating and senseless.''

"—'Twelve Maidens'?''

"Twelve Maidens, hon. They cut 'em up looking for their twelve cranial nerves. More a vivisection than an execution. I hear your father avoided seeing the scannings, the wimp. Anyway, I can see that all *my* teaching's been in vain. And what about this war we're supposed to be avoiding? You'll have done a good deal toward the killing of billions, sweetie, if Aresia takes this as hard as she ought. Eighteen years!'' She spat upon the intricately in-laid wood of the library floor. "And, for your insolence in this matter, three more people, all innocent, die today—and you'll be there to see it.''

"I—Merry, I—'' The Princess Linsang shuddered, reaching out to her old friend. Merry, softening at once, opened her arms. The girl's so *young,* she thought; with her power, at her age, would I have done anything else?

And Linsang, daughter of the Regent, wept in Merry's arms as she had so often done through her eighteen years; Merry, who had not wept at all after her own third year (there'd been no one to respond), comforted her royal charge while gazing abstractedly at the little spotted catlike animal for whose graceful species, *Prionodon pardicolor,* the linsang, her noble-born mistress had been named. The creature was made anxious by the Princess' weeping; it twitched its tail and darted its great lustrous eyes about.

Every bit as willful, mused the secretary, and every bit as beautiful.

On yet another of the Regent's myriad palisades stood Dyson Tessier, Doctor of Synes, member of the Seneschalate of Troy and lately steward of His Regental Puissance's Sweep Catuvel. Released but an hour before from a week's security quaranty aboard a Regency galliot and ordered to Summer Semerlinga for questioning, the young man found that despite his years of training he could not conceal—from himself or any other—the trembling in his hands. And this was *Summer* Semerlinga—think of how he'd feel on her icy twin, Winter Semerlinga with its snow leopards and white bears, but forty kilometers away and in both season and spin the opposite of this golden place. Still, at this moment Dyse wished he were in the Deep on some sailing with Catuvel, or on any other Island but Summer Semerlinga! Ordered before his Regent for the first time, he knew a visceral hollowness that was in some way greater than any other fear he'd known; for few, very few, of the Regent's millions of servants ever see their master or his family, and of those who do, most are either members of the First Security Maniple, have otherwise spent decades in the Regency service, or are doomed to die.

Alone on the sun-swept stone terrace, Dyse savored his disquiet again and again. Did Lothar IV prefer pain or drugs to lubricate the tongues of his servants? And what, indeed, did the Regent. Pantocrator of the Path of Jove, *look* like? No Regent, of course, permitted the scanning or other representation of his person before death, so that the first encounter with such a man had an eerie touch even without the influence of the incredible surroundings of his personal cylindrical world Semerlinga.

But Dyse had been sent quite unescorted onto the bright "mountainside" of Semerlinga's flowery Sunward pole—no guards, no black-clad interrogators from the First Maniple. He had been instructed to wait at this place a kilometer above the "valley" floor, standing next to a lichen-covered statue of Margrave II, great-great-great-great-grandfather of the current Regent. He'd waited for almost an hour, listening to some far music wafted to him on the wind, wondering how he would conduct himself. There was, after all, nothing to hide—Catuvel, the Regent's pet, would already have offered her master a look at the dying of the Aresian Senator from a multitude of angles as would the encyclopedia Pantolog Five, and by this time the precise nature of the fatal poison would likely have been discovered. Why, then, call a new subseneschal before the Regent himself?

A rustling behind him brought Dyse about as two men in orange-piped black—the uniform of the Psychological Operations Corps, interrogators of the First Maniple— approached along the flowered path. The senior of these saluted, hand over heart, saying, "Our respects, Doctor, and the Regent requires your presence now."

"Thank you, gentlemen. Shall we?"

Very good, thought Dyse to himself, not a tremor in my voice. All walked along the terrace for a half kilometer to a stone stairway following the gentle coriolis curve of a waterfall downward through the palisades and lilies, olive trees, climbing grapevines and orchids. Down, down, and weight pressed on Dyse's shoulders as they approached the "valley" with its full mass. Then out again, along another terrace that curved back, a shoulder of the Sunward-end "mountain," rounding which they came startlingly upon a structure of some white material—bone?—delicately grown, almost lacy, with curving windows overlooking the length of the Island's floor below.

In front of this place there was a broad veranda of stone (All this stone! Need the Regent never conserve his matter?) on which were arranged five comfortable-looking carved wooden chairs—no restraints, no instruments of torture, nothing worse than the overwhelming smell of blossoms.

"Here, Doctor," said the senior officer formally, "please make yourself comfortable." The Sunlight from Semerlinga's distant mirrors glinted off the silver shark-totem of the Maniple on the man's collar.

The three sat, leaving two empty chairs like beacons for Dyse's apprehensions. Two maidservants, orange-clad and scantily, approached with tray tables of various bottled beverages and platters of bite-sized delicacies. Placing these before the seated men, the girls stepped back and made obeisances—seemingly directly to Dyse—and returned to the structure beyond. Then two silver bells, one at each end of the terrace, rang, in pitch a fifth off one another, and a man and young woman were striding toward them.

What is the first impression of the person of true might? Is it one of awe, or of honest fear, or of admiration? For Dyse, now, it was but a sensation of the nearness of death as Lothar IV, Regent and Pantocrator of the entire civilization of the Path of Jove and the Outer Rocks, ambled across his terrace with a small dog under his arm to look upon his servants and the vast golden realm of Summer Semerlinga beyond. Of undistinguished height and spare, but powerful build, the Regent positively beamed at his young seneschal, grinning an easy grin of well-spaced white teeth. Like all of the portraits of his ancestors before him, the Regent was yellow of hair and blue of eye—it was rumored that only persons of similar coloring were permitted to marry into Stirps Semerling. The Regent's face was tanned and lined handsomely in a manner appropriate to a man of six healthily lived decades, and his cheer seemed infectious. Dyse could not help but reflect inwardly that the fat, alcoholic Homar, Prince of the realm, must be a great disappointment to this man.

"M'Lord Regent!" Dyse and the two interrogators rose, slapping their fists across their breasts in unison.

"My daughter Linsang—Doctor Dyson Tessier." The

Princess, her long gold hair plaited in a single braid with embroidered red ribbon, nodded at Dyse. "Doctor," she said. Her fine-featured face was drawn, almost haggard— she looked, in fact, more like one whose life is forfeit than like a Princess Royal in the company of her father. Silver lupine leaves glistened on a silver chain at her throat and on a brooch that held her orange cape over her left shoulder.

"Well, siddown, siddown, gennelmen! And, young Doctor Tessier, how glad I am to meet you! My Mama Catuvel (that's what we *all* call her, you know) tells me that we've done very well indeed, taking you on as we have."

In view of all his morbid anticipations (the Regent's reputation among his servants was not a pleasant one), Dyse actually gulped as he murmured a halting "Thank you, m'Lord" in response to the evident jollity of Lothar IV and the unexpected meeting with his daughter. The palms of Dyse's hands sweated, and he became silent.

"Why, see, gennelmen, our young steward seems a bit discomfited here. Well, Earth"—Dyse winced at the obscenity—"executive sessions are always tough at first— shall we have a nibble here and there?"

The Regent and his officers leaned over their trays, pouring themselves some of a white wine ("Right from Summer Semerlinga here, boys," the Regent observed happily) and gathering to themselves tiny sandwiches and stuffed grape leaves. *Drugs,* thought Dyse, but he did the same. The uncomfortable-looking Princess took nothing.

The Regent winked. "Doctor," said he, "I'll bet you're afraid of drugs in your food, right? Well, no drugs here, not a chance—today. Cheer up, boy—this isn't an interrogation. Don't mind these goons"—he waved at the interrogators—"*we* have more information for *you* than *you* could ever hope to give *us!*'' Laughing at himself, Lothar IV swallowed a sandwich in a single lusty bite before continuing.

''Ravenous. Simply ravenous. There, that's better. Eat up, men. Now, Doctor, permit me to tell you what we've learned of this assassination of yours—after all, it *is* yours, your having been steward on board at the time. Well, anyway''—he belched and sipped some more wine—''my first thought was that we'd taken on an overzealous young seneschal—you understand? I thought, Here's a boy straight out of Academy, ambitious, bright, finds in his care an old enemy of my stirps, thinks to please his master, arranges a bit of indigestion for my enemy, right?''

''M'Lord Regent, I—''

''Right. Only a fleeting idea, my own mistake. Of course, Catuvel and that damned arrogant encyclopedia of yours (damn all six of the Pantolog Series, and damn the Sisters who grew 'em), plus the older staff, cleared that right up first thing. Next thing, who *was* responsible? The matter-brokers? The priests? Naah—they'd know better than to grab a hot iron like that. And we'd scanned everything—*everything!* Fairleigh's men had, too, of course, and there seems to be no *way* anyone could've gotten to the Senator's food.''

The Regent reached for another sandwich, the interrogators remaining silent and immovable in their black and orange, the Princess twisting and untwisting the end of her long braid in her lap.

''Well, Doctor, you're a bright lad, and you'll no doubt have guessed by now what happened. There was a bug, a biting syne, in the neck of his banj! The damned thing was less than a quarter of a millimeter long, but it burrowed

right through the palm of his hand—some damned hemo-
pulmonary poison, *drowned* the bastard in his own blood!''

Lothar IV grinned that spotless grin of his and winked
again at Dyse. ''Oh, Earth, Doctor, I probably sound a bit
lighthearted to you, right? And in one respect I ought to
be—I hated His Excellency the Senator as much and as
cordially as he hated me. But hundreds of millions of
lives—lives of whole nations, not to mention mine and
that of my dear Semerlinga—hang in the balance right
now, and thousands of politicians on both sides of the
Rocks are yelling for my head. Most notably worse, the
Imperium at I Aresia is calling for retribution, material
retribution, as the only alternative to war. Not only have
they killed the entire Stirps Spier, my cousins of the
hereditary hostage house, but they demand some as yet
unspecified but no doubt magnificent payoff—lest they
send their raptores our way to initiate the very war we'd
hoped to circumvent. I suppose I'll have to go along with
whatever they demand, if only to save face and lives, but
I'm going to try to temper their greed in advance by using
the old scapegoat trick.

''And my daughter here, she was to be the link that
might have preserved the peace for a time. She could've
gained us a bit of leverage in the Aresian hierarchy through
her hold on the Senator. And here's the rub, of course—
that banj of Fairleigh's was a gift to him from Linsang
herself, as you know and as his men know and as anyone
else knows. Looks as if my little girl wanted to surprise
him with a good deal more than a fancy banj, eh? Not
enough discipline, I guess—ought to have all her tutors
throttled.''

Linsang looked as if she would speak, but at a look from her father remained silent.

Dyse, too, started to speak, but the Regent prattled cheerfully on. "Face it, boy, my posterior had best be covered, and fast. I'm going to take this rap on my own shoulders, or at least the shoulders of a few of my workers—we can't have Linsang's work publicized, after all. We have to begin with some public record of action, though, even if it be meager action. So, working from my original hunch about an overzealous servant, I've arranged a little tableau here for the pols, jolt 'em a little, show 'em some Regency retribution for the killing of the Regent's esteemed son-in-law-to-be, right? I hope you don't mind, but you're a promising lad, and I want you to see how things are done on Semerlinga when we cover our posteriors. At the same time, I can show my little Linsang the consequences of her meddling with the affairs of her betters."

The Regent nodded at his officers, one of whom inclined his head in the manner characteristic of one possessing an Okumura mycelium—although the frequency on which the First Maniple and its syne accessories operated was not within Dyse's Okumura range. Immediately, there appeared from the elegant structure behind them an odd procession of synes and men—three quadrupedal scans, their long holographic snouts protruding ridiculously from their small globular heads, strode out on spindly legs, followed by two First Maniple corporals leading three chained men—three servants, in fact, of the chef Levon of Catuvel. Recognizing them, Dyse moved to stand, but a chilling look from the Regent's black-clad senior officer stayed him.

"You know these poor fools, of course, Doctor. You

also know as well as we do that they had nothing to do with the killing of Fairleigh. No one *else* does, however—not yet—and we've destroyed all evidence. We've even, ah, adjusted the body of the Senator so that it looks as if he took his tasty in his dinner rather than through the hand.

"So, young Doctor, we're going to advertise the 'fact' that we discovered a plot in our own kitchens on Catuvel, and we're going to have to do some fancy apologizing. Our apology, of course, is going to be made public, and we are going to seem to eat some weighty brownies in the process. I'm afraid that these three cooks are to play an important part in our apology's imaging and publication."

The scans arrayed themselves in front of the Regent, so as not inadvertently to collect an image of his person, and the Regent himself stepped aside and nodded again at the Okumura-equipped officer, who inclined his own head. The cooks, drugged, seemed not to see Dyse or anyone else. They did not strain against the thin silvery chains that held their hands loosely to heavy leather belts about their waists. But when the two synes called by the officer this time appeared, the chained cooks noticed at last. Saliva ran from the corners of their mouths, and there came an intestinal smell to the balmy air as their sphincters loosened in a reflex of fear and loathing far older than humanity itself.

As a young man, of course, Lothar IV had been required to read the Annals of the Hand of Man. In the Second Codex of the Annals, he once read a quote: "Washington and Moscow are come to blows at last, and with them all of Earth must die; by fire, by knives and by venom airborne are we doomed, for the talons of these beasts are steel, and their breath Death itself."

Whatever manner of animals—or weapons—Washington and Moscow might have been, the then Rising Regent had found this reference to them oddly appealing. When, on the death of his father, Lothar became Regent, he desired to adopt some new trappings to fit his position. Having the Semerling flair for the unusual, the new Pantocrator of the Path of Jove decided that a pair of matched synes-companion, named—of course—Washington and Moscow, would be to his liking.

Applying to the Sisterhood of the Nucleotides, he expressed his desire thus: his companions must understand (though not speak) the speech of men. They must answer to the Okumura link of the First Security Maniple. They must be lethally armed and defend the person of their Regent with their lives, if necessary; and, even in repose, they must be of an aspect which alone would strike fear into the hearts of men.

And so, according to their ancient custom, the Sisters grew Washington and Moscow, exacting in exchange two megatons of carbon, two megaliters of oxygen, and certain promises. Delving into their records, the Sisters found the tale of the Dinosauria, a lost race of birdlike beings that inhabited dread Earth long before the advent of human beings. They learned of the Deinonychid, a beast that walked on two legs like a bird but that possessed, in place of wings, terrible three-fingered taloned hands. The Deinonychid, it was said, could traverse seventy kilometers in a single hour on its long legs, each of which sported two running-toes and a scythelike inner talon with which the monster kicked its prey to death.

The Deinonychid and its fearsome kind inhabited the Earth in a time when all mammals were but shrewlike midgets, insect eaters. Within the inmost recesses of the mammalian mind, therefore, survives an ancient racial memory, a black fear of the birdbeast Dinosauria. Knowing this, the Sisterhood grew for Lothar IV two twin Deinonychids, or copies of their supposed form (none of their nucleotide sequences, after all, having survived the demise of the Dinosauria some sixty-five million years ago).

Man-high, smooth-coated in short blackly iridescent feathers, red of eye and each wearing a diamond-studded Regency orange collar, Washington and Moscow were delivered to Lothar IV by the Sisterhood. Thenceforth, they accompanied Lothar IV everywhere he went, standing outside his chambers when he slept, beside him as he ate. They became his trademarks, and his joys, and the agents of his Regental wrath as well.

And it was Washington and Moscow who emerged from the lovely pavilion before which Dyse and his master now sat. It was Washington and Moscow whose gaze, like deepest garnet, darted eagle-like from face to face of all present, resting at last on the beloved form of their Regent, who grinned his boyish grin. This was his joke on the world of men, his prank at the expense of peace of mind.

"Earth!" Shouting this oath, the Princess Linsang ran back into the pavilion, disappearing into the hallway that led to transport and to her own quarters several kilometers away.

"Ah, excuse my daughter's manners, Doctor." The Regent again. "She saw one of these, uh, little scenes one time—an execution—when she was four. It impressed her deeply. I know how to use it."

Of the others present, only the scans remained unmoved;

even the Regent's little dog whined and hid its head beneath its master's arm.

"Well, my hearties!" Lothar IV stroked the long muscle-bulged necks of his arcane synes-companion, and Washington and Moscow whistled softly from somewhere deep in their throats. They bobbed their long toothed heads and flicked nictitating membranes birdlike across their stony eyes as they stood there beside him. "Shall we snack? I need some records of your lunch for my esteemed counterpart the Aresian Emperor; do eat politely, pretty ones, and slowly." Again the Regent winked; the scans turned to the three terrified cooks, the guards stepped away and Dyson Tessier closed his eyes as Washington and Moscow raised the feathery crests at the backs of their narrow skulls and advanced to the task of sacrificing their Regent's three scapegoats.

So justice was served in the matter of the assassination of Carraghan Angetenar Detering Fairleigh, Senator from Abarricanna Blee to the Court at I Aresia.

Chapter 4: In which we embark on the Trickster's Sailing

> Has anyone supposed it lucky to be born?
> I hasten to inform him or her it is just
> as lucky to die, and I know it.
>
> —*Song of Myself*, Whitman the American

THE FRAGRANT BREEZE of Summer Semerlinga stirred its leeward pole as well. There, in a sparsely furnished cell of the sort favored by members of the First Security Maniple, windbells stirred and tinkled, their song embracing a great black-bearded man more than two meters tall who stood in silent contemplation of a simple portable altar. Two beeswax candles illuminated the incense-wreathed little shrine within which stood a black cube on a

48

pedestal on which was inscribed in old Engli the epigram above. Their author was the European Whitman, himself six millennia dead. The altar was one to the Trickster Gagarin, First Man in the Deep. Therefore, of course, the supplicant before this altar was a fighting man, the Sailing of Gagarin being the same Sailing as that of all who must live and die in the Trickster's realms of luck and the sword.

The giant, Captain Spider Quick-to-Change Melliden, knelt and, placing his hands before him on the matted floor, touched his forehead to them. He had until tonight been detailed to the public bodyguard of the Regenta Catharine but had just been informed that he would receive new orders this evening. Thus it was the Litany of the Receiving of Orders on which he prepared to meditate— one of the many litanies of that Sailing in which fighting men had taken their only solace for untold centuries. He sought to clear himself of ego, to welcome the hand of the Trickster, to reaffirm the transfer of his self-protective instincts to the protection of his Maniple and Stirps Semerling.

The hand of the Trickster is incarnate in all military orders, and the Litany opens with the Trickster's Ride:

> Lord Gagarin reached to the sky, and cried—
> Cried out from the Mouth of Earth—
> Out of the Earth I sing! he cried,
> And out of the Earth sailed he.
>
> And see! he rides among the Rocks
> And laughs across the Deep;
> Out of the Earth I sing! he cried,
> And out of the Earth sailed he.

And then the Litany of the Receiving of Orders:

"What am I? Am I not but a sequence of orders, their accomplishment in the name of my Regent? Trickster, intercede for me in the path of the Horsemen; lead them a merry chase for me, that they may not yet prune my branch of the Tree of Life; let not the Horseman War, the Horseman Famine or the Horseman Death truncate the pursuit of my duty until it please you, Lord Gagarin. Kiss the Nucleotides and make them blush for me. Extend my service, Lord Gagarin, for luck is yours to—"

A quiet knock—two, three—on the door to the cell. A First Maniple officer. The giant rose to his feet with agility surprising in so large a man and said, "Sir."

Colonel Busork Tek of the First Maniple entered, genuflected briefly before the shrine, waited and returned the giant's salute. In his hands he held a scroll sealed with three lupine leaves and the shark totem of the Maniple.

"Here they are, Spider Quick-to-Change," said the colonel. "Big tidings—you're assigned to quite a detail. All sorts of security clearances—you'll have a week's battery of tests, but it looks like the Trickster moves alongside you . . . *Major* Melliden."

A brand-new Former Captain Spider Quick-to-Change Melliden accepted the scroll in the detached manner appropriate to one receiving a promotion. Breaking the seals, he unrolled the crackling gray document and read:

12 Sol in the Year of the Hand of Man 5747 Post-Closing:

By order of His Majesty Lothar Belexon Semerling IV, Regent of Troy, Pantocrator of the Path of Jove, greetings.

On receipt of these Orders you are promoted to the rank of Major, Office of External Affairs, First Security Maniple of the Domestic Regiment of the Houses of Troy Prime. You are detailed to the suite of His Puissance the Regent's subseneschal Dyson Teague Tessier, with whom you are to share social-interface functions in passage aboard His Puissance's beloved friend the two-minute sweep Catuvel.

In passage with you will travel the Princess Linsang Rockaflar Semerling, security demanded by the Emperor Baltan II of Aresia in transport of the body of his minion Carraghan Angetenar Detering Fairleigh to cycling into the ecosystem of I Aresia. Maintenance of the security of the Princess is your primary function.

Also in passage with you will be the Limestone, only compensation acceptable to the Emperor Baltan in the matter of the assassination of his minion while in the care of the Regency. Maintenance of the security of the Limestone is your secondary function.

Also in passage with you will be two priests, His Eminence Canopus Cardinal Tamilaria and the Right Reverend Father Huxley Vereker, both of the Nunciature Pollicis of the Hand of Man to the lately aborted summit at Troy Prime; a twelfth Vice-Syndic of the Hamtsan Brokerage, Ammihud Lewic; and an envoy of the Four Bonds of the Tetravalency, the Honorable Albemarle, Lord Durrell, Third Bond, plus the associates of these four honored guests of the Regent. Maintenance of the security of these men is your tertiary function.

The subseneschal Dyson Teague Tessier possesses a Doctorate of Synes and an Okumura link of serving-syne frequency. **You are to monitor his interface with the Regent's synes including the sweep Catuvel, two-minute class, for First Maniple analysis in the matter of Doctor Tessier's possible promotion. The monitoring of Doctor Tessier's performance is your quaternary function.**

At 0800 hours on 13 Sol you will report to First Security Maniple headquarters on the Regent's Island Puppy VI to meet Doctor Tessier and receive further briefing.

"Congratulations, Major," said Colonel Tek, smiling a rare, tight smile through his own broad black beard. "May you sail close to Lord Gagarin—with a war in the offing, we need him now. You may be braided into his trajectory somehow. Perhaps you made him laugh this week."

"Perhaps. Sir, I can't consider any detail associated with that assassination to be a delight—there're many I'd prefer." The new major did not feel up to his ritual First Maniple name, Quick-to-Change, today. His work was until now *preventing* assassinations, but he did not wish to muck about in those assassinations already accomplished. Furthermore, at forty-six he was *accustomed* to serving the suite of the Regenta Catharine, directing his attention entirely to her safety. Haughty she might be, and given to intrigue on behalf of her fat son Homar, but she was also learned and even entertaining at times.

Spider Melliden had no fears for himself, of course, and none for his family—he *had* no family, Writs of Generation being issued to no Trojan military below general grade. The scion of generations of generals, he was by destiny devoted to the Trickster and to the Regency Stirps.

Still, his new orders in this time of crisis were sure indications that his trajectory was to change radically. Oh, Lord Gagarin—

Colonel Tek interrupted Spider's reverie, saying, "Oh, you'll be dossed a lot this week, but here's the latest on the killing. Seems that the Princess herself did her fiancé in—but no one's supposed to know. See, the Regent followed up on his original hunch, staging a poisoning of the Senator's food and framing and executing some cooks. But the Aresians insist that the Princess herself be sent along as security for the compensation—the Limestone—that they demand. They're all girded for war, you know. So's the Regent, but he went along with it. Quite a blow, losing the Limestone. Your work's cut out for you. You may be furthering the Trickster's Ride, too. We believe that this young steward may be a catalyst. But let's hustle for Axis—you can catch a few winks on Puppy tonight."

The men emerged from First Maniple quarters into the evening light of the "valley" floor. Here waited a cariole, the dapple-gray mare in its traces a syne who greeted Spider respectfully as Major—a yet unaccustomed major to be sure. Embarking, they were carried a kilometer along the leeward rim to a lift, thence to Axis to be propelled along the hundred-kilometer freefall center of the astounding cylindrical paradise that served as the Regent's summer home. Much to do, now—and tonight he must complete his Litany. Plus a Litany of the Bolt, for there was war in the offing, full war for the first time since the Great Black more than a millennium before. Gagarin, sail with us all.

"The number of bondspeople kept at the archipelago of Troy Prime was limited to forty million some three centuries ago. This multitude, inhabiting the twelve densely populated Islands derisively known as Puppy, or the Pups of Troy, exists entirely for the amusement of Stirps Semerling, members of which decide whether their bonds-people should live, reproduce or die—and in what manner.

"The Bureau of Bondsmen's Affairs on Puppy VI, population six point seven million, is the only place in all of the Pups at which higher Regency functionaries may ordinarily be found. Here all bondsman records are kept, and here we have to go to arrange personnel matters with the First Security Maniple for your next task aboard Catuvel."

So said a bedraggled Pantolog Five, licking himself meticulously all the while he passed this information over their Okumura link to Dyson Tessier. But Dyse hardly listened, so great was his irritation with the creature. An hour before, on Summer Semerlinga, two house servants had brought the encyclopedic cat, collared, to Dyse with stern warnings that no more trouble would be permitted from this or any other of the six cheetah-encyclopedias of the Pantolog Series.

It seemed that, upon completing his interrogation before the First Maniple, Pantolog had wandered through the forests and onto the grassland belt of Summer Semerlinga. Here, Dyse was told, the syne had encountered for the first time in his short existence a small herd of impala being stalked by a real (female) cheetah. Before he could be halted, the damn fool encyclopedia had (1) struck up an acquaintance with the wild cheetah and (2) murdered two impala—behavior most unusual for a syne, and most forbidden.

"Well?" said the cat. "We Pantologs are a new series. We have no backup recording. And it was the Regent himself wanted us grown to look like cheetahs—how was anyone to know the strengths of the instincts of my genetic matrix? Least of all my poor self—''

"Your poor, poor self," muttered Dyse. "Look at me—a year out of school, Doctor of Synes, and the very syne with which I'm supposed to be closest linked has gone off to screw around like a damn tomcat."

"Don't blame *me*," the encyclopedia demurred. "Blame the Sisterhood. They *grew* me—maybe they wanted to have some sport at the Regent's expense. They don't like him any better than—''

"The Horsemen crush you beneath the hoofs of their mounts, you mindless wordbox! How'm I going to keep you from a recycling? Flybait—the Regenta'd love to have that spotted coat of yours as a jacket."

"Yes, dear Master, perhaps I'm a bit less synelike and reliable than I ought to be. Still, it was my finest moment—something about those antelope, something about that movement of theirs, seemed to seize me like a vise. And that lovely *tabby*—what a creature! No mere syne she—she made me real for a minute. You know, it took *both* of us to kill the impala, and what glory! I *can't* have been meant to be a mere encyclopedia. But I'm not a real cat either. I'm a mishmash, a Chimaera, an evolutionary error on the part of the Sisterhood."

"The Sisterhood rarely makes errors, cat."

"They did this time, Doctor, I feel certain of it. I am not a smooth functioner in the service of humankind, including yourself, Honored Master."

"As I know all too well. You do seem to be losing your sense of decorum—*all* of your senses, if I'm a judge. As for this 'Master' bit, though, I guess we'll get a taste of 'mastery'—or thralldom—pretty shortly. I see the Pups of Troy ahead.''

The looper in which they traveled, an unintelligent but lavishly appointed two-passenger Regency affair with a thirty-second period of revolution, addressed Dyse in normal speech: "Doctor, we approach Puppy VI; I'll begin contracting my radials now to match its period. Please make yourself comfortable for the adjustment. You may watch the approach through your leeward ports.''

Ahh, great huge feeding-toroids—a dense population. Puppies V and VI, linked in counterrevolution with one another, were neither of them cylinders closed at the ends like Semerlinga and other Islands of the free. No, these were long tubes, axes open to the Deep, within which life would be low-ceilinged and close. No mighty vistas, no "sky" kilometers above for the thralls on these grim Islands. The Regent spared his bondspeople no extra room or matter. Thank the Horsemen, thought Dyse, that I'm a Doctor of Synes rather than a serf to the Regency!

"I've often wondered," he said over the Okumura link to Pantolog, "what it is that causes people like the Regent to maintain places like this. He makes no use of any service these people might offer—he just watches them as they overpopulate and fight and produce squalor.''

"Permit me a quotation from a long-dead Pollex of the Hand. Honored Master.'Twas Mao XII who said, 'Why, in a society equipped with such superb servants as synes, must there be such an immense serf class? I, gentlemen, must presume that it is due to the human need for hierarchy. Human power is power only over humanity; thus the rulers of men grow entire Islands simply that they may stuff these Islands with miserable thralls. So long as men are men, I do not foresee an end to it.' Honored Master, you are a man; I imagine that your understanding of this sort of thing is well beyond mine.''

Outside, the great twin tubes of Puppies V and VI loomed against the Deep, their orange and white body walls dwarfed by the vast feeding-toroids that captured the Sunsea to feed the wretched millions within. The looper, contracting her muscles and drawing herself to her center of mass, approached a contracted sphincter along the rim of VI, closer, closer—an instant of freefall and then the gentle contact and return of mass. Six chitinous jaws about the rim of the Island sphincter gently clamped six chitinous knobs on the looper's own sphincter rim, and the lips of the two muscular valves met in an airtight kiss—and opened.

Dyse gasped—as did Pantolog. The mahogany and leather interior of the looper filled with an odor of death so intense that Dyse's stomach did a momentarily uncontrolled jig before his years of training took over. There were dead men here, plenty of them, and they were not being cycled into the Island's physiology. What goes on? How can humans live in such a stench?

"Here we are, Doctor," said the looper in her sweet girl's voice. "Thank you for your honored patronage."

"Good afternoon, Doctor Tessier," said a new woman's voice over Dyse's Okumura link. "I am Puppy VI, and am honored to have the privilege of sharing your Okumura frequency. Please forgive the condition of my small atmosphere, but bondspeople are many here and their ways sometimes regrettable. Do bear with us—I regulate the air of the Bureau of Bondsmen's Affairs most carefully, and you'll be refreshed shortly."

"Thank you, Puppy." Dyse reeled through the man-

high sphincters, a disgusted-looking and still bloodstained
Pantolog following.

"There's the source of the odor, Honored Master, to our
right. I, ah, neglected to warn you that the bondsmen
regulate their affairs in their own manner."

Dyse looked to the right, and started in horror. On a row
of ten iron spines set firmly into the Island's keratinous
substrate were impaled the bodies of ten people—nine in
varying stages of decay, the tenth still breathing hoarsely.
Each body bore a crudely lettered sign in pidgin Lubret:

**Pildo Manure-collector, insulted the Citizens' Brigade-
master**

Targo Woodscraper, struck his wife Malda

**Malda Woodscraper, shouted, bothered the Citizens'
Stickmaster**

and the like, all down the terrible row of human wreckage.

The space was vast and low, a ceiling twenty meters
above studded with great compound syne-eyes. Within this
space, its gentle curve on either side disappearing upward
into a stinking fog, roofless makeshift boundaries and
walls of assorted organic scrap divided the ground space
into squalid territories—family "homes"?

Glancing significantly toward the glossy eyes above,
Pantolog remarked carefully, "The Regent sometimes en-
joys partaking of the affairs of his thralls."

"Such is the Regent's august pleasure," said Puppy VI.
"Please board my cariole; you'll find it pleasant enough."
An enclosed cariole with a huge bay syne-horse awaited

them. "I am honored. Doctor," said the horse as they stepped aboard. The sphincter of the cariole sealed itself, and the air within rapidly sweetened as contact with their fetid surroundings was broken.

The horse began a ponderous trot through the junk-strewn miasma of Puppy VI. As if from nowhere, a ragtag couple of dozen springbolt-armed men, loincloth-clad, sprang into view and bracketed the vehicle in two trotting cordons.

Dyse gaped frankly through the glass. "Some sort of citizen guard, no?"

"Correct, I believe," said Pantolog. "It's the custom on bondsman Islands for Regency military to allow the natives their own internal organization. I doubt most Regency military could breathe this air for long."

In less than ten minutes, during which they threaded their way through the huddled affairs of thousands of scantily clad or naked people, the cariole reached a bulkhead stretching from Puppy's floor to her ceiling. A great sphincter, over which the Regency lupine leaves were embossed in corroded iron, opened for them as their filthy human escort dispersed as quickly as it had appeared.

The sphincter was an airlock, but not to the Deep. As the inner sphincter opened before him, Dyse saw trees—a formal meditation garden, with what he recognized as the black cube of the Gagarinian sect of the military centered in a carefully raked space of white basaltic sand. The cariole's sphincter opened, the great horse said, "I am honored, Doctor," and Dyse and Pantolog stepped out. The horse and cariole vanished back through the bulkhead sphincters into the terrible world of Puppy VI.

Here, all was different. There were no eyes in the ceiling—no ceiling, in fact, but a glassy dome through which a gentle mirrored Sunlight played over the elegantly pruned and obviously ancient evergreens of the garden. The air, like that of Summer Semerlinga, smelled of blossoms. It was a courtyard garden, entered from within the garrison through two tall oaken doors standing open.

"Doctor Tessier." Two giants stood within the doorway, hands over hearts in salute.

Related, thought Dyse, saluting in return. He recognized the speaker as Colonel Busork Tek, to whom he'd been introduced at Semerlinga. The other could almost have been the colonel's twin. Well taller than Dyse, bronze of skin, both men wore thick black beards, their eyes glistening darkly from beneath bushy black eyebrows—genetic markers of the First Maniple officer sept. In their black uniforms the two seemed like great bears. Both momentarily regarded Pantolog, then the colonel spoke again.

"I'm honored, Doctor. Please forgive the conditions outside. May I present Major Spider Melliden? He is to be your executive officer on your ride back across the Rocks."

"Major. I'm looking forward to your assistance."

"Aye, Doctor," rumbled the huge major. "Our work is laid before us. My superior here has prepared a small meal that should cheer you after the inconvenience of your arrival."

Pantolog, having located this meal with his acute nose, strutted through the courtyard doors into the adjacent space, another formal garden, and smaller. Here an elaborate black ironwork table awaited them, and the sight of the spare but excellent military fare—a bit of wine, some tiny steaks sizzling on an hibachi, breads and a light salad, did much for Dyse's lately upset stomach. Members of the officer sept of the First Maniple were as well trained in the arts of cooking and light conversation as they were in the arts of the killing of men. Within a half hour, Dyse was at ease again, his muscles relaxed as they'd not been since the assassination.

"Well now, Doctor," said Colonel Tek. "You're wondering about our reasons for calling our meeting here on Puppy VI." He sat back in his chair, his broad leather baldric creaking. "We of the First Maniple have through professional necessity spent centuries acquainting ourselves with the ways of the ruling Stirps. You yourself know something of those ways—you'll recall, for example, a certain three cooks, not to mention the nature of life on Puppy. Our garrison here is immune to the Regent's many sensors. Quite immune. Outside, throughout the remainder of this Island, not so. But, dedicated as we are to the security of the Regent, we have ample opportunity for insulating our own security from his. Now, Doctor, please examine the medal on Major Melliden's necklace."

"It's Engli, isn't it? My Engli isn't too smooth, although I recognize the word 'Earth.' "

"Yes, Doctor," said Major Spider Melliden. "An Engli quote, from an Ascendancy poet of immediate pre-Closing; perhaps this unusual encyclopedia of yours can translate it."

Dyse inclined his head, and across their Okumura link Pantolog spoke: " 'A day will come when the Earth will scratch Herself and smile and rub off humanity.' I have no link with the garrison library—wrong frequency, I'm not military. It *is* Engli, though, and in late Ascendancy style. Sounds a bit, ah, heretical to me, if I, a simple syne, may comment on the religious affairs of men."

Dyse looked at his new executive officer with suspicious

interest. "I recognize the quote, I believe—is it not a Batesian one? Are you connected with Batesian heretics?"

"Not Batesian, Doctor," said Colonel Tek. "The quote is indeed Ascendancy, by a poet of the Second Engli Empire named Jeffers whose sentiments, those that survive, have long appealed to those who follow the Trickster's Sailing."

"The worship of the Trickster is sanctioned by both Regency and the Hand—but I find it difficult to believe that they would countenance this image of the Earth as a smiler."

"Doctor, the regard of fighting men for the Trickster's Sailing has been established for thousands of anni. During that time we've evolved many of our own religious opinions, opinions which in no way interfere with duty. Certainly, we have parallels with Batesianism—as we have, more openly, with the precepts of the Hand. But a fighting man's life must not involve needless self-sacrifice, nor, we believe, can any man's.

"Mind you, Doctor, the Trickster's flight from the surface of Earth may not have been a flight from Earth Herself, but from conditions produced by humankind's activities on Her surface. Note well the well-meaning Puppy VI and her sisters, organisms whose behavior is always most laudable; but note also the conditions prevailing among the men and women who must live here. These are not conditions reflective of the minds of the Pups of Troy, but of the mind of the ruling Stirps that we all serve."

The huge colonel stood, walked to a small portable Gagarinian shrine. "Fighting men deal mainly with conditions produced by humankind. The Deep does not kill, nor, we suspect, did Earth. The work of Har Bates was declared heresy by the Hand some four and a half millennia ago because he suspected the same—and died because he voiced that suspicion aloud.

"Now the Deep is full of the retiaries and raptores of men whose whims also support the likes of the Pups of Troy. Those retiaries and raptores, let loose to do their gene-stamped tasks, will make of the kindly Deep an aggregation of Pups, a new Great Black, indeed a new Closing that might prove permanent. Gagarin's Sailing is a Way that requires of its followers an avoidance of such needless waste."

The colonel picked up the black cube of the Trickster's Ride, turned it over in his hands speculatively. He smiled. "We do have reasons for discussing this with you, young Doctor. We're not trying a conversion on you. Your mission on the return across the Rocks is to serve as Regency interface with your passengers. Major Melliden's is to provide security—ostensibly. But you are a young, intelligent man, quite adaptable, I learn from your dossing, and can be expected to understand another thing."

"A thing outside my own duty, Colonel?" Dyse's old suspicion of the First Security Maniple swelled, and memories of its methods filled his mind.

"Perhaps, Doctor, if your duty be not to humankind but only to our Regent. We of the Sailing believe that the Trickster is our only ally against the Horsemen, the Horsemen who wait to ride across the Rocks at this moment. Can you recite their counting, you who were raised within the doctrine of the Hand? They are, after all, your deities—if I may."

"The Horsemen's Counting, Colonel? Certainly, although you know it well yourself:

" 'First is Famine, Hunger's Waste;
      Second War, his thrall;
      Third is Pestilence, of Earth,
      And Fourth is Death for all!' "

"Yes—and do you know the origin of the Horseman Pestilence?"

"An Earthly concept, I believe—something about the Earth's perpetual scourging of humankind. It's linked with the 'insects that suck men's blood, the worms that devour from within,' of which we read in the Second Codex of the Annals."

"Doctor," said Spider Melliden, "the Hand has educated you well. We, on the other hand, believe that the Third Horseman was Earth's response to humankind's own excesses."

"And what has this to do with our orders, Major?"

"Doctor, you see looming before you a war—a war of resource. Do you learn nothing from your glimpse of life on Puppy? From the very name, 'Puppy'? Resource here is kept limited by the pleasure of our Regent, who also permits his thralls to reproduce at will—no Writs of Generation, no regulation except when it is his pleasure to see some death. This same pleasure, and that of his counterpart the Aresian Emperor, will be unleashed to destroy the Islands of both peoples unless the Trickster intervenes. As fighting men, as agents of the Trickster, if you will, we hope to avert the inevitable. Otherwise, we too will be sacrificed to the Second Horseman, War. Uselessly, Doctor, because of the mental inertia of our species as a whole."

"But the diplomatic urge remains intact—we have the option of summits."

"Summits?" The major sneered behind his beard. "Summits like this last farce? Summits are the playthings of the Regent and his ilk. They play with the lives of billions. Material resource, the domain of the First Horseman, is at stake here. We of the Trickster's Sailing have identified certain resources that may break his gallop. We may—"

"You claim to be able to circumvent the Forces of Selection?"

"The Trickster's purpose, young Doctor. Recall his story—how, at the height of the Ascendancy, he sailed into the Deep and found it to be a place well suited to Man. The Hand would have it that he fled Earth, which as the source of evil would destroy humankind. We, on the other hand, suspect that Man—not Earth—unleashed the Horsemen on the Ascendancy. We suspect that this was done by the princes of Earth in the same manner that it would be done by our princes in the Deep. Control of resource, limitation of resource, is the province of princes and of the First Horseman.

"It is instructive, Doctor, to consider the patterning of resource through history. The Four Resources—Matter, Space, Energy and Time—are unequally distributed, are they not? On Earth, for instance, we suspect that human numbers and appetites reached the limits of Earth's capacity to provide Space and Energy for them. Lord Gagarian sailed into the Deep and found abundant Space and Energy. On the other hand, the Deep provides little small-body Matter, a resource with which Earth was abundantly gifted. Our princes "lay claim" to small-body matter among the Rocks, and distribute it according to whim and profit. This is a workable situation until the limits to their availability are approached. Then the princes must fight for their wealth. And we in their service.''

"Why, you sound like a pirate of the Hemispheres!'' Dyse, astounded, imagined Batesian worms gnawing at the heart of the fabric of his society. *"Are* you a heretic? One to be reported to—''

"To whom, Doctor?'' asked Colonel Tek. "To the First Maniple? *We* are the First Maniple; report us!''

And now Dyse saw himself trapped. The Trickster seemed a living presence here, devious and yet somehow inanely humorous, laughing at a young steward enmeshed in the flux of history.

"Well, Doctor!'' Smiling, reading Dyse's anguish, Colonel Tek relented. "You see the Trickster at last. He has always been at your side, though—was with your father, whose service to Lord Teague gained him the Writ of Generation that permitted your conception and birth, was with your mother when she chose for you the name of a prophet of old.''

"Prophet? My name is a family name, little more.''

"Doctor, there was during the Ascendancy a prophet bearing the name Dyson. He foretold the exploitation of the matter resources of the surfaces of moons and other large objects. Resources, Doctor, that exceed by many millions of times those of the Rocks that are now so carefully hoarded by the princes and matter-brokers. We hope to discover some of his works, in so doing perhaps unlocking the secret of stealing from Gravity the materials humankind needs to survive in any sort of dignified manner. The works of Dyson the European were alluded to in the Book of Bates; we have reason to believe that these works survived the purges that destroyed Old Wirtanen two thousand anni ago. Yes, we seek access to large-body matter.''

"But no man, no syne, could survive the twisting of Gravity on such a body! Your heresy is bending your minds.''

"An angry young man.'' Colonel Tek laughed momentarily, then said: "You know, perhaps, that we of the First Maniple are reputed to be of what has been rather crudely described as 'mindless courage'? Doctor, our purpose is not ruthlessness but the avoidance of needless sacrifice. We are human—we are not, after all, monsters of the Chimaeric Wars. We would sail with Gagarin and see humankind saved from itself again. We would find resources for Man, and we believe that we have.''

"You sneak about like any of the Regent's skulking eyes. How would you propose to subvert Gravity to survive these planetary surfaces?''

"Think on history, Doctor,'' the colonel said. "How could Lord Gagarin have led the Filtration into the Deep? How was the Filtration accomplished? Certainly the peoples of Earth possessed no synes, but they must have constructed some sort of jetted implements to counter Earth's Gravity—which, by the way, is so great as to equal one mass in force. With no synes, they must have done it with Machines, their legendary tools and vassals. We read that Machines were not alive like synes, but that they were not dead either. They must have worked; else the Peoples of the Deep would not exist, nor men of Earth. Our kind would have become extinct at Closing.''

"You're suggesting, then, that humankind can rob Gravity and live?''

"Doctor, be not obtuse. Life *evolved* on Earth, lived

there, we're told, for some four billion years. Certainly, Earth Herself may be inhabited by the Third Horseman. But the other planets are composed of sterile matter like that of the Rocks. It is only a question of human courage and the will of the Trickster whether we exploit these riches and survive, or allow our rulers to snuff us out as the princes of the Ascendancy snuffed out the men of Earth.''

''You say again that Earth Herself did not motivate the Food and Oil Wars.''

''No more than will the kindly Deep motivate the coming war, young Doctor. The Second Horseman is Man's Horseman. Only the Third Horseman can be said to be of Earth—She used him in an attempt to control Her offspring Man much as a human mother chastises her child with the flat of her hand.''

''Are you testing my loyalty? You speak almost as Batesians, as heretics!''

''Again, Doctor, you are an intelligent *man*. Please don't shout. Your loyalty is—or ought to be—to humankind, not merely to a temporal ruler, though in his service you find yourself. We hope on this voyage to contact another force working (we believe) on behalf of humankind, and we believe that you, steward, can facilitate that contact. There are legends suggesting that the unknown rulers of the Batesian Heresy are in possession of records of the modes by which the peoples of the European Ascendancy transferred matter from the surfaces of the Earth and Her Moon to build the Cities of O'Neill at Earth's Lagrangian Points.

''Because none of the writings of Saint Gerard himself seem to have survived the destruction of Wirtanen more than two millennia ago, we must look to the Batesians for assistance. One of them, Durrell of the Tetravalency, will ride with you and Major Melliden on your passage across the Rocks; Catuvel is ostensibly to return him to his home port amid the Middle Belt. Your task as steward is to engage the man in conversation; in so doing attempting to draw from him any information that could lead us to Batesian records, for he *is* a Batesian—perhaps the only one we can locate in the short time remaining to us. The Earthly records taken in the great Batesian exodus of two millennia ago may unlock the secrets of the nonliving Machines, thus obviating the necessity of war. Major Melliden's task is to understand and relay to us something of what Lord Durrell says under your adroit handling. We have confidence in you, Doctor; we feel that Lord Gagarin sails with you.''

"So—you wish me to deal with a heretic to discover the whereabouts of legends, with the Regent's eyes and ears all about me.''

"Again, Doctor,'' said the colonel patiently, "*we* are the Regent's eyes and ears.''

Major Melliden grinned through his bushy beard. "We tell the Regent all he *needs* to know. He has no desire to acquaint himself with, ah, heretical doctrines. Know well, Dyson Tessier, that your fate is in your own hands. You can do no better than to take a moment to reflect that we all ride with the Trickster's Sailing. Now, we have dosses here on the Princess, your principal charge, and on your coming tasks. For these dosses you ostensibly met with us today; understand them well, all the while remembering that what was said here will cost you a lingering death in Regency style should it escape to the wrong ears. We are, after all, the First Maniple, and our ways are well known to you. With this new familiarity, perhaps we can abandon formality. Please, now, call me Spider. I will work better that way.''

Spider Melliden handed Dyse the little dosses, which curled up in his hand. Later they would speak, telling him of his passengers and the potentials for disruption on the coming voyage, but for now they might sleep.

Colonel Tek stood, signifying that the interview was at an end. Dyse and Pantolog did likewise, turning to leave by the oaken doors into the outer meditation garden.

As he prepared to meet the cariole that would carry him back across the hellish world of Puppy, Dyson Tessier glanced at the glistening black cube of the Trickster's Sailing on its pedestal surrounded by raked white sand. An odd spasm seized him momentarily from somewhere within his chest. To Pantolog, ever watchful, it seemed that the young steward bowed his head ever so slightly to that enigmatic symbol of Gagarin's Ride.

Chapter 5: In which, having embarked on the Trickster's Sailing, we ride with Catuvel

Catch me a piece of the whirling Deep,
A line to a far-off port;
Roll me away through the bright Sunsea,
And pay me your motion-court, my loves,
Pay me your motion-court!

—Song of the sweep Catuvel, two-minute class,
  to the driver-synes that accelerate her at
  the beginning of voyages

OF COURSE the summit, or what was left of it after Senator Fairleigh's assassination, had been a disaster. All Aresian representatives to the Regency court had been recalled across the Rocks in protest, crippling the thing to begin with; then the pirate Whip had managed to disappear, a feat which—given the heavy guard all over Semerlinga— was miraculous.

The two priests of the Nunciature Pollicis, clever men both, had immediately perceived that no cooks had assassinated the Aresian Senator. In the manner of their kind, they had taken the opportunity presented by public suspicion to cast aspersions on the Batesian, Durrell of the Tetravalency, who in indignant response sequestered himself with his aides in the little Tetravalency trading Island from which all carbon-brokerage for Troy was conducted. Further, Durrell threatened the Hand of Man with a cutoff of carbon trade, intensifying the starvation fear rampant throughout the Plate.

In addition, millions of new retiaries and raptores, some large enough to destroy entire Islands, were ordered from the branches of the Sisterhood of the Nucleotides serving the two Trojan Points. In return, the Regent had been forced to pay the Sisterhood enough matter so that they were already reputed to be growing an Island of some sort whose orbit would be set significantly oblique to the Plate. The Sisterhood, always looking to its own preservation as growers of synes and preservers of life's diversity, evidently foresaw war and hoped to establish operations far from the unstable politics of the Plate. The Sisterhood, reflected Dyse, was as good a political barometer as any.

In the two weeks after his disturbing First Maniple interview, Dyse had learned much of the Princess Linsang who would travel aboard Catuvel. Not only was she beautiful, as he had learned at the execution of the cooks; she was also a scholar and accomplished historian.

Again, as her part in the assassination had amply shown, the Princess was skilled in the ways of intrigue and death. On the Dodecade of the School of Assegai, the light javelin, she stood at ten, two steps below the Tip. With her hollow-tipped stylet-anlace, she could pick and crack a man's button at seven meters, and with springbolt or knife she was lethally acquainted with the Vertical and Horizontal.

Like the animal for which she was named, the Princess Linsang was an agile hunter, a Diana at eighteen. Certainly she was a far better candidate to assume the Regency than was her weak brother Homar *princeps*, but it was a Regency she could never—for having been born female—rule.

The Princess would be accompanied by her secretary, America Berecynthia, herself a formidable being. Born and raised on Sappho in the leading Trojan Point, she had been selected by the Regenta at the birth of Linsang to accompany the Princess as aide throughout her life.

Indeed, all personal servants to the women of Stirps Semerling were Sapphonic; the Island Sappho had been grown for this purpose centuries before. In addition, a number of Sapphonic girls were said to be tapped yearly by the Sisterhood of the Nucleotides in some connection with their arcane dealings in the fundamental molecules of life. No man had ever set foot on Sappho; no man had ever even *seen* one of the Sisterhood—and Dyse was forced, as he listened to the murmuring dosses, to reflect that the world of men was in many and mysterious ways netted within a barely visible fabric that was the far more durable world of women.

At a pre-voyage state dinner over which the Princess presided, Dyse had met this America Berecynthia. Named after the Second Engli Empire of the European Ascendancy, she seemed as imperial as her name; austere, quiet, handsome in her forty years, the secretary nonetheless somehow reminded him of that pirate Whip who had so suddenly disappeared. It wasn't in her appearance, of course, or in her conversation—she said little—but in a certain indefinable *readiness,* a hawklike attentiveness, that Dyse found the resemblance. The doss, of course, contributed nothing to this feeling; it spoke only of eighteen years of dedicated service to the Princess as nurse, tutor, secretary and general companion. But the feeling remained, and the inscrutable Sapphonic power of America Berecynthia's level gaze had done nothing to set him at ease.

Dyse had also listened to the doss of Major Spider Quick-to-Change Melliden, who would be his closest human associate on the funereal voyage. The major's presence might be resented by the two priests of the Hand who would accompany them; Gagarinians recognize no priestly hierarchy, the Trickster's Sailing being an intensely personal Way in which the individual's mind, rather than any theocratic intermediary, dictates his actions. Not a Way suited to the Hand's authority, and priests suspect any such Way.

But for all his seemingly seditious conversation on Puppy, the major's doss reflected a dedicated service to Stirps Semerling. Bred of countless generations of his like, he was a velite—an elite hand-skirmisher—as deadly and efficient as the most celebrated of his sept, and his doss portended a distinguished career furthering the ends of the Regency. Which, then, was deceptive—the doss or the major? Ah, but the doss was a product of the First Security Maniple itself; what, then, *was* the First Security Maniple?

Again, as had happened so many times in the past days, an image of the black cube of the Trickster's Sailing invaded Dyse's overwrought mind.

Still, he had shared many hours with Spider Melliden in the past weeks. The giant warrior had taken to calling Dyse "Doc," and amused him with his military humor as well as providing much aid in planning and security work.

And then there was Albemarle, Lord Durrell of the Tetravalency, always cordial, always talkative with Dyse. The Bond, carbon-broker, Batesian heretic, had few dealings with anyone outside his own entourage. Still, he seemed to enjoy a moment here and there in Dyse's company—and now Dyse was to manipulate him for information. Would the Bond Durrell perceive his motives, of which even Dyse himself was not certain? Did he, in fact, really know anything about the legendary Machines?

Three big Regency loopers carried the company of voyagers toward Catuvel, lying four hundred kilometers to Sunward of the archipelago of Troy Prime. With Pantolog's disrespectful wit quelling his disquiet, Dyse made light conversation with the Princess, her Sapphonic secretary and Spider Melliden, all of whom shared his looper. The Princess carried on her person the Limestone, consolation gift from her father to the Emperor in the Path of Mars.

Perhaps the greatest treasure known to humankind, the Limestone did not look like much—a walnut-sized brown stone of curious texture embedded in a Tetravalency-grown diamond. Nonetheless, through the centuries the thing had remained an object of awe and sometimes fear—some said that the Third Horseman, Pestilence, resided somewhere within it. Indeed, according to all of legend and history, the Limestone was the only thing of Earth that remained in the possession of the Peoples of the Deep. Through nearly six millennia of changing fortunes, it had passed from hand to hand until coming to Troy long ago with Stirps Carraghan, from which it had been taken by the Semerlings when they took power. Its progress had often been accompanied by bloodshed, and some said that ill luck was generated by the Third Horseman within its Earthborn substance. But, for all that, it seemed a small thing—albeit of much value—and Dyson Tessier did not put much stock in legend and superstition of this sort.

As the loopers made their way to the waiting Catuvel, their passengers were treated to the spectacular sight of a new Island being grown for the Princess Linsang's future pleasure. The thing was in its spinder stage, with Deep-adapted arthropods laying metaproteinaceous lines to bind its growing skeleton against the vacuum of the Deep itself. As they passed this infant Island, America Berecynthia treated them to an explanation of its growth—she was well schooled in some of the ways of the Sisterhood of the Nucleotides.

"The principle of physalian development was known since perhaps before the Synthesis, for its namesake is a sort of sailing jellyfish-like being, *Physalia physalis,* that was common on Earth and still lives on watery Islands like my own home Sappho. We call it a 'man-o'-war,' because, like all men of war (Major Melliden), it stings viciously when touched. But what we see as a jellyfish is actually a colony of zooids, little animals, each of which is specialized to a certain function within the whole."

"As in a colony of ants?" said Spider.

"Not precisely. Individual ants are free to move about and to perform many functions in their colonies, but the man-o'-war's individuals are locked into their specialized functions for life—one becomes a float for the colony, others function as stinging tentacles with which the colony captures its food and defends itself, still others function as digestive 'organs' or reproductive 'organs.' But each remains an animal in itself; one might say that the physalian egg 'hatches' a number of times, generating a group of animals whose functions gradually specialize as they subordinate themselves to the whole colony of which each is part.''

''And how does this jellyfish creature fit into the growth of Islands?'' Spider asked, watching the partially skeletal form of the growing Island outside as it whirled past their looper viewpoint.

''Well,'' said Merry, ''Islands are grown from physalian eggs—actually Seeds. The Sisterhood creates the nucleic-acid sequence, which contains all the information required to complete the Island's growth. They then bind this information into an egglike sac along with all of the elements and compounds necessary to the growth of a living form from its nucleic code. When a Seed is laid on a Rock, it first sprouts a large pair of leaves that collect energy from the Sun to fuel the ensuing steps.

''Then a number of chewing arthropods hatch from the Seed; if the Seed were to be considered a plant at this stage, the new antlike arthropods would be its roots. They begin breaking the Rock, swallowing it, passing it into digestive systems that divide its substance according to content. This substance is then fed by the chewers to the Seed itself, which rapidly grows and begins to extend its skeletal spars outward into the Deep.

''The next stage is the spinder stage that we see here.

The Seed hatches a generation of spinders, thousands of them, who lay the metaproteinaceous lines from spar to spar. Along those lines will soon extend vinelike stems which will gradually produce the knitted skeletal wall characteristic of Island surfaces. Ultimately all openings in the integument will seal themselves against the Deep, at which point the hollow skeleton is complete. Princess Linsang's Island here is due to be about seventy-five kilometers long and some eight kilometers in diameter.

"Meanwhile, of course, the Rock from which the Island is growing will be disappearing; any extra Rock substance is extruded to the skeleton's Deepside, and volatiles and liquid water are then released by the Seed (which must be fed these foods by its chewing arthropods) within the skeletal enclosure. Nerves and blood vessels grow along the interior, over which more arthropods born of the Seed will then spread soil. It is up to the Princess, of course, to decide what sort of organisms and ecosystem her Island will support.

"Finally, the Seed resorbs its original leaves and begins growing mirrors and feeding-toroids. By this time the nervous system is an electromagnetic one rather than a biologic one as in the original arthropods. The Seed itself becomes in the end the mind of the Island, maintaining her ecosystem and looking to her minions outside. She disperses her mind into a series of ganglia throughout the Island's body wall, so that the Seed itself can no longer be said to exist as such." Merry looked about apologetically. "I hope I'm not talking too much."

"Certainly not," said Spider. "Fascinating! And what of loopers, and sweeps?" He looked about him at the elegant Vessel in which they rolled toward Catuvel.

"All Vessels are grown from physalian Seeds. It's the information coded into their nucleic acids that determines their form and function—just as the same code determines whether an organism will be a man or a mushroom. But the physalian steps are essentially the same, and in all cases the arthropod members of the colony ultimately cycle themselves into the Island ecosystem again—they feed themselves to it, so that it may reuse their substance in its overall metabolism."

"Delightful tale," said Spider. "The arts of growing synes must be far more entertaining to the mind than the arts of war."

"Perhaps—to the mind of the Seed. Certainly, once planted, a Seed goes through its development with no more human interference than a dog's fertilized egg requires to produce an adult dog. And in any case it is the minds of the Isles of Mothering themselves that sequence nucleic acids; the minds of the Sisters could never, being human as nearly as we can guess, contain the information necessary to sequence even a single bacterium."

Thus the short passage to Catuvel passed pleasantly enough, and finally she herself came into view, floating against the curve of Jove. Her radial muscles were contracted in preparation for acceleration so that her center of mass rested like a tumor against the lacy elegance of her vast living quarters with their gardens and ponds and singing birds. Beneath her shell clung a half dozen forty-kilometer drivers, their great leaves spread to bask in the sun, their abdomens extended like immense strings of beads into the leeward Deep. Already, those abdomens were aligned along the invisible line that was to be their trajectory; they would accelerate Catuvel for several days at one mass, finally releasing her to extend her radials and unfurl her mirrors, sweeping off into the Rocks like a second hand on some gigantic two-minute clock while the drivers curled their abdomens up and returned, sailing on the Sunsea wind, to Troy Prime to await their next task. Even now, as the three loopers carrying her passengers approached, Catuvel would be cooing to the stupid oxlike minds of the drivers on her belly, singing the sweep song that prepared them for their mighty effort, urging gently, soothing them as their leaves soaked up the Sun's bounty.

Catuvel, thought Dyson Tessier, you're my best friend yet. And they reached her then, each looper touching one of her sphincters in a movement so precise that none within could detect it. Like oxpecker birds on a rhino in the Regent's game park, the three loopers clung to the sweep while sphincters opened in a life-protecting bridge across the Deep.

Chapter 6: **In which the paranoia of Dyson Teague Tessier is fed a hearty meal**

> But let the frame of things disjoint, both the
>   worlds suffer,
> Ere we will eat our meal in fear, and sleep
> In the affliction of these terrible dreams
> That shake us nightly. Better be with the dead,
> Whom we, to gain our peace, have sent to peace,
> Than on the torture of the mind to lie
> In restless ecstasy.
>
> —*Macbeth*, Shakespeare of the Engli

THE AMPLE COMFORTS of Catuvel being sufficient to have rested and amused the official company aboard

after twenty-two days of travel, Dyson Tessier was at last
able to persuade all of them to dine together. There was to
be music—none for the banj, incidentally—and for novelty's
sake the meal was centered on food from fresh and salt
water. Sappho being an unusually watery Island, and America Berecynthia and her Princess having laid in a large
Sapphonic store of comestibles, there were salmon broiled
with hoisin sauce, lobsters with butter, clams, crabs, fat
scallops, sautéed squid, caviar, and a dozen other aquatic
treasures in addition to appropriate wines and vegetables.
Even the air was Sapphonic, the Great Hall being flooded
with a briny smell and a sound as of the distant crying of
gulls.

Sated and mellowed with wine, Canopus Cardinal
Tamilaria remarked on the starry Deep rolling slowly past
the vast leeward windows of the Hall. "On Earth, it's
said, they called oceans of water the Deep. How appropriate,
this meal and view together."

"Let us, then, not of Earth, drink to Her who spawned
us." The Princess Linsang raised her goblet of wine and
smiled about the great oaken table.

"To Earth?" The Cardinal frowned. "An unholy senti-
ment for one so wellborn and beautiful. I must demur, as
must my colleague Father Vereker."

"Ah, Lady," said Spider Melliden, "from Earth sprang
my patron the Lord Gagarin. I drink with you, and happily."

"And you, Lord Durrell?"

"Indeed, Lady. Earth was our mother, for better or for
worse. The words of Har Bates, founder of the—heresy"—
he winked broadly at the Cardinal—"suggest that this is a
toast that would do me honor."

"And I cannot." Lewic of the Hamtsan examined the

Princess' face for response, saw none. "The Hamtsan Brokerage provides clean oxygen, and sterile; 'tis said that the oxygen of Earth was tainted."

" 'Tainted'?" Dyse glanced at Spider Melliden, who sat unmoved.

"Tainted," said Lewic. "Earth is said to have produced tainted oxygen, or even to have withheld it, in order to slay humankind."

"For what little it's worth," said America Berecynthia, "some of my sources differ from yours, m'Lord Syndic. I was educated to suspect that human beings played a part in the tainting of Earth's air—perhaps by destroying forests and oceanic algae. I would have to drink to Earth."

Dyse, caught completely by surprise, looked again toward Spider. This time the giant's left eyebrow rose somewhat, and he shifted in his chair to look with new interest on the Princess' secretary.

Father Vereker, historian, saw his chance. "On the other hand. Mistress Berecynthia, you are a Sapphonic. I cannot help but suspect that historical sources on an Island that does not permit visits by priests might be tainted themselves. Certainly it is unusual that one born of the serving septs, like yourself, would presume to contradict her superiors at the Princess' board."

"Aye, good Father!" Spider heaved his vast person cheerfully toward the priest. "And is it not then equally inappropriate that I, a mere officer in service of my Regent, should contradict a priest of the Hand? You failed to mention that."

The Cardinal took up the refrain. "Yes, Major. The Hand maintains the most extensive records surviving on the subject. Too, by reason of our training in the Way of our faith, we are able to determine enough of the nature of Earth to perceive a certain evil in Her motives. It would be most presumptuous of me to believe that a soldier—even a velite as honored as yourself—would understand much of the ethic attributed to Earth. Earth was not a moral being in any positive sense. But then, perhaps soldiers are not as directly concerned with morality as must be the religious.''

Durrell of the Tetravalency grinned a grin as sparkling as his inevitable diamond. ''Morality. Well then, Cardinal, with your permission and that of my other friends, may I recite one of the Bharrighari Allegories? In brief, of course. It tells of the morality of the Hand in days gone by.''

''Why, certainly, m'Lord Durrell. I would be delighted.''

''Ah, thank you. It is said in the Allegories that before the Chimaeric Wars an august Pollex of the Hand, Marxian III, once diverted his attention from the persecution of the Batesians to ponder the mythos of the Europeans. There he seems to have found an allusion to a monster, half man, half horse, called a Centaur.'' He paused, looking brightly about the company at table.

''Go on, m'Lord Durrell, please,'' said the Princess.

''Yes. Well, Marxian desired to see such a being, and, being a powerful man, purchased one from that branch of the Sisterhood that served the Hand—still serves the Hand. But when the Centaur attained maturity, he beheld himself a monster, a monster with the mind of a man. Revolted, his man-half slit its own throat; the horse-half lived on for a short time, twitching, to die at the feet of the Pollex who'd brought the thing into being. In all fairness, I should add that the Pollex Marxian in turn slew himself —though suicide is a sin within the Hand—to erase from his mind the blasphemy of his Centaur.''

The Cardinal, scandalized, turned to Linsang. "Lady, please remind this, ah, carbon-broker that it was Pollex Shibuya III who proscribed the growth of any human Chimaera."

"Yes, Cardinal," said the Princess, "but later, much later. Some two millennia later, was it not? And throughout history the Pollices have often been given to moral excess. I speak, of course, as one confirmed within the Hand."

Why, thought Dyse, between this Princess and her secretary, Spider may learn more than ever I could wring from Durrell. Spirited one, this—that rapacious Semerling spirit, true, but spirit. He turned again toward Spider, but the big man's beard hid any emotion as he spoke evenly: "Your Eminence Cardinal, do you know much of this 'tainting' of the air of Earth? Or do you, m'Lord Syndic?" to Lewic. "I found a most amusing children's book in Catuvel's library, which, by the way, I recommend to all present. In it, I read of some ogres, or trolls, of what is called the Sodality of the Tainted Crossing. Would they have anything to do with the tainting of Earth's air?"

"Ho-*ho*, my dear soldier," laughed the Cardinal, "reading tales for babes at your age! Well, allow me to assure you that this Sodality did not taint anything but itself, if, indeed, it existed. It is said to have worshiped the Third Horseman, Earth's henchman—but those are fairy tales. The Batesians are said to know something of the Third Horseman, being folk with interests in such scatology— perhaps you'd better ask our friend the Lord Bond Durrell, here."

Durrell of the Tetravalency laughed. "Such 'scatology,' honored Cardinal, is surely not worthy of the attention of a priest of the Hand. After all, the Third Horseman was 'Spawn of Earth,' no? Left behind in the Filtration, Cardinal? Six thousand anni in the past, nearly? Yes, I believe that he was an Earthly Horseman, the Earth's response to human tomfoolery. But I would not, as an adult, seriously consider a group of ogres worshiping Pestilence. And you, Major Melliden, do not worry yourself with thought of ogres; children's tales are much alike, whatever their content.''

Evasive one, this, thought Dyse, we'll try him another time. He spoke: "My encyclopedia Pantolog Five, here, was educated in the records of the Hand and others; let's consult him.''

Over Dyse's Okumura link, Pantolog's whiny tones flowed in: "Sodality of the Tainted Crossing. Reputed to be a brotherhood of monks with Batesian leanings, the Sodality is said to have originated some five millennia ago during or shortly after the Synthetic Wars. They are said to have been of a conservative bent, resisting the rise of syne technology and clinging to the old nonliving technology and regions about the Lagrangian Points of Earth-Moon System in which the ruins of the Cities of O'Neill are still said to be located. If, indeed, the Sodality existed, it is said to have been led by a *flamen* or priest whose succession is trucidate; the successor, to succeed, must murder the incumbent.

"Some say that the Sodality, by virtue of its extreme conservatism, maintained Machines using the lost magic of the Europeans, although by what means and to what ends is uncertain. Because of the ancient interdict by the Hand of Man against approach to Earth's orbit, little more can be said about Sodality; indeed, most sources doubt its existence altogether. Reference must, however, be made to its place in folklore as a haven for certain uniquely deformed—both physically and mentally—specimens of humanity whose existence would not be tolerated among civilized peoples.'' The Okumura link became silent then, and Pantolog continued lying on the barbaric rug beneath the dining table, perfectly still, attentive, as Dyse related most of this material to those about him.

Princess Linsang spoke: ''I recall tales of the Sodality myself—they were quite thrilling when I was a little girl. Merry, you told me some of those stories—can you recall them?''

''Only a few, Lady. A long time it's been since I told them or you listened to them. Still, it is said, as Pantolog notes, that the Sodality understood Machines, and that Machines both carried life from Earth into the Deep and, on Earth, served the Europeans in a multitude of ways; they were as many as synes, but not alive. They were like stones, made of stones.''

Stones? Like the Limestone? Dyse, who was less than convinced of the Limestone's Earthly origin, had had an opportunity to view it closely within its clear diamond shell. It *was* odd-looking, seeming to be composed of thousands of tiny seashells. But could not someone have fashioned the Limestone with small shells from a sea-Island like Sappho? Still, it was said that there were no living animals that possessed such shells, that they were the skeletons of Earthly creatures extinct for many millions of anni. Perhaps Machines sprang from such unusual stuff—

''I doubt that Machines are of the Limestone,'' said Merry. ''More likely, they were of metal, and of *petroleum*, blood of Earth, fuel of the Ascendancy. And no one knows what petroleum was, either. So we remain in the dark.''

Dyse, preparing to ask another leading question of Durrell of the Tetravalency, was suddenly alerted by his Okumura link to Catuvel.

"Sorry to intrude, Doctor," said the motherly voice, "but I must discuss a matter of importance. Please excuse yourself and follow Pantolog. Remain cheerful for your guests, but ask that Major Melliden attend you."

Dyse and Pantolog rose as one. "Ladies and gentlemen, I must slip out for a moment. Do excuse the interruption, and permit me to steal the major." He bowed, as did Spider, and the two left the room in pursuit of the trotting cheetah.

"Doctor, there is a great deal of unusual activity here. We're crossing a Kirkwood Waste, so the Rocks are rarefied in distribution at present; there aren't many Trojan retiaries here. But my own retiaries are picking up indications of mass and movement all around my sensory perimeter; we have a mika's sensory diameter at present, and all this stuff is remaining just out of my reach. Some big things, too, that appear to be blackbodies; no visuals available. I fear, Doctor, that we're being followed—and by a gigantic force."

Dyse relayed this information to Spider, who said, "Aresia? They could mount such a force, but why? There's enough trouble already; besides, we'd have known weeks ago if they were moving so much mass."

"Doctor," said Catuvel, "it's not Aresian. It has a feel of the *outré* about it—a feel of the Hemispheres."

"Pirates? Surely no pirates could penetrate your raptorial net, Catuvel."

"More than pirates, Doctor. Something *big*. And malevolent, if I'm any judge; the mass seems concentrated at the leading edge of my sensory perimeter. I increase the radius forward, and they move beyond. They're waiting. Doctor, I have no idea what's out there, but it's coordinated and it's huge—perhaps dispersed a mika thick, and in immense numbers. My whole sensory sphere seems surrounded by masses precisely matching our trajectory. I've mobilized all reserve retiaries, twenty thousand in all, and may have more information soon. My raptores are in defense-net formation, and I have two of my twelve galliots armed and manned awaiting Major Melliden's instructions."

"Done," said Spider when Dyse passed this information on. "I'll see to it, Doc, and you take the dinner con. Wish me luck."

"Ride with the Trickster." Dyse watched the giant trot off into Catuvel's military bowels, then said over the Okumura, "Catuvel, what's your next move?"

"Well, I can't change trajectory, of course. My only option at present is to try to pierce their sensory net with a few of my smaller retiaries to get some inkling of what's out there. That's all. You keep the diners happy—they're almost done—and send them off to bed. You, too, Doctor. You're tired."

"Right." Dyse betook himself back to the Great Hall, his mind reeling. Throughout his life, the Deep had seemed the most constant, the most reliable aspect of experience. Now Something unseen lurked invisibly out there, hundreds of thousands of kilometers distant. Something that smacked of Man, the least constant and least reliable aspect of existence. And that Something was watching Catuvel.

Chapter 7: In which the manner of Man in the Deep is shown to be one with the manner of Man in all places and times

The raptores and the bolts of battle
Will ever winnow Men from cattle.

—War anthem of the Holy Fist of the Hand of Man

THE NEXT TWO DAYS saw a gradual increase in tension as Catuvel revised ever upward her estimation of the size of the lurker beyond her perimeter. She learned but one new thing during those days; that the lurker (as they called that vast invisible aggregation of organisms) was augmenting itself from off-Plate, both from the Hemisphere of the Hook and that of the Cross.

"If those aren't pirates," said Dyse to Pantolog, "then *I* am a pirate."

"Any pirate, dear Master, would agree wholeheartedly," responded the cat, whose recent switch to a preference for shellfish seemed to have intensified his characteristic sarcasm.

On the first day after contact with the lurker, Dyse had alerted all his official wards of its presence and separately probed each (with Spider's aid) for information about its nature. But, though the priests and Hamtsan Syndic made some pointed references to Batesians and carbon-brokers, and though Durrell of the Tetravalency in turn happily mentioned the Holy Fist of the Hand of Man, no concrete information was forthcoming from anyone aboard.

Some hundred female military servants to the Princess Linsang, led by America Berecynthia, moved incessantly about Catuvel and commingled noisily with the twenty security men attending the two Nunciature priests, the three attendants to the Hamtsan Syndic and Durrell's staff of fifty Tetravalency men linked by their own private Okumura mycelia. The net effect was to bring Catuvel to a state of warlike pandemonium. Only the two First Maniple velite centuries under Spider Melliden seemed disposed to keep out of sight. They were assigned battle stations which they assumed, and silently maintained.

Everywhere were assegais, swords, knives and bolts, and Dyse could not help shuddering, imagining the legends of the projectile launchers of the Europeans, so much on his mind lately. Those weapons, *firearms*, were said to be Machines that might discharge of their own accord and would have pierced the fragile body walls of any Vessel. What if we still had *those?* We'd all be dead by our own hands, in seconds. Even a bolt, ill aimed in a light Vessel, could pierce her wall and kill her, or evacuate her living contents into the Deep; but Catuvel assured him that no springbolt aboard could possibly break her own integument.

Without, Deepside, twelve galliots manned by First Maniple velites dispersed themselves among the raptores hovering in a sphere of fifty thousand kilometers' radius about Catuvel. Each was manned by twenty men and each carried a thousand or so jetted projectile-raptores whose lives, like those of all raptores, were dedicated to piercing and destroying in the name of the Trojan Regency. Possessed of enough intelligence to hunt independently in packs like wolves, Catuvel's raptores could also hunt doglike in conjunction with the men in the galliots now cruising Catuvel's raptorial perimeter. Each was willing to die protecting the sweep; withal, in the gleaming facets of their three-lobed compound eyes, those raptores reflected nothing of life's instinct for self-preservation.

And the lurker, vast, diffuse, grew ever larger. Catuvel dispersed the thousands of hoplites of her mirrors, preparing them to assemble in decoy masses should an attack begin. And it would certainly begin soon; no verbal contact with the lurker had been made, a fact suggesting that it was preparing not to rob but to destroy. And why? Why waste the incredibly rich matter-resource within? No one knew; all waited.

By this time, Dyse had abandoned any notion of pirate dealings. It was not believed that pirates possessed enough matter to mount such a force as that now arrayed against Catuvel. Indeed. Catuvel's records suggested that in all the history of the Deep no pirate attack of this magnitude had ever been mounted. What was it, then? Lightlink messages flashed both to Troy and to Aresia elicited promises of help, but both were far away and neither could identify the lurker. Already, it was said, a jetted Trojan flotilla had been launched; but its arrival was a week hence, and the time for Catuvel seemed short.

Dyse, Spider and Pantolog sequestered themselves in Catuvel's sensory-interface chamber, a blister on her belly within which she converted information from her retiaries to sounds and visuals readable by human beings. Here they monitored the great transparent gelatinous corneal screens on which the sweep modeled the deployment of her thousands of symbiotes. On-screen, she represented herself as an orange point about which hovered a series of diaphanous spheres color-coded according to function—red for her raptores, blue for her retiaries (the blue of the retiary fields intensifying as these flashed word of mass and movement beyond) and twelve green points marking the manned galliots over whose dispersal Spider presided.

Without, the Deep wheeled by in a stately minuet of stars. No life was visible there to the naked eye, and but for Catuvel's sensory interface an uninformed observer would never have suspected the colossal arrays of Deep-swimmers that opposed one another across hundreds of thousands of kilometers of silent vacuum.

The sensory-interface chamber was circular, comfortably lined with fine padded leathers and delicately wrought fruitwood. Catuvel kept a pair of gold-edged metachitin basins sitting beneath twin sphincter nozzles filled with liquid stimulants—creamy coffee for Dyse and a minty distillate of the leaves of First Maniple coca for Spider. A larger sphincter below occasionally extruded a fresh-grown sausage-shaped beefy musculature for the encyclopedia, and servants brought additional food and water on command. It was a place of tactical insulation from the human activity boiling across Catuvel—it permitted a comfortable alertness and a quiet surrounding.

Spider had hung his burnished dress helmet over a small carving of the Sword-and-Helix; his folding Gagarinian shrine, black cube of polished ironwood mounted in a carved hinged triptych of zebrawood, admonished them with those disquieting words of the long-dated Whitman:

> Has anyone supposed it lucky to be born?
> I hasten to inform him or her, it is
>   just as lucky to die, and I know it.

After staring in silence at these words for some time, Dyse spoke: "It's been days, but you will have noticed the Princess' interest in this matter of the Earth and all. What do you think?"

"I did," said Spider, "and also noticed it in her secretary. Can we be on the same trajectory? Seems a bit risky to approach a Semerling too boldly, but I can't help being reminded of Mistress Berecynthia's Sapphonic origins. She knows something of the ways of the Sisterhood, and the Sisterhood fears war—fears any dealings with, ah, normal folk. Perhaps they have their own motives, but I suspect that the peoples of the Hemispheres—the Batesians—and those of the Tetravalency foresee the consequences of a Trojan-Aresian war with more misgivings even than we, and that Mistress Berecynthia hopes to contact them because she shares similar fears."

"So her mission is perhaps to gain access to the records of Wirtanen, paralleling our own," said Dyse. "Pantolog," he added over the Okumura link, "give me a rundown on the Sisterhood of the Nucleotides, any connections they may have with Sappho, anything else we might use."

"Have you a few weeks, dear Doctor-Pirate? I could go on—"

"Condense it, then, and leave out the feline wit, if you can."

"Yes, beloved Seneschal, Doctor, yes. The Sisterhood of the Nucleotides originated sometime during the Synthetic Wars; it is said that during these wars a group of female technologists were the only ones able to isolate themselves from the, shall we say, uncertainty of the times, and maintain the apparatus necessary for the enumerating of nucleotides in nucleic-acid chains and the interpretation of the living code. This original enclave of females saved the first Isle of Mothering or syne-growing Island from possible destruction. Because they remain the only guardians of lifegrowing ritual, the Sisterhood has continued to this day to steer clear of physical contact with other folk.

"The Sisterhood has jealously guarded their life-molding ritual ever since their origin—over a period, you know, of more than five millennia. As you know, no one has ever seen a Sister of the Nucleotides. No one approaches an Isle of Mothering, for the Sisters then threaten to destroy both the Isle and themselves. Needless to say, such an act would have catastrophic consequences. Note also that no Isle of Mothering orbits anywhere within ten mikas of any other Island or settlement of any sort, no matter under whose employ. And, of course, because of their monopoly on syne-growing ritual, the Sisters are able to extract vast quantities of matter from anyone purchasing synes or Seeds. They probably possess more matter than any but the greatest of Stirpes.

"There are eight branches of the Sisterhood within the Plate. There is one associated with each of Jove's two Trojan Points, both of course in the employ of the Regency; there are two in the orbit of Mars, both in the employ of the Aresian Imperium. The Holy Isles also employ an Isle of Mothering, and each of the major matter-brokerages—the Riders of the Cloud of Oort, the Tetravalency and the Hamtsan Syndicate—probably employs one also. Those of the Wirtanen Federation were destroyed by their own Sisters during the destruction of Apollonia by the Hand about twenty-two hundred anni ago. The Sisters mean what they say."

"What of the Hemispheres, Pantolog? Would there be a Sisterhood out there?"

"I have no information on that, nor has Catuvel. No one even knows *who* lives out there, precisely—most Hemispheric folk see good reason to remain inconspicuous to Plate peoples, what with the likes of Stirps Semerling and the Hand rampaging about."

"And Sappho? How, precisely, is she connected with the Sisterhood?"

"Precisely, omniscient Doctor? Sapphonic women are almost as secretive as the Sisters themselves; they reproduce only by purchases of semen from selected males, mostly members of the military septs, and no male of whom I am aware has ever visited or wished to visit Sappho. On the other hand, Sapphonic women are known for scholastic and military ability, hence their favor with the Regency as attendants for Semerling ladies. Otherwise they stick to Sappho, it seems. Incidentally, there is an Aresian counterpart to Sappho; her name is Isle Atalanta. Both of these Islands are said to offer seven candidates per annus to the Sisterhood, a number that seems far too small to support the populations of eight Isles of Mothering—if, indeed, those Islands really are inhabited by a Sisterhood of human beings.

"Some legends suggest that the Sisters manipulate their own genes in violation of the Shibuyan Anti-Chimaeric Bulla of thirty-six hundred anni ago. Perhaps they are immortals. Perhaps they are monsters. No one knows except the Sisterhood. And possibly a Sapphonic woman or two. But your friend Mistress Berecynthia would probably say no more on the subject than would one of the Sisters."

"So," said Spider on hearing all this recounted, "the Sisterhood possesses vast matter resources, and it taps Sappho and Atalanta for recruits—or whatever. What of ideology or religion?"

"Here I may be of more use," observed the cat to Dyse. "You will recall the Batesian Heresy, to which our guest Lord Durrell and his Tetravalency servants are the nearest adherents. Its founder, Har Bates of Wirtanen (who was killed by the Hand some forty-five hundred anni ago), broke with Hand ideology by suggesting that Earth, rather than having been an evil being, ought to be regarded as Life's Home, and one kindly enough at that. No one has ever tested this theory, of course, for the Holy Fist put an end to any approach to Earth Herself and no syne could ever pierce Her thick atmospheric membrane or survive Her bacteria anyway. Remember the Third Horseman.

"We can say objectively of Earth that She is a forest

planet three quarters of whose surface is covered by water. In the days of the Ascendancy, it is said, large parts of Her land surface were nearly devoid of life; these were called *deserts*. The Hand says that Earth produced *deserts* to destroy human life; Batesians claim that human life consumed the landscape, itself producing *deserts*. You can understand, then, the fundamental differences that make the Nunciature priests and Lord Durrell such entertaining mealtime combatants.

"Now, back to the Sisterhood. As you know, they personify the Four Nucleotides as four dancing young women; these, they say, are the First Women of Earth, their dance, the Fourfold Saraband, representing life's evolutionary unfolding. They accompanied life into the Deep, and, under the care of the Sisters, they perpetuate life to this day. Earth must thus seem to the Sisterhood a place as beneficent as She does to the Batesians. Certainly, were the Hand not as dependent as everyone else on the Sisterhood, there would be a persecution of some sort. But the Sisters bother no one with proselytizing, and they are the only ones who understand the Dance of the Nucleotides. So they remain safe.

"In all, there is probably no connection beyond that of commerce between Tetravalency and Sisterhood. Both groups *are* secretive, however. All human beings seem secretive to me, but then I am nothing but a miserable syne with the emotions of a cheetah."

"Doctor Tessier," interrupted Catuvel, "my screens."

Dyse and Spider turned to the displays. At the leading edge of Catuvel's blue sensory sphere, a broad arc of brighter blue marked an intensification of mass concentration.

The lurker was moving, on a front some two hundred thousand kilometers in diameter.

"Contact is made at the leading perimeter," said Catuvel's calm voice. "I have visuals from some retiaries, but they're being killed by the thousands. I'm ready with visuals—a moment ago it was all blackbodies, but—"

On the screen nearest Dyse appeared a glistening spear, Catuvel's scale showing it to be about fifty meters long. Even as they watched, the spear assumed colors, all the colors of the rainbow. The head of the thing was, indeed, a head—the elegantly fearsome shape of the skull of some nightmare bird, a lacy skull ten meters long. Its eye sockets, rimmed with crimson, were transparent, and within could be seen the shadowy figures of men. The beak was striped yellow and green, as was the long trailing propulsive abdomen whose ample feed-bladders were fat with propulsive hydrogen. The creature's leaves were furled for war.

"Chebek!" Spider's black eyes seemed to start from his head. "It *is* pirates! How could they mount such mass? It's—"

The image of the chebek disappeared as something killed the retiary that had been observing it.

On another screen appeared four more orange points near that marking Catuvel; she was directing her reflective hoplites to form decoys. And a message went out to all her minions: Strive and Survive!

On the broad mapping screen, the bright blue of Catuvel's leading sensory surface began to fade. "They have millions of badans out there, Dyse! They're eating those poor retiaries alive!" Spider scrambled from the chamber to join his men and coordinate his dozen galliots. By now, a host of purple points, more chebeks, hundreds of them, had appeared within Catuvel's sensory sphere. Two days away, yet, but the tiny badans accompanying them would be far faster.

And such badans! As any of them approached a retiary, Catuvel was able to produce a visual for Dyse. But only for a moment—the little retiaries were dying like flies out there. Badans, of course, are the Hemisphere people's answers to raptores. Like the latter, badans are living projectiles equipped only to kill; but these badans were of far greater variety than the raptores accompanying Catuvel. Ranging in length from half a meter to ten meters, some were equipped with long piercing proboscises, others with gnawing mouth parts for breaching the tough integuments of large Vessels—like Catuvel. And there was a glimpse of one big one with long crescent-shaped blades, four of them, extending outward almost a hundred meters from a muscular thorax.

"Doctor, that badan is going to try to cut my radial muscles. Those people wish to kill me." Catuvel paused, then: "But I don't think they want to kill *you*. Here, the mapping screen." On that screen appeared three bright points of purple.

"Well?" said Dyse.

"Caracors. Hundred-meter man-carriers, fast, probably comfortable quarters for fifty apiece. They're holding back— avoiding violence for the moment. It looks like a ransom run after all." Catuvel was silent for a moment, then her screens went dark.

"Doctor, I am engaging my first raptores. Major Melliden will be seeing to his men. You see to the Princess, and remember me with kindness."

Pantolog was nowhere to be seen. Dyse ran along the

long portrait-hung galleries of the leeward arc of Catuvel toward her heavily defended and armored royal apartments with their separate physiological support systems. Already, the Princess and her suite had sequestered themselves there; velite-soldiers with venomous doglike quadrupedal raptores and syne-flies leaped from Dyse's path and saluted as he sprinted past the great toothed protective sphincters of the Princess' quarters.

Within, people milled about in seeming confusion. All wore springbolts at their sides, and Deepskins—the living integuments that protect human bodies from the Deep's vacuum—were being passed about. Once in the Deep, the creatures would unfurl wide photosynthetic leaves from their shoulders to catch the Sun and convert exhaled carbon dioxide back to oxygen while the rest of the Skin created a closed ecosystem of metabolic functions that could maintain a man for weeks, if necessary, on the waste products of his own body. And each Skin possessed a voice box in order that those wearing them could converse in the Deep. Skins for the hungry vacuum, Skins for war, Skins with eyes of transparent metachitin on a reflective featureless silvery orange face.

Dyse found the Princess already in her Deepskin. A small orange-furred doss clung to her shoulder whispering in her ear information from Catuvel concerning the frightful events without. Linsang was armored with a syne-breastplate whose assorted talons twitched in response to her excitement. In her right hand she held a springbolt whose grip was carved in her own likeness, in her left an assegai whose brass haft tip was similarly fashioned. Beside her stood her secretary, busily unboxing poisonous dragonflies from their anesthetic cage. The insects flitted into the air, hovering about the Princess as their genetic instructions dictated.

Linsang's face, still uncovered, betrayed little of the fear she must have shared with all others aboard Catuvel. This Princess had sometimes seemed to Dyse a mere excitable girl, yet for the moment she appeared as unperturbed as might one awaiting a good breakfast. She smiled a bit as the steward approached, saying, "Ah, Doctor, I was worried. We'll be better off together here—I'm not so confident without being able to hear that Seneschalate accent of yours nearby."

"You look a very pillar of confidence to me, Lady," said Dyse. Eying her array of weaponry, he added, "It's my confidence that's done well by your presence. I feel better already."

The Princess agreed. "Our trajectory's broadened, I think, if we sail together. Broad enough, I hope, to confound the Ride of the Horsemen." She smiled for a moment, looking up into the face of the tall steward, and then her face reddened a bit as she lowered her eyes. "I suppose that to you, Doctor Dyson Tessier, I'm a mere job, a spoiled brat maybe, a Semerling whose family kills for fun? A venomous little animal to be protected from other dangerous beings?"

She paused, watching America Berecynthia give orders to the Sapphonic guards around the chamber. Dyse unslung a pair of springbolts from his own syne-armor, prepared to move on when Linsang laid a hand on his arm. She seemed to sense the nearness of the Forces of Selection, wanted to talk, to clear a mental space with her steward.

"Oh, I know the history of the Seneschalate Sept— the selective processes, the requirements for Writs of

Generation—you know, Doctor, that while your sept is classed as a serving sept, you're by the nature of that Seneschalate genetic history at least as broad in potential trajectory as any ruling Stirps. You'd have to be; Stirps Semerling would have perished in its own excesses centuries ago without the regulating influence of the Sept of Seneschals. In a way, I suppose, we're parasitic on the Seneschalate that we created—it maintains us.''

"Lady, there'd be no Seneschalate Sept and no Dyson Tessier, were it not for your Stirps. As for what you say about the ways of your Stirps, of course, I cannot—''

She interrupted: "Doctor, remember, I'm just a woman to them—I can't hold matter or power except in the name, carried through male descent, of Stirps Semerling. I'm property. On this voyage, I'm a sort of ransomee, no? A bone thrown to Aresia to ensure the safety of the Limestone, and that of my father and brother? Know you, Doctor''— her voice became sharp, bitter—"I'm all too well aware that both my House and Aresia value the Stone far more than they'd value any Semerling daughter, else I'd never have had the leisure to study as I have—I'd have been grooming through my life for Semerling goals, Semerling potentials. I'm comparatively free because I'm worthless to the Stirps except as a bargaining chip. But give me a moment's credit—as a bargaining chip, I've lived with the ever present knowledge of my real worthlessness, and I've tried to compensate with my choice of military training, my love of history, my interest in the sailings of all the Peoples of the Deep, not only that of my own Stirps. I'm a human being, Doctor, I'm *alive*. Do give me that.''

The Princess' blue eyes glistened, perhaps partly with fear for herself but more likely with the pain of the moment, her odd social juxtaposition with her father's subseneschal here in the path of the Horsemen. Dyse's Priamic training had never quite encompassed such a meeting with his Princess, and he found himself rubbing the palms of his hands together behind his back, twining and untwining his fingers as he tried to look deferential and concerned.

And the woman spoke truth—the ladies of Stirps Semerling were indeed a class apart, a second class, one given by necessity to more deviousness even than the men of that ferocious House. Now, this pale Princess seemed to be attempting a bridging of the impassable social gulf between herself and a subseneschal, for what purpose— other than the fear of the moment—Dyse could not divine.

"Uh, Lady," he said, "I'm proud to share the moment with you, I'm, uh, comforted that we're able to, ah, face the Horsemen together. With your permission, I'll see to our guests now."

And without waiting for his Princess' permission, Dyson Tessier nervously strode to the corner where stood the two priests and Ammihud Lewic, Vice-Syndic of the Hamtsan, with his three huge bodyguards; of Lord Durrell and his men there was no sign. Some sixty Sapphonic attendants to the Princess completed the company, milling about the royal quarters; they were prepared to die, if necessary, at their Princess' side.

Okumura link: "Doctor, my bow crescent is pierced and evacuated. A platoon of Major Melliden's men is dead. The major is not with them." Such a strange calm to the voice of Catuvel in his brain.

"Ladies and gentlemen," Dyse called to those unequipped with dosses, "we're hit. Pirates. Catuvel believes it's a ransom run, but the attacking force may well kill her."

The Princess grinned fiercely, eagerly. "Not while we're here, Doctor. Put on your Deepskin!"

Unthinking, Dyse obeyed. At Priam, the examiners required one to don his Skins in less than a minute; Dyse couldn't have taken more than forty seconds this time.

A soldier, her face plate open, saluted him. "Where is the encyclopedia? We have a Skin for it, and there are more about the sweep."

"He disappeared from Sensory Interface. Haven't seen him, but keep that Skin ready!" Oh, Arts of Fist and Foot! Having no hands, the cat could not put on his own Skins!

There was a dull explosion somewhere, and Catuvel's entire skeleton shuddered.

"Doctor," she said evenly, "my Great Hall is pierced and evacuated, along with the main leeward gallery. All internal sphincters now closed."

Pantolog, then, was probably lost—as must be anyone else, Skinless, in the vast halls and corridors now rendered airless.

"Doctor, Major Melliden's galliots are engaged at between two and eight thousand kilometers. Of twelve, ten— now seven—remain alive, and I fear they'll be overcome momentarily. At least forty manned chebeks are within their perimeter, closing faster, far faster, than—" A pause, then: "Doctor, five large badans are approaching me at forty kilometers per second, arriving—"

There was a splintering crash as a tall glass-faced bookshelf swung outward from the walls. The photophores, Catuvel's living internal lighting system, dimmed and brightened again as everyone and everything bounced and whirled into the air in a torrent of flailing arms and legs. Freefall—

the radial musculature was cut, and the vast delicate hull of Catuvel shot undirected away from her center of mass.

Not quite freefall—people and objects began settling slowly toward a wall-become-a-floor. In what was now the ceiling, the sphincter-blocked entryway, its concealing oaken doors broken away, stared down like some atrocious eye. Fraction of a mass—the hull must be end-over-ending it through the Deep.

Dyse took account. Old Cardinal Tamilaria appeared to have broken an arm, but he was alert. The scholar-priest Vereker stood by his superior, springbolt at the ready. The Hamtsan broker, choosing as always to remain weaponless, crouched surrounded by his three trained mute giants; of all in the chamber, only these four men wore no Skins. The Princess and her secretary, both bristling like porcupines with armament, steadied themselves in a cloud of dragonflies whose flight appeared ill adjusted to the light sense of mass remaining about the somersaulting hull of Catuvel. Linsang's furry doss lay partly crushed, dying at her feet. Now there would only be waiting.

Okumura link, Catuvel: "Doctor, without the sensory array and ganglia at my center of mass, I'm blind to the Deep. I can still see within my hull, though. I am unable to locate Major Melliden; he did not leave my person unless in the wind of evacuation. Lord Durrell and his personnel were blown out of the leeward gallery, in Skins— they may be safe. I cannot find Pantolog Five, although last I saw him he'd found someone to help him with Skins. He may also have been expelled in the evacuations. I am almost completely evacuated outside the royal apartments. My internal sensory and mental functions continue intact, though." The voice was so even, so *calm*.

"You're on Okumura, Doctor," said Princess Linsang. "What can you tell us?"

Dyse repeated the information, adding, "We'll be boarded any minute. They'll have badans to gnaw through these sphincters, and men to deal with us."

"Aha! We're well taught to deal with men on Sappho," gloated America. "Dealing with men is a little specialty of ours."

"Filthy pirates," growled Lewic of the Hamtsan. "They eat human flesh, I'm told. Do your worst, Mistress Berecynthia, but I fear we'll all end up as lute strings and banj heads."

"Or ransomees, m'Lord Syndic," said Dyse. "You'd bring a good deal of oxygen from your cohorts."

"No, Doctor. We of the Hamtsan do not deal in ransom. This the pirates have long known. I am useless to them alive, and they will be delighted to make sport of me for many days."

"M'Lord Syndic!" Cardinal Tamilaria, cradling his injured arm, half walked, half floated among the huddled crowd to kneel by Lewic. "Surely there is hope. The Hand will handsomely ransom me, and I will demand ransom for you also. I can do it."

"Ah, Cardinal, you are not a mercantile man. The pirates have no love for matter-brokers, particularly the Hamtsan. You will recall my conversation with that red-toothed savage on the night of the assassination. Perhaps you could trouble yourself to ease my mind with the Rite of Passing?"

"M'Lord, you are quite unhurt. Come to your senses, man! Where is your *will?*"

"My will for what, Your Eminence? My will to live? It

is well away in the Deep, at present, perhaps riding with a megaliter of oxygen to Troy, or the Holy Isles. Now, the Rite of Passing? Please, Cardinal, a favor to an old man.''

''I must refuse, m'Lord Syndic. I will not be party to this silly display.''

''Very good, then, Your Eminence. Princess Linsang? Lady, know my gratefulness for the generosity of your House. And you, Doctor Tessier. Your company's been a pleasure.''

''M'Lord Syndic,'' Dyse protested, ''listen to your Cardinal! You're healthy and unhurt, and there are three caracors approaching whose facilities will more than accommodate you. It's a ransom sailing, m'Lord!''

''Doctor, you're a young man. For me there is no ransom. Please bear with me.'' The Syndic rose unsteadily to his feet, the light mass in the room causing him to float a bit as he stood.

''Tell my relatives at the Hamtsan Brokerage that I passed quietly. Ask them to say me the Rite of Passing. I salute you all, and may the Horsemen ever smile on you.'' With a wave of his hand, he silenced a clamor of opposition.

The Syndic stood at attention, then, a tall man, handsome in that pale Hamtsan way. He nodded once, and before anyone could make a move to stop him bowed his head to one of his mute giants, who instantly placed at the nape of his master's neck a springbolt muzzle.

Phut!

Ammihud Lewic, twelfth Vice-Syndic of the Hamtsan Brokerage, settled slowly to the bulkhead, a short broadhead dart protruding from the bridge of his nose. In the next instant the three giants bowed to the company at large, slow motion, low mass. Then, bowing to one another, each pointed his springbolt upward beneath his own chin and discharged. In a last dreamlike falling, all came to rest protectively over the body of the Syndic.

Linsang, Princess, spread a cloak atop them, an orange velvet monument to the honor of Ammihud Lewic and his duty-bound men.

There followed an hour of silence, during which Catuvel flooded the royal apartment with a scent of roses. I wonder, thought Dyse, about an intelligent syne's understanding of humanity. I wonder if my Pantolog is alive. I wonder what *he'd* say. No, I don't. I know. He is as much cat as syne, and he'd only be amused—especially at the Cardinal's regard of suicide as sin. But he'd take pride in the Syndic's strange courage, that I don't doubt.

Okumura: "Doctor, we're boarded. Two twenty-man platoons, more following, clothed in green-trimmed Deepskins. They're heading for the royal apartment with a badan—one with a toothed proboscis. They seem to know my anatomy and exactly what they seek."

"Thank you, Catuvel. You've done well." Dyse rose unsteadily in the light mass, hand against the floor-that-was-a-wall.

"Attention. Catuvel tells me that we're boarded, and that a syne will shortly bore through the sphincters protecting these apartments. We may now lay down our arms."

"Hah! Surrender, Steward? Where are your Priamic arts?" The Princess rose in turn, fastening the faceplate of her Deepskin. "They may want me and the priests alive, but they'll kill everyone else in the room, including you! Steward, fight for your life, and I'll join you. Merry, to my back!"

"Yes, *ma'am*," shouted the secretary, leaping to her

feet so forgetfully fast that she executed a half somersault in the low mass. *Duty,* thought Dyse, and gave in.

There was a low grinding noise and various thumps as something went to work on the meter-thick metachitin sphincter in the "ceiling" of the chamber. In all their Deepskins, an accented voice spoke:

"We are in total control of this sweep. We want the Princess Linsang and two priests of the Hand of Man. We want them alive. Are they within?"

"I am," said Linsang, and her voice was carried to all of the Skins and the listeners within them.

"How many share your quarters? And have you the Limestone, bread of Earth's body?" The soft foreign voice hissed a bit in all their ears.

"Only my secretary," she lied, "and the priests under my protection, and the Limestone, of course—it's under my protection also. I suppose you'll collect quite a ransom, pirates."

"Our purposes are our own," said the accented voice. "We are in vacuum here. Are your Deepskins conscious?"

"Yes, warthog, come on in. We'll live." Linsang motioned her assembled forces to positions of concealment among the tumuli of junk in the room. Only America and the priests remained unhidden.

Over his private Okumura to Catuvel, Dyse ordered the photophores dimmed and waited in the dark while the Princess stood beneath the sphincter. The leathery skin bulged, then tore outward, the room evacuating in a great FOOMP and flying whirlwind of clothing and documents.

A toothy legless two-meter badan floated down and bounced slowly on the opposite wall-turned-floor, followed by a faceless green-clad man, springbolt ready, and another, and another, and another.

"Lady Princess," said the strange hissing voice, "please to come with me. And these priests. You." The green-clad figure pointed at Merry. "Who you are?"

"She's my secretary, scorpion-pig," snarled the Princess in what seemed to Dyse a deliberately childish tone. "She goes with me."

"Stand aside, please, seketary," said the accented voice.

"Yes, SIR!" shouted Merry, most impressively Sapphonically, and discharged a concealed springbolt into the man's faceplate.

A swirl of low-mass movement. Another green-clad one grabbed the Princess, whose syne-armor erupted into his abdomen. Blood flew, vaporized into a frozen pink mist. More men, a green cataract, fell through the rupture in the "ceiling," and the Sapphonic amazons burst from concealment in a weirdly silent welter of flying bolts, taloned armor and knives. Someone in silvery green shoved the priests aside, someone in silvery orange shot the green man. Someone in green landed feet first on the back of the fearsome America Berecynthia, knocking her away from the equally fearsome Princess; something seemingly quadrupedal in orangey silver darted past the green man, somehow in the process opening his belly to the vacuum. Dyse, cracking a green-Skinned skirmisher's faceplate, leaped to the Princess' side. Back to back, they faced a growing circle of greenly Deepskinned figures.

Movement ceased.

"You are ours," said an oddly familiar voice in Dyse's Deepskin. "Please be still. Doctor Tessier, we meet again. It is my pleasure."

"You—the Whip! Warthog indeed, you scum, you Earthborn—"

"Doctor, I am fatigued. You likewise. Rest, please." The faceless green figure immediately before Dyse raised a springbolt and discharged it.

A buzzing numbness, a maelstrom, through whose whirling mists Dyse saw the tiny peg stuck in his sternum— no broadhead, but a miniature feathered hypodermic needle around whose entry hole the viscous sealant of his Deepskin already congealed. He saw, too, the slow-motion approach toward his face of the floor-that-was-a-wall, and the broken intricacy of its trampled carving. Rest.

Chapter 8: In which we meet Hunger personified

What is a ship but a prison?

> —*Anatomy of Melancholy,*
> Burton the Engli

UP, UP through the misty maelstrom toward light, yellow light, a yellow face—a mask! A round thing, black and yellow, with golden black-rimmed eyes, a—a—Dyse's consciousness returned in a flood of adrenalin, and his muscles tensed for flight. But astonished recognition overcame the hormonal reflex—the weird mask before him was the spotted, self-satisfied face of none other than Pantolog Five, his own encyclopedia!

Over the Okumura link, the creature purred his greeting.

"You've rested very well, Doctor. Through five weeks and three days you have slept. Myself likewise, although with my quicker metabolism I awoke two days ago. The food is not the best here, but I have eaten more of it in compensation."

Dyse was lying on a low couch, its musculature embracing him comfortably. "Must get up," he said through the Okumura link. He tried to rise, but his muscles seemed paralyzed. "Drugs—"

"You're not drugged any longer, honored Doctor. You have been unconscious for more than five weeks—you expect too much of your muscles, which have been still throughout that time. It took me some three hours to regain full coordination; it'll take you an hour or two longer. There are stimulants, though, to speed the process. I have made the acquaintance of this splendid physyne, Swo Yeak, who has attended our, ah, hibernation, and he will see to your requests."

A new voice, accented, spoke in human tones through a set of physyne vocal cords. "Honored Doctor, I am at your service. We may provide massage to quicken your recovery, if you like; your cells show traces of theophylline, caffeine and other vegetable-based stimulants to whose use you are accustomed. I can provide these also."

"Uh, ah, thank you, Swo Yeak." Dyse painfully turned his head to regard a quadrupedal physyne rather resembling a huge fat fox—its assorted medical appendages were hidden (thank goodness!) beneath a thick red fur. The thing regarded him attentively with yellow eyes, slit-pupils widening a bit as Dyse struggled to move.

"Please, Doctor, patience. Your physiology is entirely healthy, but as with all things of beauty a physiology requires a certain meditative appreciation of the whole of its parts.''

Accented or not, all physynes seemed to share this tendency to lecture . . . legend said that in the days of the ancients there were *men* of medicine. Had they lectured like physynes? And what am I doing here alone with a pair of damned professorial synes?

"Pantolog—the others? Where are they? Is anyone left? Where are *we?* This Swo Yeak is no Regency physyne!''

"One at a time, Master. First, I know regrettably little of anyone else's whereabouts save that of Major Melliden, who remains sleeping in the care of Swo Yeak, here.''

"Honored Doctor,'' said the physyne, "the soldier will awaken in approximately four hours and twenty-two minutes from this moment. He has more years than do you, and his metabolism is somewhat slower. Also, he is a considerably larger man.'' Swo Yeak paused, his long nose pointing for a moment toward the floor. "I have never examined people of the Plate before; my masters rarely take living foreigners with them. Are all so large as yourself and your soldier companion?''

Pantolog broke in: "The Plate has more material resources, Swo Yeak. The people of the educated classes eat more. Now, I saw a place called Puppy once, one of the Trojan Regent's bondsman Islands, where the average individual human size was far smaller than that of—''

Dyse forced himself up on his elbows. "Pantolog! Where *are* we?''

"Forgive me, honored Doctor. You might have learned something. Oh well, we are on a caracor, well jetted, of ninety-seven meters' length and ten meters' diameter, with whom I do not share an Okumura link. My friend Swo

Yeak does, but he is not permitted to share it with me. I
have seen no human activity aboard, although I have seen
only a small portion of this Vessel. Still, Swo Yeak and I
have amused ourselves by looking out the viewports and
attempting to determine our location.

"As nearly as I can judge, we have been following a
trajectory that, from our present point of view, places the
Sun in the constellation Centaurus. Named, incidentally,
after the European Centaur mentioned in that fable of Lord
Durrell's. At any rate, we are probably about fifty-five
degrees off-Plate in the Hemisphere of the Hook." The cat
winked at Swo Yeak.

"Also, dear Doctor," he continued, "we are decelerating at one mass, our caracor having done a flip; the surface
on which we stand is the forward side of a large bulkhead.
I know nothing of our destination, though. We are farther
into the Hemisphere than most civilized folk would care to
penetrate."

"I am permitted to add, Doctor," said Swo Yeak, "that
your time of sleep was coordinated closely with our time
of travel. We will reach our destination, my home, in
twelve hours, forty-seven minutes, approximately, from
this moment. During that interval you will come to feel
much better. Furthermore, the caracor in whose care we
travel is named Hunger. Two of her sisters, Avidity and
Drought, accompany her, each at a distance of fifty thousand kilometers. Hunger is well disposed toward you,
Doctor, never fear."

"No doubt," growled Dyse. "I'd like to see a human
being or two—even that treacherous Hook."

The physyne spoke again: "Doctor, human beings are
awakening all over this Vessel. No doubt someone will see

you soon, once I am satisfied that your condition will permit a comfortable interview. As for my master whom you call Hook, he rides the caracor Avidity, who travels with us. Do have patience, Doctor.''

''Patience. Coffee.'' Dyse was now able to sit up and swing his feet to the floor. Blood rushed to them—for a moment they felt ready to burst before the veins in his legs controlled the flow. He was naked, but the physyne extruded an appendage from where its ribs ought to have been, a powerful four-fingered clawed arm over which was draped—!—an entire set, clean and unwrinkled, of the formal vestments of Dyson Tessier's Regency stewardship!

''We felt, Doctor, that on leaving Catuvel so unexpectedly we ought not to bring a messy steward.'' Pantolog laid his ears back smugly.

''Then you were conscious throughout the boarding?''

''Indeed, honored Doctor. I fled Sensory Interface when it became apparent that Catuvel would be pierced. I found a servant who assisted me with a suitable Deepskin. The servant, unfortunately, was killed in the piercing. I, ah, made my way to the royal apartments behind a number of our captors who were carrying a syne of the sort that can chew Rocks—I felt that those folk would surely admit me, even if you and the Lady Linsang would not. I was not disappointed; the green-clad ones were very obliging, although they knew nothing of my presence.''

Dyse tried to stand, flexing his toes. He wished to dress, and to know more. ''Were you there for the final fighting, then?''

''Yes, Doctor, very much so. As a matter of fact, I even participated, in my small way.'' The encyclopedia's Okumura voice took on a purr of conceit.

"How can an encyclopedia participate in battle, even such a vainglorious one as yourself?"

"Recall honored Master, that on Summer Semerlinga we learned that I am not simply an encyclopedia. The matter of the Regent's antelope and my female conspecific, you know. When I came uninvited to the battle, I saw green-clad men inconveniencing my human associates. I have these dewclaws"—he lifted a foreleg, displaying a two-centimeter scythelike talon where the thumb of a man would be—"and so has my Deepskin, somewhat magnified. And the anatomy of a man is very like that of an antelope— same soft spots. I therefore saw an opportunity to gain some practice as a cheetah, for I find that I love being a cheetah more than anything else—if a mere ridiculous syne can be said to love."

"Preposterous," said Dyse, dressing all the while. "Preposterous. Synes are too specialized in—"

"Forgive me, honored Doctor," interrupted Swo Yeak, "but my associates report that your encyclopedia disemboweled some eight fighting men before being restrained by a tentacled badan. Most unusual. Indeed, his life would not have been preserved but for this behavior. In some ways he is like unto the Chimaeras of the ancients."

"Or the Centaur of Marxian III," said Pantolog, "except that I am incapable of destroying a being so superb as myself."

"Perhaps sometime I'll offer to do it for you, and save you the trouble." Dyse moved toward a water basin which was extruded by Hunger from her body wall. She was obviously watching his every move; jewellike sets of compound eyes completely ringed the chamber's perimeter. Beside the basin was a razor of unusual make, and a bar of translucent green soap. He had grown quite a beard in his five weeks of sleep.

After lathering his face, Dyse spoke again. "What of Catuvel? Is she still alive?"

"I'm unable to say," said Pantolog. "Swo Yeak tells me that she was left; no scavengers were set on her by our attackers, for the purpose of the attack was primarily the capture of the Princess Linsang—oh yes, and the Limestone, with which they also nabbed the body of Senator Fairleigh. Although I do not know who mounted that huge attack, I can certainly say that it was worth their effort. Quite a haul. Of course, they had reason to flee the Plate quickly, so they paid little attention to Catuvel, who was, in addition to being too large, quite helpless. Others will attack her, though, I fear, unless some Trojans reach her quickly; she is a treasure of matter, and the Deep is full of hungry scavengers."

Dyse bit his lower lip. Catuvel, my friend, I hope to see you well again . . . .

Without, fifty thousand kilometers away from each other and from Hunger, the caracors Avidity and Drought paralleled their sister at identical deceleration. Chromatophores in the integuments of all three commenced coloring their surfaces through the hours, yellow and green spangling them in intricate patterns as they slowed themselves. From their thoracic bulges grew broad leaves, two apiece, each leaf turned toward the distant face of Brazenface the Sun in a search for food and warmth. As they decelerated, the sisters spoke over lightlink one with another:

"Hail, flesh of my flesh! I, Hunger, salute you—it is

good to break silence and resume visibility. The blackbody cloak is a somber one.''

"Hail, Sister Hunger. The blackbody cloak is good, though, among the minions of the Plate.'' This was Drought.

"Even so. The Platers would devour us. Now, though, I'm glad to show my colored robes to Brazenface and the people of our home.''

"Hail, flesh of my flesh! I, Avidity, salute you. My Plater wards are well awake, along with my masters. The Platers seem most ill disposed toward me—they are two priests of the Hand and two females, ferocious ones, of the Regency of Troy. I am pleased that they are disarmed; they would as soon pierce my flesh as consume the food and drink I provide them.''

"Justly so. They are prisoners. In other circumstances they would imprison our masters, and under far less pleasant conditions. They will soon learn patience.''

The Deep, even in the Hemispheric waste, is full of conversation.

Within the skin of Avidity, the physyne Fea Yeak made obeisance—uselessly—to his royal charge. "Lady Princess, our destination is thirty minutes away. You will be experiencing two seconds of freefall before linkage. Avidity, our caracor, asks that you forgive that inconvenience and do us the honor of returning to your couch when notified to do so.''

"Yes, doggy, I'll lie down when told to, and roll over and speak, too. Will I be fed a cracker?'' Linsang Semerling had been awake for some five hours, sharing with her secretary quarters identical to those housing Dyse and Pantolog fifty thousand kilometers away. Her captors had raided her wardrobe, so that she was clothed in clean and neatly pressed dinner dress.

"Listen, Linsang," said Merry, "don't pick on the physyne—it's doing its best by us."

"The miserable thing hasn't told us a thing about our whereabouts in the past five hours. Is that its best?"

"Regrettably, Lady, I am but a physyne under the command of my masters." The creature paused, listening as might a fox for a mouse in the grass to some Okumura link before continuing: "I am instructed to advise you that the after sphincter of this chamber will now open, permitting Avidity's other two Plater guests to join you."

Instantly, a sphincter dilated through the floor, and a moment later the aged Cardinal clambered through, followed by his scholarly assistant. Both were clothed formally—their captors had overlooked nothing.

"Lady Princess! Mistress Berecynthia! There's little to fear, I hope—they're treating us well enough, and I'm sure we'll, ah, be bought back shortly. Have you any idea where we are?"

The Princess curtsied, said, "None, Your Eminence. But your arm! It was broken, wasn't it?"

The old man smiled. "The grace of the Horsemen placed me under the splendid care of the physyne Fea Yeak during our long nap. He took care of the arm. In fact, I feel a new man all over—more fit than I've been in years."

"Lady Princess, Your Eminence, my master, Saker the Swift." The physyne lay down on the floor, and through the sphincter climbed a small green-clad man. A tuft of hair on the back of his head, his only hair, in fact, was braided in dozens of tiny jeweled rings; his tunic and trousers were of green silk, and he wore an ivory-white syne-armor jerkin.

Recognizing the little man at once, both priests instinctively reached for weapons that they did not, luckily for them, possess. "Offspring of Earth! You crooked little ape! Your name was Hook once, was it not?"

"Lady Princess," said the Whip, clicking his armored heels together. "Your Eminence, Father. Forgive me for your, ah, temporarily reduced circumstances. Yes, my name is Hook—to such as the Hamtsan brokers of oxygen. I wished of the late Vice-Syndic his intestines, if you will overlook my regrettable indelicacy, ladies. These intestines I was able to locate, too, although unfortunately the Syndic was not alive to donate them personally as I might have wished. He died in sin, did he not, Your Eminence? And so he lived. But that is past. My name among my people is Saker the Swift, and for the moment you are my people. I am both honored and enriched by your presence." The softness of his voice, his accented Lubret, reminded the Princess of the hissing of a snake.

"You slippery little worm! How did you escape Summer Semerlinga?"

"Lady, after the unfortunate extinction of your fiancé, I understood that your father the Regent planned to offer me up to Aresia as partial compensation—the Aresian Emperor, after all, has no greater affection for my folk than do you of the Path of Jove. Still, I felt that I was an insignificant and unworthy gift, and to spare your father further humiliation betook myself elsewhere. We of the Free Deep are well experienced, you know, in betaking ourselves elsewhere.

"Your father was then forced to seek another form of

compensation; the elaborate deaths of your cousins of the House of Spier, and also of some cooks, seemed not to have appeased his Aresian counterpart. So he was forced to offer *this* pretty, for whose safety I am now responsible.'' And the Whip pulled the Limestone, glittering in its diamond shell, from a pouch at his belt.

"The Limestone! You took it all, pirate, didn't you?!''

"That which was worth taking, Lady. You note also that we preserved your secretary's life, and even brought some of your underwear, that your temporary stay at my home might be more comfortable. I am here to inform you that we will arrive at my birthplace within fifteen minutes, and to offer my own meager welcome.'Tis best that we all couch ourselves now; my friend Avidity, to whom you owe your sustenance these past weeks, will dilate a port through which you may observe the approach from your couches. Lady, Your Eminence, Father Bishop, I must be elsewhere. I will see you again soon.''

Pocketing the Limestone with a sharp-toothed smile, the Whip descended again through the sphincter in the floor. "*Too* soon, I'm sure," muttered Merry. "Linsang, we'd best hit the couches.''

Each of the four ransomees lay in a couch, the gentle muscles of the couches cradled them, and opposite their positions the integument of the wall of Avidity dilated to reveal a four-meter port through which the starry Deep glistened like a sequined velvet cloak. Avidity's movement was changing, and the stars passed slowly across their view. Here and there a syne moved by, a driver or a caracor, leaves spread wide. They were come to a place of commerce.

And then their rotation caught them a vision of an

Island, a blackbody Island, ovoid, a somber egg whose longer axis spanned some twenty kilometers; then its opposite-spin twin, linked to it across annular musculature thirty kilometers long. Each was ringed by feeding-toroids so large that only the ends of the inhabited eggs protruded from their life-giving sheaths. Beyond, leaves and mirrors hundreds of kilometers across collected the waves of the Sunsea.

"Small Islands and huge feeding-toroids," said Merry. "Lots of people, *lots* of people. Linsang, I can't imagine where we are!"

A caracor passed the viewport, then another. They were paralleling Avidity's movement, and all neared the growing Islands as one, gradually matching the near Island's perimeter rotation. A set of appendages extruded by the Island swung into view, each appendage equipped with a compound eye with which it would locate the appropriate catchjoints on the approaching caracors.

Closer, closer, a momentary exhilaration of freefall, and the three caracors were united with the Island's revolving black skin. A voice spoke—the physyne Fea Yeak, who had wedged himself into his own couch: "Ladies and gentlemen, welcome to my home and that of your hostess Avidity. The ancient Islands of Wirtanen II."

Chapter 9: In which hersey speaks aloud

What lives out in the Hemispheres?
What brooding vengeance swims there,
And guides the starving chebeks in
To feed their cold despair?

—8th Versicle of the Litany of Assegai,
from the Trickster's Sailing

"DOCTOR TESSIER, again I am honored." The Whip Saker the Swift clicked his heels together. "Do forgive us for your separation from your executive officer, but Major Melliden is, after all, a fighting man. Like him, I am most careful. He rejoins us momentarily."

The Whip opened a gate carved from a flat sheet of

some bonelike material, leading Dyse and Pantolog into a meditation garden. It was the only space containing vegetation that they'd seen in their entire day on this teeming Island, and the odor of its old pines and jasmine vines was a relaxant to their overwrought minds. This oasis was tiny—its walled enclosure was but ten meters on a side and grew outward from the curving rim of a domed rotunda that dominated the entire vista presented by this strange Island of Wirtanen II. Within that palatial dome, they'd been told, they would eventually learn something of the fate that awaited them. For now at least there was the soothing smell of the garden and tea in the offing.

The square of the garden centered on four lifelike ivory statues, dancing female nudes, whose interlinked hands together supported a black cube. A cube, withal, exactly like that of the Trickster's Sailing, minus the latter's inevitable Engli inscription.

"Here is your officer." The Whip clicked his heels again as Spider Melliden entered the garden gate escorted by two green-clad men over whom he towered like a fir tree.

"Spider!" Dyse jumped to his side, grinning.

The giant laughed, a deep and roaring laugh. "How these little fellows searched me, Doc! Probed for Okumuras, looked up my ass for—who knows? Maybe they thought I had an assegai hidden in my gut—why, look here!"

The black cube, resting on the hands of its four erotically disposed nudes, extracted from the giant velite an automatic genuflection before he recalled his alien surroundings.

"What've you little buggers to do with the Trickster's Sailing?"

"Trickster's Sailing, Major?" The Whip looked thoughtfully at the black cube. "The Trickster—is he that Plater men of your ilk invoke under torture, no? I know nothing else of it."

"*This* is Lord Gagarin's Ride!" Spider gestured at the cube. "How come you by it, midget?"

"The Principle of Heisenberg, Major," said the Whip, showing his pointed teeth in a polite smile. "Heisenberg was a European; it was he who framed in words the nature of Uncertainty with which we of the Free Deep are fated always to be on intimate terms. It has no bearing on your Trickster of which I am aware. But we will shortly be in the presence of a person who may enlighten us as to any connection between the two. In the meantime, here is tea."

Another green-clad man entered, carrying a tray on which stood an elaborately engraved decanter, small cups and some plates of the unrecognizable colored gelatinous cubes on which all folk of Wirtanen seemed to subsist.

"Gah! Poisoned," Spider said, spurning the cubes. He nonetheless joined the others in taking a cup of the steaming tea—the presence of the black cube in this garden had already convinced him that, whatever the barbaric Whip had called the cube, Lord Gagarin yet sailed alongside.

Pantolog spoke over his Okumura to Dyse. "Doctor, this cube is most interesting. As they call this place the Islands of Wirtanen II, we can of course reason that it is a stronghold of Batesians. But the presence of this cube amongst both Gagarinians and Batesians suggests common origins, no? This place is full of delightful mysteries—and plenty of matter, considering the desolation that characterizes off-Plate space as a whole."

"*Stolen* matter, no doubt," said Dyse over the silent link to the encyclopedia. "Stolen, probably from—"

"Forgive me, Doctor," said the Whip, "but I cannot help perceiving a certain rudeness in your employment of that Okumura link with your beast, here. We kept the thing alive because it is a curiosity; among other things, it transcended its specialization and attacked men. It may still do so, in which case it, you and your executive officer will be liquidated into our ecosystems—and we are a hungry folk. Do take care with your syne."

"Doctor," Pantolog intruded, "these four nudes, are they not suggestive of—"

"Not now, you damned fool! Listen and look around you—*learn* something!"

And look around the encyclopedia did, learning all the while. He saw that this Island was most unusual by Plate standards, for instead of being grown as a long cylinder it was shaped like a long egg; while its central volume was in Deep vacuum, the fifty-meter-high living space within its rotating shell was transparently roofed so that, looking up, one might clearly see the opposite side five kilometers away at the equator.

No waste of air *here,* thought the encyclopedia, nor of any other matter. Every square meter a living area, except at the leeward end of the ovoid, through which sunlight poured from outer leeward mirrors to an odd axial mirror, there to be reflected downward into the living space. No Island-long expanses of Sunlight alternating with forested "valleys"—no forests, indeed. Probably matter poverty, for millennia.

And yet there was leisure here, leisure to create. Everywhere were aesthetically intertwined carvings of vegetation, for rest to the eye in a place almost completely devoid of living plants. Individual structures, grown from various fruitwoods, bone and ivory, were densely sculpted with inscriptions from what Pantolog recognized in some cases as ancient Plate history—but oddly twisted history, seeing as they were Batesian-inspired inscriptions rather than derived from the Annals of the Hand with which his own learning-centers had been infused. And the inscriptions, many of them, were in the language of Old Wirtanen, itself lost from the Plate for millennia save in the minds of scholars like Pantolog. Lucky that such as the Whip here were able to converse in Lubret, if not the Trojan branch of that Platewide language. And such an interesting Lubret the Whip spoke, with its odd blend of Wirtanen accents and primordial Eurasian roots! Withal, the dead, the almost-forgotten, seemed to Pantolog to whisper again here, touching him across thousands of anni of history.

The conversation between the three human beings in the garden remained strained for some minutes as Dyse and Spider sparred vocally with the Whip. Then a pair of pointy-toothed hairless green-clad pirates entered the garden and addressed themselves to Saker the Swift, heels clicking.

"Honored Whip, the Chancellor will see you and your guests."

"Ah, Doctor Tessier, Major Melliden. Now you will be questioned, and perhaps you may ask questions of your own." The Whip stood, motioning his three wards through an ornate portal into the adjoining rotunda.

They entered a long, arched passageway, its vaulting fruitwood ribs meeting at their apices in knotted bosses of Sisterhood-grown ivory linked by a tracery of intertwined

Batesian carving. Entablatures above a multitude of side
portals bore representations of long-gone persecutions and
migrations; the Hand of Man was pictured in these scenes
as a mailed Fist—the Holy Fist, agent of a thousand
pogroms in the dim past.

And into a great circular hall, eighty meters in diameter
at least, over which soared the dome they'd seen from
without. Some forty meters above, at the dome's apex,
colored light filtered through a rosette of stained glass
mounted in a lacy skeleton whose lines portrayed the
scarred face of Har Bates himself. The soft light seemed to
bring that face alive, pouring into the hemispherical space
a multicolored luminosity that showed the floor to be a
great mosaic mapping of the matter-rich Plate that bisects
the Systemic Sphere.

At the center of the hall's immensity there lay a flat
smiling representation in brass of a man's face—the Sun,
Old Brazenface Himself. Then circles, ever wider, of planetary orbits, a broad circlet in gold for the Rocks, all the
way to the path of cold Pluto at the vast room's rim. On
this map the Trojan Points of Jove were orange metal
inlays of lupine leaves; the Aresian archipelago was a
triskelion of knife-wielding arms. All of the planets were
in a line from Pluto at the portal to Old Brazenface at the
center; opposite the Sun from Earth, in Her orbit, the Holy
Isles of the Hand were marked, not with a Sword-and-
Helix, but with that ever present mailed Fist.

Earth Herself was a knot of four women, dancing about
a black square, all inlaid in a blue circle half a meter in
diameter.

Eighty meters opposite the portal by which they entered,
astride Pluto's Path, stood a small carved dais on which sat

an old woman, black-clad and hooded. Toward her, across the entire Plate in miniature, walked Dyson Tessier, Spider Melliden and Pantolog Five with their green-clad escort. Inward, inward, across each planet to Brazenface's circle, and outward again, across the paths of Mercury, Venus, Earth—marred with the gray-mailed Fist—Mars, the Rocks' wide gold expanse, Jove, Saturn, Uranus, Neptune, and onward to a point halfway between the Paths of Neptune and Pluto, where they were stopped before the tiny wizened woman, who sat immovable, dwarfed by her seat and by two green-robed men at her sides.

At her feet, on a small red-cushioned wooden pedestal, lay the Limestone in its cubical diamond shell.

The Whip clicked his heels, the sharp sound echoing for some seconds through the cavernous space around them. "Chancellor, we are honored. Our guests of the Trojan serving classes."

The diminutive creature on the dais beckoned them closer, and in perfect Lubret spoke: "Doctor Tessier, Major Melliden, welcome to my home. This is the Hemispheric Hall of the Islands of Wirtanen II, and I am privileged to be Chancellor here. I am Niagara, Falling-water, if you wish." Her voice was thin, itself like falling water. She can't be much over a meter tall, thought Dyse.

Trojans both, Dyse and Spider slapped their right hands smartly across their hearts. "We are honored, Chancellor Falling-water," Dyse began—but Pantolog, ever unpredictable, began trotting toward a carving remarkably like a cheetah that formed part of an animal tableau surrounding the base of the Chancellor's dais.

"Doctor Tessier, your encyclopedia is being closely watched by the Hemispheric Hall, who will destroy it and

you if it attempts one of these unusual homicidal episodes.''
The Chancellor did not move as she spoke, but Dyse
noticed the dilation of several small sphincters within the
sculpted arms of her seat. Springbolts within, no doubt.

Pantolog, too, understood and froze.

"Doctor, your syne is most acute. You may, if you like,
use your Okumura link with it in my presence.''

Dyse listened for a moment over the link, then: "My
servant, Pantolog Five, thanks you. As an encyclopedia,
he is motivated primarily by curiosity, and well under-
stands the futility of any aggressive act here.''

"Excellent, Doctor,'' said the diminutive Chancellor.
"We have a saying here, though: 'Curiosity killed the
cat.' ''

"We have the same saying, Chancellor. Indeed, curiosity has come close to killing this one several times.''

"You understand me then, syne. Speaking through Doctor Tessier, please answer my questions. You are of a most
interesting yellow color. Are you perhaps a representation
of the cheetah, swiftest of quadrupeds?''

"Yes, Chancellor Falling-water. More than a representation; I *am* a cheetah, with an artificially augmented mind
and an Okumura link of course. My, ah, 'homicidal episode'
is more of the cheetah than of the encyclopedia. I regret
the damage to your minions, but at the time it seemed
necessary.''

"Within the framework of your origins, syne, you acted
commendably. You do seem, however, a good incarnation
of Heisenberg's Principle. I can't believe that you were
designed to behave in such a manner in defense of your
masters—you are, after all, an encyclopedia.''

"No, Chancellor, of late I often feel the design of my body, Sisterhood-grown, at odds with their intent."

"Well spoken, syne, although few of your ilk know anything of the intent of those who grew them. Do you know anything of the Book of Har Bates?"

"Access to that Book, Chancellor, was eliminated long ago from the Plate by the propaganda ministries of the Hand of Man. I know nothing of it that has not filtered through the fingers of that Hand."

"As I thought. Know then, syne, since your lives are forfeit, that one perhaps like you figures in a verse of the Book. From that portion entitled *The Extension of the Lines of Probability,* written not by Bates himself but by some of his followers after he was murdered. It is to the verse in question that you owe your current position, and the position of these men with you, among the living for the moment. You are said occasionally to be given to excesses of self-regard; rein these excesses in now, and ponder these lines:

> "When off the Plate
>   The Limestone, that alone of Earth
>   Recalls to us Her frame,
>
> "Returns to you, my wanderers,
>   Look you then for a mind of gold,
>   A Beast in all but name."

The Chancellor leaned forward, her pointed chin cradled in a tiny withered hand, her elbow resting on her knee. Onyx-black eyes fastened on Pantolog, glittering in their deep sockets, examined him minutely. Then she moved swiftly, her black robe rustling as she pointed at the Limestone before her.

"What say you, syne, to your presence here in conjunction with *this?*"

Pantolog's black-tipped tail twitched in agitation. "Chancellor Falling-water, I have little to say. Those lines sound to me like prophecy, and prophecy has a way of fulfilling itself in the minds of those who attend to it. Myself, I was given little sense of religion, if you'll forgive me, by my growers, and it was none of my doing that brought either the Limestone or myself here."

"I'm certain of *that*, at least." The Chancellor smiled slightly, the leathery skin at the corners of her eyes crinkling. "And you'll know nothing of the verse that I repeat now, with your indulgence:

"The resource of the Deep may fail, but in your hour of need
The Earth will call you, Heisenberg's children,
    with bread of Her body.

"With an awakening of Machines, whisper back:
    She'll have had done with revenge."

Niagara, Falling-water, picked up the Limestone and turned it over in her little hands so that colored light sparkled from its casing into Pantolog's face.

" 'Bread of Earth.' Not much, is it, gentlemen? A bit of rock, with little sea-shapes on its surface, all grown into a Tetravalency diamond. Our Book says that of Earth this alone survived the Synthetic Wars, that it was preserved by the earliest Sisterhood and passed by them to Har Bates some forty-five centuries ago. Then your Hand stole it from him, setting it before him so he could see it as they unraveled his intestines.

"Some later Pollex of your Hand bought its casing from the Tetravalency—it's said that the Stone was susceptible to the acids of people's fingertips. For services rendered the Hand by the rulers of Troy during the Great Black, Lenin X of the Hand presented it to Stirps Carraghan; from that stirps it was stolen by the Trucidate Stirps Semerling. Now it returns to us, the 'heretical Batesian pirates,' while on its way back across the Rocks to Aresia . . . if only it could speak!"

Spider, who was infected by a growing superstitious awe of these circumstances—the cube of the Principle of Heisenberg, the Limestone, the Book of Bates's strange words—slapped his hand across his chest. "Chancellor Falling-water, with your permission, what do *you* make of all this? I am only a soldier—I have no knowledge of significance, least of all of the Limestone—save its great worth."

" 'Only a soldier,' Major? Your decorations mark you as a velite of the First Security Maniple of the ruling house of Troy, and thus one of great resource. You also, I believe, follow the Sailing of Gagarin—that which my soldiers call Heisenberg's Principle. The Principle of Uncertainty, Major, and it is Uncertainty that stares us all in the face at present.

"Allow me, Major, a momentary look into the future of the Peoples of the Deep. All of them—yours, mine, all who live and call themselves human.

"Let us suppose that your Regent sees fit to go to war with Aresia, or vice versa, over the matter in the Rocks. I believe this will happen shortly. Now, every single Rock's position and orbit is known to both of the great Plater states; every Rock therefore has a Trojan or Aresian retiary hovering about it, and every such retiary has one or more badans—raptores, you call them—within easy lightlink call. The Rocks, in short, are a wasp's nest of synes set to fly at both of the states hoping to inherit them.

"Once released, the array of Plater organisms inhabiting the Rocks would destroy both Plater states. We'd have another Great Black, Major, one worse than before; the millions of raptores left among the Rocks, feeding on the Sunsea, patient, mindless, directionless, grown to kill, would remain alive for centuries. They would attack any living thing, and the belts of Rocks would become uncrossable, a place of terror, a sad but fitting memorial to the Trojan and Aresian tyrannies.

"Worse even than that, the Hand would have remained carefully uninvolved, and, being the only great power to do so, would in essence inherit the Plate. Its Fist would crush the remaining fragments of humanity in a grip that would take millennia to break."

"Ay," said Spider, "I see your meaning, Chancellor. But surely the Islands of Wirtanen II, with such as Saker here, would—"

"Major, think you that Wirtanen II could oppose the Hand unaided and survive? The priests of the Hand have for centuries exacted tithes from their followers, accumulating vast reserves of matter in anticipation of just such a war as we face now. They intend—have long intended—to become the sole masters of humanity.

"And here, Major, is another uncertainty that faces us. For security reasons our orbit is long and elliptical, and perpendicular to the Plate. We are now moving rapidly

Sunward, and our crossing of the Plate between the orbits of Earth and Venus will take place in less than two anni. We make such a crossing once every one hundred and thirteen anni, and have not yet been tracked by any Plater force—else we would no longer exist.

"In this time of Plater mobilization, however, we may well be noticed as we cross the Plate. Then the Hand, Major, will surely net us in a web of raptores as we helplessly follow our ancient path. We will be destroyed—except, of course, allowing for the Principle of Uncertainty, the Sailing of your Trickster. Your Trickster brought you here—you, Major, the Limestone, this 'Beast in all but name' and a steward with the name of Dyson."

"Dyson of the Machines?" Dyse inhaled abruptly, held his tongue and breath.

"See, Doc, you remember our conversation on Puppy!" Spider almost laughed, recovered himself, said, "Chancellor Falling-water, what do you know of Dyson?"

"That he foretold the mining of planetary surfaces with Machines—self-replicating Machines. Such a mining would be the only option for humanity if the Rocks were left full of creatures who deal death."

"Y'see, Doc," said the grinning Spider, "Lord Gagarin sails with you!"

"And his methods are indeed tricky." Dyse stared at the Chancellor. He had been enjoined to engage Durrell of the Tetravalency in conversation about the Batesians, but the Trickster had brought him to the heresy's very core.

Niagara Falling-water leaned forward again, spoke to Dyse. "Doctor, you see hereabouts the cube of the Principle of Heisenberg. About it dance the Four Nucleotides. Do you know them as you seem to know of the European

Dyson, whose name you carry? I believe that their dance is the bridge of your coming.''

"Only indirectly, Chancellor. We're taught that they're deities of the Sisterhood.''

" 'Deities.' Yes, Doctor, and more. They construct and direct the process we all call Life. Their dance is called by the Sisterhood the Fourfold Saraband; in it they weave the living way about the hoofs of the mounts of the Horsemen— *your* Horsemen, you of the Plate. It is their understanding of the Nucleotides, Doctor, that enables the Sisterhood to grow the synes with which we are all symbiotic. The Nucleotides dance Diversity, without which there can be no life.''

Spider spoke: "Chancellor Falling-water, do you know much of the Sisterhood?''

"Major, your lives are mine. Know that I, Niagara Falling-water, am a member of the Sisterhood of the Nucleotides. The only one you will ever see. Look at me well, and tell me what you see.''

"A woman, one in a position of power, one with much experience and knowledge. A woman, though, none other.''

"And you, Doctor Tessier?''

"I can say nothing else.''

"And you, Beast?''

"I, too, see a woman,'' said Pantolog through Dyse. "But my nose tells me that you are not made as are other human beings; your body chemistry is different.''

"This syne, so fortunate to arrive in conjunction with the Limestone, is indeed a perceptive being. 'A mind of gold, a Beast in all but name.' We never really understood that.'' The Chancellor stared speculatively at Pantolog for a long moment. "Gentlemen, I am very old. I was born at about the time your Regency so arrogantly 'laid claim' to the Outer Rocks. In my youth, I knew that a time approached when the men of the Plate would array themselves one against another as did the Europeans so long ago—with consequences as disastrous to life in the Deep. I set my life to study of the problem, electing to spend it among the libraries of the Islands of Wirtanen II. Many of the Sisterhood find solace here; the Plate, after all, is ruled by men.''

"Are men such poor rulers?'' asked Dyse almost in spite of himself.

"Men strive against one another with weaponry, the men of the Hemispheres as well as those of the Plate. It is a fact as old as humankind itself, which age our records suggest to be some three million anni. Only a moment of that interval has been spent in the Deep, and we perceive no change in the pattern. Note that the ruling stirpes of all states are trucidate stirpes—their successions are all too often determined by bloodshed.

"Here men engage themselves largely in the pursuit of matter or the defense of our small home; too, they are often scholars. Women, on the other hand, serve the Nucleotides; they attend the Fourfold Saraband without which our lives would cease to be. Here we have no trucidate successions; our order is continuous, and peaceful.''

"One guesses then that, had Earth been ruled by women, there would have been no Closing—by your words, I mean, honored Chancellor?'' Dyse framed his words within a respectful question.

"Likely so, Doctor. Earth Herself is a woman. She gave birth to a living system of such diversity that some ten

million species may have lived there before the European
Ascendancy unleashed the Horsemen.

"Our records, which are perhaps more ample than those
of the Plate, indicate that at the time of Closing the surface
of Earth was congested by some six thousand million
human beings. Their numbers had already pressed hundreds of thousands of other species into extinction. There
is a pair of verses by Har Bates bearing on that terrible
time:

"A cry and a lamentation went up from the
women of Earth to their princes:
'Deliver us, O princes, from these births;
Stay them, for our children are too many
to move about at will, too many to live as
human beings.'

"But the princes responded:
'Nay, ye are but women, whose cause is best
served by silence. Bear many children,
thou wives, that they may serve us and purchase
our goods, and in their own turn multiply and serve.'

"Such princes commissioned the destruction of their
own Ascendancy, gentlemen. Think you not that I hate
men; I hate no human being, save any who seeks to
narrow the diversity of the living substance." The Chancellor seemed to shrink even smaller in her massive carved
chair as she sat back and looked from Dyse to Spider, and
to Pantolog. Then she lifted the Limestone again from its
cushioned pedestal, turning it over and over in her ancient
hands.

"My own living substance, incidentally, narrows with age. I am tired, too tired to continue this interview. Your arrival in such unusual circumstances has earned you an extension of your lives that would not otherwise have been permitted; you are three very interesting beings. I have much thinking to do, and must take counsel with my friends and with the mind of the libraries of Wirtanen II, before I can plot your trajectory. But you will play a part, I think, in the preservation of Life's diversity. You may even discover a means of mining the great moons for matter, of circumventing the wrath of Gravity. I cannot yet say precisely how this would be, but your place in the Book compels me to believe that your trajectory may knit the future sailing of our kind. Go now, knowing that about you is danced the Fourfold Saraband. Please excuse my abruptness."

Saker the Swift then motioned Dyse toward the portal, Spider and Pantolog following. Back across the Hemispheric Hall they walked, toward and across the brassy Sun at its center, outward across the planets in their orbits—Mercury, Venus, the Earth with Her dancing maidens, Mars, the bright ring of Rocks, Jove, Saturn, Uranus, Neptune, Pluto; and the soft polychrome from the face of Har Bates above dappled them in a moving embroidery of light.

Chapter 10: **In which a trajectory is plotted**

A priest of the Hand is worth two birds any day.

> —Saker of the Forty Badans,
> grandfather of Saker the Swift

"I AM HONORED, Princess Linsang. Never has a member of the mighty Stirps Semerling visited our meager home before. You're perhaps annoyed with me for delaying this interview for two days, but I am old and slow and needed a day in consideration of the fruits of a prior interview with some interesting members of your Trojan serving classes." The ancient voice was sibilant, a sound of water falling in the distance.

"*I* am honored, Chancellor. Would it be presumptuous

of me to ask, which members of our serving septs?''
Linsang Semerling stood on the Path of Neptune in the
Hemispheric Hall of the Islands of Wirtanen II; beside her
waited her secretary, America Berecynthia. Under guard
on the Path of Uranus behind the women knelt Canopus
Cardinal Tamilaria and his colleague the Right Reverend
Father Huxley Vereker. The priests knelt because their
green-clad guards had ordered them to do so, and they
remained in this unseemly position because each felt the
bright tip of an assegai between his shoulder blades.

''It would, at this moment, be presumptuous. You'll see
them soon enough. Tell me, Princess, have you fared well
here on Wirtanen?''

''Chancellor, I've fared as well as a prisoner might
expect. We've had food, though what food I cannot guess;
we've had clean quarters, and ample. We've had no
freedom.''

''Freedom to do what, Princess? Freedom to call on
your father, that he may overcome us, destroying you in
the process?''

''Freedom to move about at will, Chancellor Niagara.''

''Ah, Princess, you're free to move about—at *my* will,
of course, for you *are* my guests—you and these priests of
the Fist here.''

''Chancellor!'' The Cardinal spoke from his position of
forced humility several paces behind Linsang and Merry.
''The Fist is only the military order of the Apost—'' He
was interrupted by a motion of Niagara's withered hand, a
slight increase of the assegai's pressure at his back.

''Odd that these priests are so much less respectful than
your Trojan servants, Princess, even though priests claim
also to serve—to serve the Horsemen.'' The Chancellor of

the Islands of Wirtanen II peered at Linsang as might a bird of prey at a mouse. "Tell me, Princess, what have you to say of the conditions you see about you in Wirtanen?"

"With your forgiveness, Chancellor Niagara, I see the inevitable consequences of life without access to sufficient matter. I see little vegetation, no open space save within this splendid Hall, I see few but war synes, and no mammals or birds at all. Only people, many people, all at least a head shorter than I."

"No birds, no mammals," the rippling old voice repeated. "No living ornaments, beasts to amuse but not to be eaten. And have you seen anything of life on your father's Pups of Troy?"

"Only on his sensory-interface screens, Chancellor. I do not—"

"Indeed. You do not go there. It would surely sully your appreciation of the good things about you on the Islands of Semerlinga. Princess Linsang, we are at least as densely populated here as are the wretches on the Pups of Troy, yet you will agree that our lives differ markedly from theirs. Why would this be so?"

"Perhaps because the flow of matter to the Pups is regulated, while—"

"Regulated!" The wrinkled old face almost smiled. "Regulated! Dear Princess, it is regulated by your father's whim. We are regulated by our own purpose, not by the whim of a barbaric satrap for whom the discomfort of others provides laughter! We are densely populated by reason of our need for genetic diversity; our small individual size permits us the requisite numbers and diversity without pressing too hard on the limits of our small material resources. But we are a free folk."

The Chancellor turned her attention to Merry. "And you, Mistress Berecynthia. Are you well?"

"Well enough, honored Chancellor. What will you do with my mistress?"

"In good time, mistress, in good time. Our dosses indicate that you were born and educated on Sappho before your purchase by the Regent's procurators. Do they not still teach patience on Sappho?"

"My patience, honored Chancellor, is in the service of my mistress."

"Even so. Spoken Sapphonically, to say the least. You know that the Sisterhood of the Nucleotides has in every annus since the growing of Sappho tapped seven children from that Island?"

"Yes, honored Chancellor. Although their fates were never disclosed, it was always said to be an honor."

"Yes, mistress, an honor, although in most cases short-lived; of those seven, six are selected for their genetic sequencing, which is used to increase the Sisterhood's own options. The children cease to exist as such in the process."

"You can't intend to release us, then, Chancellor; you know that I'd warn my Sapphonic sisters."

"You might, should Sappho survive the warlike whim of the rulers of Troy and Aresia. And the seventh child? What think you is *her* fate, she who is not sequenced into the minds of the Isles of Mothering?"

"Dare I even guess, honored Chancellor?"

"Be aware, then, Sister, that I am myself a child of Sappho, born there almost four centuries before your own birth. I was the seventh Sapphonic child of your year 5344 Post-Crossing."

"Four centuries! Impossible!" Linsang's voice echoed

through the Hemispheric Hall, her shock magnified by the immensity of the place. Behind her on the floor, the priests stirred in surprise and horror as they recognized the Chancellor to be a Chimaera.

"There is little that is impossible, Lady Princess." The Chancellor smiled at the young woman before her, thinking for a moment back on her own youth in centuries past. "Most folk die before their first century is over. The rich may purchase organs, and physynes to install them, as their own organs fall prey to entropy. Such persons may approach a century and a half, though they usually choose not to do so—human life, after all, becomes a burden after its first century. A burden, Princess, a vast weight—have you ever heard of the man Sisyphus, from the European mythos?"

"Sisyphus, Stone-roller, fated forever to roll a great rock to the top of a hill, only to have it roll back down just before he attains his goal?"

"The same. Princess, my physiology is altered in favor of a long life, which I have had. But I looked as I do now before I'd reached the end of my first century. Life became—has remained—a Sisyphean burden.

"Why? Why, for the continuity of awareness, a thread linking the generations. My life knits a span of history much as the Okumura mycelium links the worlds of syne and man. Like that mycelium, my life is an artificial thing. But it serves the understanding of history, without which human beings must perish in a morass of their own stupidity. Written history is subject to the tampering of men like your two priests here. *I* am not, nor are my sisters.

"Now you will be wondering about your own paths, you and these priests here." The Chancellor beckoned to the Cardinal and the Bishop. "Rise, men of the Fist, and join these ladies."

The priests stood uncertainly and walked to the Princess' side. Chancellor Niagara nodded at one of the green-robed men beside her; he stepped behind the dais and brought forth the little cushioned wooden pedestal on which lay the Limestone. Niagara picked up the Stone, the multicolored light from Bates's portrait above reflecting off its polished casing into her black eyes, and thence to her audience.

"This, you know, is an object for possession of which many would gladly offer their lives, oddly enough. Now it is in my possession. I could ransom it for many megaliters of oxygen, hydrogen and nitrogen; with it I could obtain countless megatons of aluminum or iron to feed the diversity of my people.

"This, though, I choose not to do. This Limestone seems to have a life of its own; it alone of Earth survives to tantalize us, and it figures in the Book of Bates, in that portion predicting this very juncture where we are again confronted with a great threat to our species. About it is danced the Fourfold Saraband, and it portends greater doings in the name of diversity than any mere matter-ramson could accomplish.

"Priests, tell me what you know of the Limestone."

Father Vereker, the historian, spoke: "Chancellor, the Limestone came into our hands when—"

"Enough. As I thought. The Limestone did not 'come into' your hands. It was taken by force from Har Bates of Old Wirtanen four and a half millennia ago—by such as *you!*" She spat the words, the watery sound of her voice rising for an instant to a torrential roar.

"And then, dear priests, your predecessors murdered

the philosopher Bates, very slowly, while forcing him to look on this Stone.

"Priests, *you* are my ransomees. Your Fist will pay handsomely for your safe return, which I will grant. I am not cruel. But the Limestone I will never ransom to Platers, though its worth be far greater than that of two cowering priests. No, the Limestone has its own place in the Dance of the Nucleotides; it will take a long journey. To ensure its safety I will see that it is accompanied by *you*, Princess Linsang Semerling."

"And you expect me to do your—"

"Princess, you will have little to do, unless you choose to take an opportunity to learn. Your place is in your name, a fierce one, and cruel, but a name that commands the respect of all Platers. No, you are but a form of insurance for the safety of the Limestone, which will travel for something more than an annus. Lest the Platers discover its whereabouts and in their greed attempt to divert it from its appointed trajectory, you will accompany it. The Platers will not—I think—be too quick yet to risk your life for a little rock.

"You will sleep out your journey on my caracor, Drought, and as you sleep the Limestone will ride on your breast. Should Drought be approached by anyone or anything, she will take her own life; she will, in so doing, destroy everyone and everything aboard. Who would be responsible for both the loss of the Limestone *and* the death of the daughter of the maleficent Lothar IV of Troy?"

Merry broke in: "Forgive me, Chancellor, but there are many who—"

"Surely, Mistress Berecynthia, there are many who have no love for Semerlings. But I have friends on the Plate, friends who will endeavor to see to the safety of the Limestone's trajectory for much of the way. Friends whose love for life's diversity is greater than their mercantile avarice. Please—'' The Chancellor gestured to a green-clad man at the opposite side of the vast map of the Plate; he clicked his heels and opened the portal there.

And in strode Albemarle, Lord Durrell, Third Bond of the Tetravalency, black-clad as ever and smiling his diamond-bright smile; beside him walked the Whip Saker.

"Chancellor, we meet again," said the Bond. "I am honored."

"As am I, old friend. The Limestone would not have ,come my way without your assistance, nor would my servant Saker have escaped the elegant prison of Summer Semerlinga.''

"A small matter of disguise, Chancellor Niagara. Dressed in black, and unsmiling, our fast friend is as unprepossessing as any Tetravalency functionary. It was his lovely teeth that I worried about—he *does* smile a lot. We had to keep him unhappy, did we not, honored Whip?''

"And disarmed," said the Whip, "which made me very unhappy indeed, as did the lack of my beloved betel nuts.''

"You! Heretic!" Cardinal Tamilaria faced the Bond Durrell across the crossed assegais of his guards. "So you provided the force that took Catuvel!''

"I helped, in my small way. Certain aspects of our voyage and of the writings in Bates's Book suggested to me that it was a good idea. Only the Hand, as Your Eminence well knows, could possibly profit by a war among the Rocks; all others would languish for millennia in another Great Black. I hope to have aided in delaying or preventing such a Black.''

Durrell turned to Linsang. "Lady Princess, I am honored. I will be providing decoys during your forthcoming journey back to the Plate. Our priests here will remain under the Chancellor's care until such time as we perceive you to have safely reached your destination. Then they will be sold back to the Hand.''

Linsang stiffened. "My destination? What *is* my destination, then—or must that remain a secret? And what's to become of my secretary?" The princess' blue Semerling eyes caught the reflection of the Limestone's casing as it flickered in Niagara's wrinkled hands.

"Lady Princess," said the Chancellor, "your destination is a place of which I know little; it is a place of legend, of children's tales. Know you of the Machines, the living-dead servants of the Europeans?"

"I heard tales, in childhood—and we have discussed them recently, in fact.''

"As I'm told. And have you ever heard of a place called Lagrangia?"

"Lagrangia! The place of the trolls of the Sodality of the Tainted Crossing! You would send me to the ogres of the Slough of the Third Horseman? You seek, then, to—"

"Pay this Chancellor Heretic no mind," shouted the Cardinal. "Chancellor, those are silly tales, and evil. What could you gain by sending a young—"

"Your Eminence," said Niagara, "your voice is unusually sharp for one standing with an assegai at his back. Yes, the tales of Lagrangia are children's tales, perhaps sillier than the reality of the place. We know that there is considerable mass in the Fourth Lagrangian Point of the

Earth-Moon System, though, and the arrival of the Lime-stone at Wirtanen II leads us to believe that it is in our interest to examine Lagrangia rather closely. I suspect, priest, that your Fist would not hesitate to destroy what-ever is at Lagrangia were it to learn that the Limestone was on its way in that direction. Lagrangia may prove to us that it is possible to continue to diversify—independent of the Hand—by using large-body matter. Legend has it that Lagrangia's matter came from the surfaces of Earth and Her Moon, carried by Machines that mined. Were we able to tap these resources, we'd be able to found a power base at least equal to that of the Hand—and the Hand is not likely to take kindly to such a Wirtanen success, eh? You can see, therefore, that it is best that you spend an annus of relaxation with us until the trajectory is completed.

"Princess Linsang, you may see Lagrangia, or whatever is left of it. Perhaps, in so doing, you will die; some tales say that whatever destroyed the Europeans lives on at that place—some form of the Third Horseman. But you have a chance to learn. Your servant America Berecynthia will sleep with you, never fear; she is Sapphonic, of great resourcefulness, and will no doubt aid you on your awaken-ing at Lagrangia. Others will go, too. You came here accompanied by an interesting set of the Trojan serving folk, as I mentioned before. They too will sleep on the caracor Drought."

"Which of my servants survived, then? Have I no choice in their company?"

"They're a most adaptable lot, and may well serve you in a time of trouble. One is the steward Doctor Dyson Teague Tessier, who in addition to bearing a compelling first name is most formidably educated. His executive

officer, Major Spider Quick-to-Change Melliden of the First
Security Maniple attached to your Stirps, will attend the
doctor. Then there is the matter of a syne, an encyclopedia,
a sort of gold-colored Beast-thing. Like a cat. A very
curious being that is of great concern to me. And knowl-
edgeable, as befits its intended function.''

"Pantolog Five," said Linsang. "I know it; it shares an
Okumura link with Doctor Tessier. I do not like it, or any
of the Pantolog Series; they have proven untrustworthy on
more than one occasion.''

"As have Semerlings, Lady Princess. Nonetheless, all
of these will sleep with you aboard Drought, as will my
friend the Whip Saker and one decade of his men.''

The Whip smiled, his pointed red teeth showing for an
instant. "I am honored, Lady Princess. Your safety, and
that of the Limestone, is my safety.''

"And if we refuse?" said Linsang.

"There is no refusal, Lady. You are guests of the
Islands of Wirtanen II.'' Niagara smiled a bit, looked to
the Cardinal. "You, priests, are also our guests, for an
annus or so. Have you any questions before I retire?''

"What of the body of Senator Fairleigh of Aresia? It
was in our care, to be returned to the Aresian court intact.
Its defilement by heretics may—''

"Yes. Well, priest, the Senator was raised within this
Hand of yours, and would no doubt request a funeral of
the sort only you, here in the Hemispheres, could provide.
You will see to the proper rites, but his body will be
cycled into our ecosystems here—we have greater need of
his substance, Heisenberg knows, than do the Aresians.
Give him a passing in your own manner; you have plenty

of time, and his corpse is frozen. I should not have liked to meet him alive.''

· The ancient Chancellor turned again to Linsang, the Limestone still glittering in her hands. ''Princess, the sailing of this Stone is the greatest event of my existence. Should it reach its destination and have the effect foretold in our Book, offering our people new matter resources to enhance their evolution, my labors will have ended—for better or for worse.

''It is the fact of this Stone's sudden appearance here, in accordance with the portion of the old Book, *The Extension of the Lines of Probability,* that encourages me; although it is intrinsically of likely small worth, symbolically it commands the attention of billions. Call it superstition, call it what you will—I think it of surpassing importance that the Limestone accompany you on your voyage. This may be the time of the reactivation of Machines that can approach large-body surfaces and survive as no syne might, in which case life may again be able to grow and diversify. Despite, that is, the suicidal follies of the great Plater states. And diversity is my goal, gentlemen. I will not, in any case, live for more than two anni longer. Time is short, now, and Drought already awaits you with sleep. I will see none of you again, save, on occasion, these priests who are to remain in my care.

''Ladies, gentlemen, my Sisyphean boulder is about to roll back down the mountain of my fatigue. I bid you farewell, and beg of the Nucleotides a safe path for you among the hoofs of the Horsemen's mounts.''

Chapter 11: **In which, having had a long sleep, we are awakened at the gate of Hell**

> *Monstrum horrendum, informe, ingens,*
> *cui lumen ademptum.**
>
> —*The Aeneid* of Virgil of the First European
> Empire

TWO MEN sat at a wooden chess table, the squares of which were light leather inlaid against dark. The chessmen were of ivory, red and white.

The players differed more from each other than did the

---

* "A monster horrible and formless, vast and eyeless."

opposing chessmen. One, about a hundred and sixty centimeters tall and hairless save for a braided tuft at the back
of his skull, smiled a smile of sharp triangular red teeth.
"Knight takes rook," he said.

"Then I'm finished," said the other, almost half again
as tall. His face was surrounded by a uniform bush of
black beard and tousled black hair. He reached thoughtfully to the board and pushed the white king over on its
side.

"You are only recently awake, Major, and yet you play
a fearsome game. In a few hours, it will be superior to
mine." The Whip Saker winked at his giant opponent.

"Ah, Saker, I'd do better to call you Hook, like your
friends the Hamtsan. Why the Trickster stuck me across a
chessboard from the likes of you, I'll never know." Spider
Melliden began resetting the chessmen for another game.

"The Trickster. Heisenberg's Principle? There was no
uncertainty about it, Major; I challenged, you accepted.
In other circumstances, we have opposed each other
with badan and raptore. I find this a far more pleasant
opposition."

"And myself, dog-toothed midget."

"A midget who consumes economical amounts of food,
furry giant. Shortly, at our meal, I expect to be reminded
that you can eat as much as any three of my fighting men.
We have no time for another game—all are awake, and
hungry. We go to the mess."

"Mess. Yes, 'mess' is the right word for this Hemispheric slop. Oh, for a haunch of pork!"

"Pork. Doctor Tessier's tusked beast. I tasted it once
aboard Catuvel, and found it most agreeable. But the
Hemispheres support no such creatures, alas, and we are

forced to make do with the lesser fare of our caracor Drought. Pray, do not despise her; she fed and cleansed you through your sleep of an annus across more than a thousand mikas of the Deep. She it was who awoke you at the proper time. Do her the honor of kindness.''

''Bah! Drought—a good name, considering her food. You're right, though, little Saker. Let's see how the others've fared.''

Drought was decelerating at one mass in reverse. The two dissimilar warriors clambered through the sphincter of the bulkhead forward—now above—them, and into her mess hall, a circular space ten meters in diameter at the center of which Drought had set an equally circular two-meter oaken table. The surface of this table was inlaid with a miniature of the map of the Plate in the Hemispheric Hall of the Islands of Wirtanen II. At its center, covering Old Brazenface and the orbits of the planets out to Jove, rested a cushion on which lay the Limestone.

Even as Spider and Saker appeared through the chitinous bulkhead that was the floor of Drought's mess hall, America Berecynthia slid through the ceiling bulkhead on a seat that was an appendage of Drought's body wall. The chair rose again on its jointed muscular arm, this time descending with the Princess Linsang. Rising, it returned with Dyson Tessier, who was in turn followed by his encyclopedia Pantolog Five, who preferred a catlike leap from ceiling to floor.

''What's this?'' complained Pantolog over Dyse's Okumura as he examined a pair of bowls on the floor. ''Cat food?''

''Shut up. The bowls are silver, at least. This is a military Vessel, no Catuvel.''

"Well I know *that*, honored Doctor. But this—this food—is none but the same Wirtanen biscuit and water. After so long a period of unconsciousness, I'd hoped for something more substantial."

"Biscuit more than good enough for you, 'Beast in all but name.' Eat, and show appreciation."

All seated themselves about the table, and Saker's men brought goblets of water which they placed neatly on the table's Path of Neptune, and bowls of the red and green bits of Wirtanen fare nestled on noodles prepared in a bittersweet brown sauce. Remaining standing, the Whip moved the cushion bearing the Limestone aside from the maps of the paths of the inner planets.

"From *here*"—pointing at the air above the table somewhat beyond the Path of Jove—"to *here*"—pointing at the blue inlay on the Path of Earth. "We've had a long journey, honored guests. You are mortally inconvenienced, of course, but we all slept through most of it. There was a chance, had there been any interference, that we'd never have awakened. We *have* awakened, however. Being a superstitious man, I suspect that the presence of the Limestone protected us, not to mention that of the Lady Princess Linsang. I salute you, Lady, and the Stone in your care." He lifted his goblet, and the others followed suit.

Then, seating himself, Saker tasted a green cube from his plate. He ate in Wirtanen fashion with two small sticks between which he lifted the cube. The Trojans took up their forks, watching him all the while.

"We have much to discuss," said Saker between bites. "First, of course, the news. Drought has been in continuous lightlink with the mind of the Islands of Wirtanen II, which, in turn, has many eyes throughout the Plater space. She has offered me an entire annus of happenings, but I've distilled them a bit for you—I ask your indulgence.'' He took another bite, chewing for a moment.

"First, my mistress, Niagara Falling-water, is said to be ill. She has, as you know, more time behind her than do most human beings; she is tired. Too, she feels—hopes— that her task in the name of the Fourfold Saraband has fallen into our hands. I fear, knowing her, that she will live only long enough to see the outcome of our own labors, whatever they may prove to be. She sends you all her greetings.''

"Greetings for her prisoners. How pleasant,'' said Linsang.

Across their Okumura link, Pantolog spoke to Dyse: "Tell our pirate that I personally found Niagara to be a fine old lady, very discerning. My sympathy, miserable Beast that I am, goes out to her.''

Dyse repeated this to Saker, leaving out the bits about the pirate and the Beast.

"Uh, my thanks, syne,'' said the Whip, eying Pantolog suspiciously. He had never been comfortable in Pantolog's presence, especially since the creature had (1) killed some of Saker's men and (2) appeared to figure in the Book. As he himself liked to say, Saker the Swift was a superstitious man. Pantolog knew this; Saker knew he knew it.

More news, between Saker's carefully chewed bites of his meal. "On the Plate, as you can imagine, a great outcry was generated by the, ah, interruption of the sailing of Catuvel. Because of the killing of your fiancé, Lady Linsang, many were suspicious of the Regent's security.

You know more about that than we do, no doubt. At any rate, this attack on such a perilous creature as Catuvel has caused some to suspect that the Regency had a hand in that, too, in order to retain possession of the Limestone. After all''—he smiled—''no ragtag band of Hemisphere pirates could have accomplished such an attack alone; and Durrell of the Tetravalency is a silent man. No one suspects him. Suffice it to say that the Hand, ever active in such matters, is aligning itself with Aresia in sowing fears that the Regency stole its priests and the Limestone back. Both of those priests, by the way, remain well at Wirtanen—as well as can be expected.'' Saker lifted another bit of food between his wooden sticks.

''Your own whereabouts, Princess, are not as yet suspected by the Platers, any of them. Some believe that you are back at Troy Prime, or hidden in the archipelagoes of the Trojan Points, and that you carry the Limestone with you. The Regent, of course, denies this; he too believes that 'pirates' could not have accomplished a successful boarding on Catuvel, as indeed they could not. He in turn suspects aid to the boarders by Aresia, as does his son the Rising Regent, who is said to be urging a strike at Aresian shipping in response. The Regent, older and perhaps wiser, is not as hotheaded.''

''Hotheaded!'' said Linsang with her mouth full. ''Blatherheaded! My brother is a predator who wishes his own Regency as soon as possible.''

''Even so. It is said that the internal politics of the Regency Stirps are undergoing considerable heating due to this friction, and that the Lady Regenta allies herself with her son Homar. I am grateful that I was not born into such a stirps.''

"Well then, Master Whip," said Spider, "perhaps I am better off here than in the Regent's service at present; the faction of the First Security Maniple serving Homar *princeps* is not that to which I belong."

"Even with this food, Major? But I digress. Your friend Catuvel, to whom I am as indebted as are yourselves, was saved by a flotilla of Regency galliots and raptores from destruction by scavengers among the Rocks. Drivers were sent to her, and she has been taken to the Isle of Mothering associated with the leading Trojan Point of Jove for healing. Most interestingly, I learn that my Chancellor has been in contact with that branch of the Sisterhood in recent months; apparently something to do with Catuvel's gradual recovery. Of these matters, however, I know nothing more."

"Things are gruesome out there, then," said Dyse. "Perhaps the Chancellor's work may come to naught after all."

"Possibly, especially within the context of our knowledge of young Homar Semerling. But our journey ends tomorrow. Look here." The Whip gestured to Drought's body wall, which dilated a sphincter to reveal a three-meter circular polarizing port bulging hemispherically into the Deep. Without, the bright pebbling of stars seemed unmoving even though Drought still sailed at several thousand kilometers a minute.

"Step to the glass, those who are interested. Look downward—our floor is Drought's forward as she decelerates."

All of Troy present left their seats and moved to the port. The Princess was first to lean into the half globe, looking along the curving outer shell of Drought lumped with sensory organs and closed weapons-sphincters.

"What do you see, Linsang?" Merry jostled to her mistress' side.

"Two lights. Point sources, as yet, but brighter than anything else around. One is white, the other a much brighter blue."

"The Earth-Moon System," said the Whip. "Home of Life, or, as the Hand prefers to call it, the place of 'worms that live within the eyes of men, and insects which suck their blood.' "

Now Dyse crowded to the glass. In a field of stars like grains of sand, the Earth-Moon pair seemed like a sapphire and a pearl set side by side—so bright, so close to one another! Of all planets in the Systemic Sphere save only cold Pluto far away, only Earth possesses so large a moon in comparison to Herself; all other moons are as dust to their parent bodies.

"They'd be much brighter, of course," said the Whip, "if we approached them from Sunward. What we see now is reflections from narrow crescents. We'd not see them at all, except that Drought has placed her body between this port and the light of Brazenface. What do you think?"

"Have you heard the tales of the Tapeworm?" Spider, having peered out in his turn, looked from face to face intently.

"The Tapeworm," said Linsang, "was a monster that invaded the guts of the people of Earth. She sent it to torment them with starvation, for whatever they ate the Tapeworm devoured within them. No matter how much they ate, they wasted away—and the Tapeworm grew."

"How about the Trypanosome?" said Merry. "It was a sort of tiny succubus that traveled with the Bloodsucking

Insects. With its aid, Earth could produce a fever that caused people to sleep forever. Or caused their spleens to burst, or their faces to erupt in lumps like those on Drought's skin here.''

"Or the Filarian, with which Earth caused men's testicles and limbs to become as great and thick as those of elephants, while keeping their minds intact to savor the torture?'' Dyse shuddered.

"Or the Mosquito, the fly with which Earth covered men's bodies? Each fly sucked blood—and sometimes a fever succubus entered from the fly, to bleed the life away over decades of sickness.'' Spider peered out the glass again.

"Or the Loa Loa, the worm that lived within men's eyes?'' As Merry prepared to elaborate, Saker interrupted.

"By your talk, Platers, the Third Horseman, Pestilence, has already joined us. But we are well as yet, and we wish only to go to Lagrangia—so far as we know. We seek the Machine that mines, not the Third Horseman.''

"Lagrangia is within the Earth-Moon System,'' said Spider. "There too may live the Third Horseman.''

"But Lagrangia is well into the Deep, Major. Some say that the Third Horseman does not ride across the Deep, preferring to remain in his hole on Earth and watch his brothers patrol the worlds of humanity.''

"Little Whip, what was it that you called the cube of the Trickster's Sailing?''

"Heisenberg's Principle, hirsute coward—why?''

"And what Principle was that?''

"The—ah, the Principle of Uncertainty. Yes, Major, I too know fear. But it will never rule me.''

Over the Okumura, Pantolog spoke to Dyse: "You humans are a nervous lot. Myself, I'm consumed by curiosity."

Dyse transliterated, said, "Perhaps my encyclopedia illustrates a healthier point of view than ours."

"Your Beast? It is no healthy being, by my reckoning, Doctor." Saker moved a step farther away from Pantolog.

"*Oho!* Our Saker the Swift fears an encyclopedia more than he fears the brooding wrath of Earth!" Spider grinned, but the Whip remained unmoved.

"Major, the Principle of Heisenberg resides more within that Beast than in any other place I know."

"Lagrangia?"

"I do not know Lagrangia. I do know, however, that for some days our caracor Drought has been accompanied by two strange little spear-things, seemingly of metal, from that place. They do not speak—they only accompany. They no doubt speak to Lagrangia, however, so we may assume that life exists there. Its manner of being we'll learn tomorrow, if not sooner."

Pantolog, meanwhile, began flooding Dyse's Okumura link with some information he had concerning Lagrangia. As the others talked, Dyse withdrew into the link for a time, then spoke: "My encyclopedia offers a few additional tidbits about Lagrangia and its supposed religion. He tells us that the ruins are said to be occupied by a fane or basilica to Saint Gerard of the Cylinders, patron of the Sodality of the Tainted Crossing. Saint Gerard, as you know, was the single most visible proponent to the Europeans of the Filtration to the Deep, if we read our histories aright. He is said either to have died quietly in his bed or to have perished in the Closing—but he is said never to have entered the Deep himself.

"Saint Gerard was a scholar in the waning of the Ascendancy. Some say that he was a young man when the Trickster commenced his Sailing—if, indeed, the Trickster was an actual person. Gerard is also said to have invented almost singlehandedly the Cities of O'Neill, which bore his European surname and were the original habitations of life in the Deep. These Cities, which were located at Earth's Lagrangian Points in the orbit of Her Moon, were Island-like—they rotated to produce mass for their inhabitants—yet they were not Islands, being not alive, but Machines. Men were sent to them as fertile eggs in sterile frozen stasis, that the Third Horseman might not gain a foothold in the Deep.

"It is believed, finally, that Saint Gerard was a citizen of the Second Engli Empire after which Mistress America Berecynthia is named—much as the Trickster is said to have been of the Empire of the Rose, the rival and counterpart of the Second Engli on the other side of Earth."

"Many thanks, Pantolog—you too, Doc," said Spider. "Say, Mistress Berecynthia, what do you know of the origin of your name?"

"A little—by the way, we're far away from affairs of the Plate. Call me Merry, if I may call you Spider. My full name's too sonorous for this expedition. About my name, my mother told me that America was the title by which the Second Engli personified their empire. She told me, my mother, that the Second Engli were a mighty people, so much so that all of them had Machines with wheels with which they might fight Earth's Gravity and travel at will across a continent some five thousand kilometers wide."

"Continent," said Saker.

"One of the areas of Earth not covered by water—a large land mass," said Merry.

"So they required Machines just to move about? Surely, the reign of Gravity must be terrible."

"Indeed. Nonetheless, so mighty were the Americans that some sailed in the dense air of Earth, lifted by great multicolored bags of helium that bore their family crests—but these, too, were Machines. In fact," continued Merry, "I find these latter rather difficult to believe."

"As do I," said Saker. "Do continue, though—tales of the Ascendancy have always fascinated me."

"Unfortunately for the Ascendancy, my mother told me, the Machines of the Europeans, while they did not eat such food as do synes and men, did eat—but they ate only one thing, that which is called *Petroleum*, the Blood of Earth, about whose actual nature we know nothing. Earth, in revenge, is said to have withheld Her Blood, and the hungry empires of the Second Engli and the Rose came into dispute over their few remaining stores of the stuff— much as Aresia and the Regency may soon dispute the Rocks.

"I was named America because that land is portrayed in legend as a bright and beautiful place. I doubt I've lived up to the name, but daughters rarely meet the expectations of their mothers." Merry smiled ruefully.

"Nor men their fathers," mused Linsang, thinking on her brother Homar.

"We'll learn more of the Basilica of Saint Gerard tomorrow, and perhaps more of these Machines of yours, Mistress Merry." The Whip peered out the glass of Drought's port again, then: "In the meantime, allow me to suggest a few hours' sleep. The first day awake must not be overdone.''

"I'm with you, tiny pirate, I'm with you.'' Spider rose. "Merry, my respects, and thank you for a magnificent tale. I'd like to learn more sometime, but I'll dream on this one tonight.''

"And I, Spider, I fear I'll dream of the Third Horseman and his worms and succubi. Such *sweet* dreams.'' Merry grimaced, and looked out the viewport once more.

Chapter 12: **In which the Third Horseman rides again**

"And what are trolls, Father?"
"Trolls, boy? Trolls are your own worst fears, come to life."

—From a fable of the Bharrighari Allegories

"A THOUSAND PARDONS, Doctor, for this interruption of your sleep; but our caracor Drought begs to inform us that we are being contacted by human agency."

"Agh—humph—wha—Saker!" Dyse struggled up from a troubled sleep to see the sharp-toothed smile of the Whip. Such a smile is an excellent stimulant; Dyse was on his feet in an instant. "They're talking?"

Saker and Spider stood before him, both dressed and armed. "Yes, Doctor," said the Whip. Over our Drought's

Okumura, oddly enough—no lightlink. We speak through my physyne Swo Yeak here. It is a form of Lubret, very poor. Swo Yeak suggests that you'd understand it better than I.''

"Good. My clothes—"

"—are here.'' Saker held out a bundle of clothing, formal dress. "You'll probably do well to look your best. We are in rotatory mass—be careful.''

They were no longer decelerating; Drought now revolved about her long axis, so that all movement of her passengers was along the hard curve of her chitinous wall.

As Dyse dressed, the physyne Swo Yeak spoke: "Honored Doctor, the Lubret we hear seems quite archaic. You, with your learning, can perhaps tell us more.'' The creature dropped into a precise vocal facsimile of a heavily accented polyglot lingo of guttural snorts interspersed with barely understandable Lubret phrases.

Pondering all this, Dyse was able to formulate a broad translation within a moment or two. "It's a greeting, Saker, from Lagrangia—you must have guessed as much. More than that, though, it's a warning to any of our synes. It seems that there is danger to synes here, and that we are to keep them 'at bay,' as nearly as I can understand. Let's find my encyclopedia.''

"Your encyclopedia, Doctor, is mashed into the viewport of the mess hall. It is looking out at a most impressive view, blocking my own attempts to see.'' Saker, armed and armored, shook his shaven head. "I cannot deal with your Beast.''

"Beast, yes, well, I'll see to it now. Swo Yeak, come along—you may transmit Drought's communications to Pantolog, and he'll translate better than I.''

"Honored Doctor, I have been doing so. Your encyclopedia does not move except to better its position in the viewport."

Dyse, Saker, Spider and the physyne walked along the hard wall of Drought to the sphincter in the forward bulkhead, lately a ceiling for this chamber. They ducked through the opening, through which they'd lately have had to climb, and into the mess hall.

The circular table was now resting on Drought's curved "floor," and the viewport was a shallow hemispherical hole in that floor. Within the hole nestled Pantolog, face between his forefeet. Hearing Dyse, the encyclopedia lifted his head.

"Oh, my Master, my honored Doctor! I *am* having a wonderful time. I'm seeing all manner of beauty here. Luckily, I haven't had to move a centimeter—your friend Saker is a superstitious man, and allows me to do quite as I will." Pantolog bared his teeth a bit at the Whip, who started back in alarm.

"Come on—what's out there?" Dyse gestured, but the cat refused to move from his glassy nest.

"Well, impatient Doctor, it seems that the person of Lagrangia is poisonous on contact to synes. Or something of the sort. At any rate, Lagrangia herself is little more than a point-light at present. But they're adamant—we can't even establish a sphincter link, or some curse'll befall Drought here, and any synes within her—although as nearly as I can judge it's not as dangerous to human beings."

"Are there any alternative suggestions?"

"Yes, Doctor. They say that human beings may approach in Deepskin, for the Deep appears insulative to the curse. On the other hand, they say, once a human being contacts them physically, he or she will forevermore be poisonous to synes. Quite a curse."

"Poisonous to synes," said Saker, "including *this* Beast?" He pointed to Pantolog.

"Apparently so," said Dyse.

"Then perhaps *I* should go." The Whip grinned his red grin at Pantolog.

"What manner of curse would befall synes?" Dyse was attempting to peer down at the Deep, but the cat kept moving to block his view.

"I don't precisely understand, honored Doctor. You know as well as I of tales of the Third Horseman— Pestilence. I do not doubt that this Horseman lives here."

"And why would he curse synes, if not men?"

"Doctor, we are told that Man evolved on Earth, beneath the very hoofs of the Third Horseman. All synes evolved in the Deep, well after the Filtration and Closing. Perhaps the Nucleotides provided Man during his long Earthly sojourn with hidden reserves against the Third Horseman."

"Possibly, although legend would seem to imply otherwise."

"Even so. On the other hand, Man is said to have lived on Earth for several millions of anni without having fallen dead before that Horseman."

"Lagrangia tells us, then, that while the Third Horseman would not destroy human beings out of hand he might travel with them back here to Drought, and then destroy her?"

"Yes, impatient Doctor, perhaps so that we might not return home to tell of this place."

"But Drought is in constant lightlink with Wirtanen II."

"As long as she lives, honored Doctor."

"So," said Spider when told all this, "we are function-ally isolated from all the Peoples of the Deep should we visit Lagrangia."

"Just so," said Pantolog through Dyse. "Furthermore, we are enjoined to explain our purpose in these parts, and to tell of the identities of all humans aboard, man for man, woman for woman. Drought, Swo Yeak and I have agreed that it is not wise to do so until you yourselves are willing."

By this time, Linsang, Merry and all of Saker's ten fighting men had joined them in the mess hall. All crowded together around the glassy depression in the curved floor in which Pantolog huddled.

"Pantolog Five, get out of there and let us *see!*" Dyse prepared to grab the encyclopedia's black-tipped tail, but Saker apprehensively restrained him.

"Honored fidgety Doctor, in good time. I have a feeling that the view awaiting you is best at a certain moment of Drought's rotation. Allow me a few seconds more." The encyclopedia stuck his head back between his forelegs, watching carefully as the Deep whirled past outside.

"Closer, Doctor, closer—NOW!" Pantolog sprang from the port, landing in the midst of Saker and his men, who scattered like quail before a springer dog.

The Trojan company leaned as one to the port's muscu-lar edge, peering into the glassy bubble and the Deep beyond. Without, for a moment, only stars wheeled by. Then light! A bit of Old Brazenface the Sun glared out at them from behind a narrow crescent of a dead gray world flecked with the impact craters of five billion years. The

Moon, Earth's barren daughter, and, beyond, dwarfed by that charred-bone arc, another crescent.

A blue crescent—no, a white crescent—or was it green? Far away beyond the dead Moon, the Home of Life—and Death—glimmered multicolored and silvery like a polished scythe blade against the starry Deep for an instant before Drought's rotation carried their view back into the comforting black of the Deep.

In a moment the awesome crescents returned, sliding across the port—and again, and again, as fifteen wonderstruck human beings tottered at the viewport's rim-sphincter.

"So," murmured Saker, breaking the frightened silence.

"So *beautiful*," whispered Linsang, "so blue."

"The blue's supposed to be from Sunlight scattering in an atmospheric membrane—a dense one." Dyse swallowed, a flux of emotion clutching at his throat and lungs.

"So much water, so much oxygen—it's said." Saker found his right hand at the grip of his springbolt, moved the hand with effort to stroke his hairless chin. His ten men made simultaneous warding movements, forefingers and middle fingers spread wide in a V.

"Such a lovely thing, to house the Third Horseman," said Merry.

"A trap, baited with loveliness," added Spider.

"Why have we come here?" muttered Saker. "Why *us*, of all the billions of folk that might have come in our stead?"

"Your Book of Bates," Spider reminded him. "The Limestone. But we need not go to Earth, friend Whip. We go to Lagrangia."

"Never to return? I'd rather go to Troy, and hand myself to the First Security Maniple."

"Little pirate, *I* am of the First Security Maniple."
Spider fixed Saker with a stare.

"Yes, large one. But you are here, with me and my
decade of men."

"Honored Whip." Windhover, second in command of
that decade, stepped forward. "Do we understand that to
go to Lagrangia is not to return?"

"We're warned that to return here would destroy our
caracor."

"Then how do you suppose Lagrangian synes live, if
ours would be destroyed by mere contact with the place?"
Merry looked down through the viewport again. "Is it
possible that they merely intend to frighten us?"

"I doubt it," said Dyse. "Perhaps there are no synes on
Lagrangia."

"But Islands themselves are synes! How could Lagrangia
herself live with this 'curse' of theirs?"

"Do we know that Lagrangia is a living Island? She
may be a Machine, like those attributed to Saint Gerard."

Pantolog spoke across his Okumura link to Dyse.
"Drought tells us that Lagrangia is a very massive object,
though not nearly so large as most Islands. Far smaller, in
fact, than the Islands of Wirtanen II, but massive—too
massive."

"Like a stone, then," said Linsang. "Like a Machine."

All looked to the Limestone on its cushion.

"Well then, since the Lagrangians have asked us who
is aboard Drought, shall we do them the courtesy of
responding?" Saker looked about the room, licked his
lips.

Dyse spoke: "Might as well. All but Windhover and the

other nine of your decade, Saker—they may be our only link to the 'real world,' if I may, of human beings.''

"Swo Yeak, handle the communication." Saker stared out the port again, beyond which the lifeless crescent of the Moon seemed to slide silently by, then the silvery blue scythe of Earth, then around through the Deep, then that blaze of Sunlight polarized by Drought's glass, then again the Moon.

Swo Yeak spoke: "Honored Whip, Drought is in communication with Lagrangia. She begs me to remind you, the doctor and his major that there will be no return for you to Drought should you touch Lagrangia. Drought would surely die. It seems that Lagrangia is infested with, ah, microorganisms that are fatal to synes.''

"Microorganisms?" The Whip's superstition grew sevenfold.

"Little beings too small for your eyes to see. Many of them live within all of us, including Drought, and within any living being that breathes air. They are essential to our digestion, and to our survival.''

"If they're already within us, why fear them?" said Saker, looking suspiciously at his stomach and fearing them already.

"Our microorganisms have lived with us for almost sixty centuries, but they are descended from a carefully selected complement of creatures permitted to pass the Filtration.''

"Ah. Then Lagrangia claims a different complement of these—microorganisms?''

"Seemingly so, honored Whip. Apparently the physiology of human beings can support these creatures. Human beings are physiologically little altered from their time on

Earth. But the living things of Lagrangia, once they took up residence in a human body, would live on and attack any synes with which that human being came into contact."

"You invoke the Third Horseman, Swo Yeak. Is there any other word?"

"Yes, honored Whip. On receiving word from Drought that the Limestone travels with us, the Lagrangians required that we pass it to them. They not only require it—they threaten us with obliteration should we disobey."

"Are the Lagrangians human, then?"

"They offer no information on that subject."

"They are trolls," growled Saker.

"Trolls they may be, honored Whip, but they seem to bear you no personal ill will. Indeed, they offer you personally the choice of remaining here."

"Me? Me alone?"

"All, honored Whip, save the steward Dyson Tessier, who is to bear the Limestone to them; they are interested in his name."

"Ah. As is our Chancellor. She is indeed one of foresight. Any more, Swo Yeak?"

"We are also asked whether we harbor a 'mind of gold, a Beast in all but name.' "

"Ah! The Book lives here also. Your friend the encyclopedia would do admirably, though it would surely die. I would not miss it."

"Not so surely would it die, honored Whip. The encyclopedia's genetic—and therefore physiological—matrix is little altered from that of a great cat. Such cats, like human beings, once inhabited Earth. I have consulted with Pantolog Five on the subject. It is a syne very desirous of understanding, and is eager to attend its master and the Limestone.''

"Doctor?" said Saker. "What do you think?"

Pantolog flooded into Dyse's Okumura: "You *know* I'll have to go, Honored Doctor. Look at the words of the Book!"

"I guess Pantolog goes. He deserves whatever he gets, I'm sure." Dyse looked at the cat, shook his head.

" 'Curiosity kills the cat' at last. Very nice," said Saker. "Swo Yeak, have Drought advise the Lagrangians that there is indeed a 'Beast in all but name' here—although our Beast may prove a sad disappointment to them.''

Swo Yeak stared at the floor for a moment, pointed ears cocked. Then: "Honored Whip, Drought advises me that Lagrangia comes close enough for human vision. Let us go to the viewport."

About that circular opening in the floor, the Princess, Merry and Spider already clustered. Far away, bright against the starry mosaic of the velvet Deep, there glimmered a light. As they watched, the light dimmed and then returned, dimmed again, returned.

"If this dimming and brightening marks rotation, the Lagrangian Island rotates at about two revolutions per minute," observed Spider.

"Indeed, honored Major," said Swo Yeak. "Drought informs me that Lagrangia is a small place, but half a kilometer in diameter. Its rotation produces a mass of one at its equatorial rim, so that we may assume that its inhabitants prefer the same mass as do human beings."

Spider, whose sharp eyes saw many things in advance of the eyes of other folk, said, "The thing appears to be a great bead, a sphere. With feeding-toroids at each end, I think. Big ones. Dense population?''

As Drought drew closer through the silence of the Deep, Spider's assessment proved correct. Lagrangia was indeed a single sphere a half kilometer in diameter, at both ends of which projected sets of toroids presumably for the growth of food.

There were mirrors, too, aimed at the presently invisible bounty of Brazenface. But these mirrors were unlike any they had ever seen, for, instead of being composed of thousands of reflective hoplites linked only by strings of light, these seemed to be but metallic foils, dead rectangular skins. How could one instruct a dead mirror? How could the Lagrangians *live?* It was apparent to the watchers that the Lagrangian sphere was in all ways unlike the Islands of the Peoples of the Deep; instead of possessing an integument of metachitin, the thing seemed completely metallic—none of the heraldic decoration and generally bright coloring of living Islands. And the metallic sphere seemed as patched and ragged as was the little clothing of the thralls of the Pups of Troy.

There was none of the glitter of commerce about Lagrangia, no glorious mirroring of reflective hoplites forming a greeting crest-salute. Just Lagrangia, looking as dead as a few megakilograms of aluminum on a trade-drift across the Deep. Still, the sphere was far from smooth. In addition to its strange patchwork of dull metal, it bore projections, eight of them about its equator, each in form rather like that of a moth at rest. Sensors? No. Galliots? Chebeks? None like any aboard Drought had ever seen. These were seemingly of metal, as lifeless as the strange sphere to which they clung. Yet of all about that sphere, only these projections bore coloring, tiny flecks of color seen from afar, lines of red and blue and yellow.

And then the orb of Earth, blue-white and marbled here and there with dark greens, passed beyond Lagrangia. Lagrangia against Earth, a linkage of contrast, the colored planet and the corpselike thing She'd spawned.

"Honored Whip," said Swo Yeak, "Drought will come to rest at a position five kilometers to Earthward of Lagrangia. There will be a moment of forward deceleration. She offers grips."

From the caracor's walls grew several dozen grips of horn, each designed for a human hand. All present seized one or two, steadying themselves. There was a pull forward, gentle, and then the rotation-mass resumed, the grips disappearing again.

"Help me with my Deepskin," said Pantolog over his link to Dyse. "My finest hour is come."

Struggling with the quadrupedal Skin, Dyse muttered, "Hour of the Beast."

Saker overheard. "Beast, it is indeed your hour. Although I fear you, I wish you well."

Dyse slipped into his own Skin, its lips sealing themselves along his back.

"And what of us?" said Linsang. "I am ambassador of my people and—"

Merry interrupted her mistress. "Doctor Tessier and the encyclopedia can't return here, Linsang. For all practical purposes, they go to their deaths. They'll be changed."

"I think not our deaths, Merry," said Dyse as he stood before the sphincter leading to the after chambers and the Deep beyond. "I think perhaps the Trickster rides with us, to borrow a phrase from Spider. His Lord Gagarin lived

about these parts at one time, we're told. And the Book of
Bates, for what it's worth, is also known to the Lagrangians.
We've long been expected, we and the Limestone.''

"Doctor," said Linsang, "you're no longer a steward."
She approached Dyse, laid her arm on the green of his
own. "You're the future, I think. Go with the major's
Trickster, and I hope we meet again."

"Always a steward, Lady. My crest is the boar's head
of Clan Tessier of the seneschalate sept. But thank you."

"Not Lady, Doctor. Linsang—and I'll call you Dyson, the
prophet." She handed him the Limestone, which he tucked
into the muscle-lipped pouch at his Deepskin's rump. "Fare
you well, Dyson—watch out for the Machines."

"Look here, Doc," protested Spider, "I at least should
come along and—"

"No, Spider, not yet. After all, Pantolog and I are the
only invited guests. We're supposed to be a mannerly
folk." Weak joke, but Dyse's knees were a bit weak too.

"You desire to fight trolls, Major, without me?" Saker
attempted a smile. "Honored Doctor, my thoughts and
wishes sail with you. And even with your Beast. You
dance the Fourfold Saraband now, I think, you two. May
your trajectory carry you to good fortune."

Dyse closed the face of Pantolog's Deepskin, then his
own. He went aft, then, and the sphincter closed off the
view of the other humans. Farther aft, another sphincter
opening and closing for them, then another, then the sphincter to the Deeproom closed behind them. Drought re-
claimed her air from that little chamber, and her bodywall
sphincter opened wide on the whirling Deep. Dyse and
Pantolog leaned out over the opening, watching the rotation,
waiting for the tangential moment when Drought's move-

ment would launch them toward the dead sphere of Lagrangia.

—"Now!"

Two figures shot out of the curved integument of Drought, who closed her sphincter after them in a final farewell. Away they dropped, their Deepskins unfurling photosynthetic shoulder leaves to trap the life-giving Sunsea. The little Deepskin jets took over, propelling the silvery green figures, one bipedal, one quadrupedal, toward the metaliic place ahead.

Closer, closer, one kilometer away, nine hundred meters—and across the great metallic curve of Lagrangia's rim they saw a figure sailing toward them.

A man in Deepskin looks like a man—seemingly winged, true, and brightly colored, but of man-shape. The thing approaching, however, was not of man-shape—although it did have two arms and two legs. No, this thing was corpulent, bulging all over with tumorlike protuberances. On its back, where a Deepskin's leaves would be, there was a great lump, a chunky growth from which tubes and rods projected weirdly. The head was a great white ball, with a reflective faceplate. It was a monster, a thing out of the Mouth of Earth.

"A troll!" Dyse's stomach seemed to attempt to crawl from his body and Deepskin back into the safety of the Deep.

"Master, the Third Horseman—I think." Pantolog seemed to admit fear at last, and the admission somehow strengthened Dyse's resolve.

A gout of vapor from the humpbacked thing, and it moved swiftly toward them, arms and legs seeming to flail helplessly. Oh, Horseman, smile on us! Dyse nonetheless found the presence of mind to wave—*he* was a human being, whatever goblin this creature might prove to be.

It came closer, its bulbous head too large even for that twisted lump of a body. It gesticulated, not sharing their Deepskin Okumura links—gesticulated toward the leeward pole of the cancerous-looking Lagrangian sphere.

"We're to follow it, Pantolog—shall we?"

"By all means, anxious Doctor—it is our host."

"Gah!" Dyse and Pantolog altered trajectory to match that of the monster before them as it paralleled the curve of its patchy metal home. The wall of Lagrangia was wrinkled in some places, as if a cosmic hammer had bent it with random blows—but repairs seemed to have been made, some several hectares in area, all in metal sheeting. Dyse recalled that the Lagrangian cities were said to have been destroyed during the Synthetic Wars; but this one lived on, somehow. Over almost six millennia it had lived, alone among the wreckage of its fellows—wherever they were.

They crossed close over one of the white metal moth-shapes they'd seen from Drought's viewport, noting as it passed that where a moth's head would have been this thing bore several rectangular viewports.

"Observation chambers?" said Dyse.

"Moth-shaped? Perhaps the moth is their totem."

"But they do not resemble moths closely—only in the shape of the winglike projections. Nor, certainly, are they synes."

"Nothing here is alive, save perhaps our monstrous guide—and it resembles no living thing with which I'm acquainted."

"Indeed not. Man-shaped it is, after a fashion, but it

looks to be of fabric and metal—perhaps it is a Machine.''
Dyse shuddered within his Deepskin.

''And why would the Europeans have produced such a
terrible-looking Machine, unless to strike terror into their
enemies? Perhaps it's an analogue of the Regent's toys,
Washington and Moscow.''

''In which case we're doomed, Pantolog. Here comes
the entrance.''

Decelerating, the bulky goblin before them waved its
thick arms about clumsily for a moment before grappling
with several crude U-shaped grips next to a circular groove
in the wall of Lagrangia. For a moment it hung there, the
centrifuge of Lagrangia's rotation causing it to hang like a
man on an exercise bar—and suddenly the groove widened,
its center swinging inward to reveal a sort of doorway,
round. No airtight sphincter, nothing seeming able to keep
the precious air of Lagrangia—if, indeed, Lagrangia con-
tained air—within.

The Deep had never seemed kinder, friendlier to Dyson
Tessier than during the moment he entered that round hole,
dark, metal-rimmed, within the thick wall of Lagrangia.
Pantolog followed, his Deepskin furling its leaves away as
he pushed himself through the hole—burrow, it seemed—
and then the goblin entered, its multiple deformities seeming to make it as inept a Deep-swimmer as either Dyse or
Pantolog had ever seen.

The circular panel slid closed after them, cutting off the
safety of the Deep. There was darkness for a moment, and
then light—brilliant light from a globe, seemingly of glass,
behind a glass plate in the metal bulkhead surrounding
them. Nothing like the soft and pleasing light of a
photophore, this globe seemed a fire, a bit of Old

Brazenface, a glaring plasma. They were in a circular chamber just big enough for the troll-Machine and its guests, the light told them. The monster pressed a green glowing rectangle in its wall.

A sudden tightening of the Deepskins told of air being released into the chamber. An airlock. The goblin turned toward Dyse then, bowing low at its wrinkly fabric waist, beckoning behind itself—where another round door opened into the lost world of Lagrangia.

Light, then, Sunlight, no, twilight—and human beings, of a sort. Trolls. White-clad trolls. Pink of skin and eye, yellowish white of hair, some pocked oddly about the cheeks, the trolls were less than a meter tall at most—the Whip Saker would have towered over all of them. They were all stooped in posture and oddly knotted in their arms and legs. They chattered and gesticulated wildly at Dyse and Pantolog, who because of their Deepskins could hear only a confused murmur.

The Machine-goblin, their escort, laid a hand on Dyse's arm and motioned to him. Then, seizing several small winged metal protuberances about its own neck, it twisted these and—pulled off its great head!

There, staring out at them from the top of what had been a white goblin, was a face identical to that of the other Lagrangian trolls clustering about in growing numbers. Pink of face, pock-marked, pink of eye, the creature sported the same shock of yellowy white hair, was indeed the same height as its compatriots. Again it touched Dyse's Skin; it then proceeded to remove its lumpy Machinelike integument bit by bit, gradually revealing itself to be nothing but another little troll in a short white tunic.

"It wants us to remove our Skins, Pantolog. Mine

first—I've more of a chance than you." Dyse ordered his Skin to shed, which it did, splitting down its back from the crown of its green head, between the buds of its furled leaves to the small of his back, thence down each leg to the heel.

And the air of Lagrangia flooded Dyse's mouth and nostrils, pouring into his lungs. His skin felt wet, his eyes watered. Smells like none he'd ever smelled before assailed his nose, which responded by filling instantly with watery mucus. He gasped, gasped again, and a twisted pink-eyed dwarf handed him a small face mask of some strange gray substance, saying, "Our respects, great winged one. Please forgive this place, which has never seen one of your like."

The dwarf spoke the same archaic Lubret they'd heard on Drought's Okumura.

A smell as of pines seemed to come from the little mask, and Dyse's nose and eyes stopped watering. "My thanks. Are you male or female?"

A wave of soft laughter rippled through the aggregation of trolls, and the one before him smiled as it responded: "I am One-Five Lce, and am proud to be your servant. I am male. Regrettably, you will undergo some respiratory and intestinal inconvenience here—if our guesses prove correct—but we have medicines. Is this the Beast in all but name? Bear you the Limestone?"

"Yes, to both questions," said Dyse through a growing nausea he could not explain.

"The Book says that the Beast would be of gold, yet this is green."

"Green-*clad*—Lagrangia may damage it."

"It is a creature of the Synthesis, then, like those of the folk who sailed away so long ago?"

"Akin to, but not exactly like them. It is also a Beast."

"I think" interrupted Pantolog over the Okumura, "that my Deepskin is dying—dying quickly. I shall have to remove it, Doctor. If I can so love the killing of impala, surely my cheetah aspect can handle this air." Before Dyse could respond, the encyclopedia's green Skin slipped down its spine, the multitude of trolls stepping back in murmuring awe. Pantolog was indeed a Beast, and of the proper gold.

Pantolog instantly fell to sneezing, great cat sneezes that shook his body from nose to tail. "Stench," he said through the Okumura link. Gradually the sneezing subsided. Carefully, the trolls began to approach again, some even reaching out to touch Pantolog's yellow fur.

He who had offered Dyse the mask spoke again: "Honored winged one with the name of a prophet, please to follow me. You are arrived at the home of the Sodality of the Tainted Crossing, and are awaited by our Prior at the Fane of Saint Gerard of the Cylinders; we are his followers. The Prior and all of us have long awaited you; for centuries we have waited. But first you must eat, and receive medicaments, you and your Beast, that your stay will be minimally uncomfortable. You are our deliverance from our long imprisonment, or so the Book says; our Prior will tell you more."

Chapter 13: In which Pantolog Five receives a gift

"We're done for! It's all up! They just hit Miami and Tallahassee and Tampa at once! The whole coast is burning! Guys with guns are pouring into the complex like ants! Look, you're all that's left—try, try to do better—oh, God, try not to mess yourselves up!"

—Last communication ever received at Lagrangia from Earth at the Closing; inscribed into the altar of the Fane of Saint Gerard of the Cylinders

THERE WAS A STRANGE INTERVAL in a sort of hutment of metal, an interval of proddings and pokings and piercings with tiny needles. An interval of little men, three of them, all wrinkled pink and white trolls, who called themselves "physicians" and who were indeed the man-equivalents of physynes—like all of the trolls of Lagrangia, they smelled odd, these physicians, and they jabbered happily in their Lagrangian speech as they examined Dyse and Pantolog. Then an interval of rest, deep sleep, and then a leafy salad—yellowish, like all the vegetation of the twilight world of Lagrangia. "I may be a Beast," whined Pantolog over Dyse's Okumura, "but I don't eat *leaves*." But he did try, and he had always been solicitous of his fat reserves; he'd live.

Now they'd walked for half an hour over a path that led down through a tangle of thick yellowish vegetation toward the full mass of the equator of the Lagrangian sphere. Dyse carried his Deepskin, dead, stinking already, the Limestone still within. Pantolog walked alongside, ears laid back, sneezing and coughing fitfully. Despite (or perhaps because of) the medicaments they'd received, they had felt ill since their arrival in this sepulchral world.

White-haired dwarfs seemed to spring from the yellow vines as they passed, all following, all chattering. Many carried gardening tools, some carried red-faced, white-haired children who cried in terror at the strange forms of Dyse, tall and dark, and the Beast beside him. Where undergrowth did not choke the place, little garden plots were visible; they were rich with strange yellow plants growing in neat rows. Sometimes a bit of the fabric of Lagrangia herself showed, metallic or occasionally of some material unlike anything Dyse had ever seen. It smelled, some of this stuff, like chlorine, and like things for which he had no comparison. He asked his dwarfed guide what the stuff was, seemingly carved or molded into planes and curves.

"It is the Plastic of the ancients," said the troll. "It is of Earth, and magic. It lasts forever unless exposed to the Deep—then it quickly disintegrates. We used it in the past sometimes for carving, but it grows rare and is now protected and revered."

At the Lagrangian equator, in the midst of a square plaza surrounded by a wall perhaps four meters high, stood a structure as black as the cube of the Trickster's Sailing, and as featurelessly cubical save one door, one great double door of some dull gray metal, on a side facing the slanting rays of the dim Lagrangian Sunlight. That Sunlight was ceaseless, explained the troll guide; the Lagrangians had long ago abandoned maintenance of the strange foillike mirrors of their world, for their matter was strictly limited and even the little jets of their goblin-armor used valuable resources. Now gaps in the ancient mirrors reduced their area, and the Machines that had governed their movement in ages past were long dead; thus there was always this twilight in which vegetation grew yellow, anemic. Twilight, twilight for more than five millennia. Looking on the tiny pale folk crowding beside him, Dyse knew an aching of compassion, a real sense of the long purgatory to which their kind had been condemned.

He also knew a growing nausea, which momentarily took command. He gagged, but his belly was empty. He could feel a rumbling in his intestines as they prepared unbidden to empty themselves. The dwarf who spoke Lubret watched, concern showing on his pockmarked face. Then: "Winged one, betake yourself to a garden. Any garden. Do not waste your feces; they represent great wealth."

Nodding dumbly, Dyse scrambled to the nearest tiny garden hacked from the surrounding yellow tangle. He

dropped the Deepsuit, squatted—and was instantly surrounded by silent pinkeyed dwarfs, all watching intently as
the contents of his colon spilled liquidly and aromatically
on the ground.

"Aahhh," murmured the multitude as one, clapping
their wrinkled hands. "Aaaahhh."

Try to ignore. He squatted for some more minutes, his
intestines endeavoring to rid themselves of every molecule.

The tiny white-haired ones clapped, saying "Aaah," at
each convulsion of his innards. Aaah, thought Dyse, aaah.

The Lubret-speaking dwarf smiled. "Winged one, our
little world does not agree with your gut. Never fear,
though. We will provide medicines." He helped Dyse,
twice his size, to his feet, and Dyse picked up the dead
and stinking Deepskin with its precious burden. Would
this place kill him, as it had the Deepskin? Would it kill
Pantolog, syne that he was? But he said nothing, folding
the dead thing over his arm and following his dwarf escort.

The Okumura link: "Doctor, I share your disorder.
'Scuse." Pantolog bolted at his cheetah's sprint, scattering
dwarfs right and left—cats do not like being observed
while contributing nitrogen to the soil. Nonetheless, several young trolls set out in hopeless pursuit, for Pantolog
was a great sensation on this somber world.

They came at last to the black cube at Lagrangia's
equator, glistening metallically within its walled plaza. A
heavy gate in the plaza wall stood open, and beside it
waited tiny white-haired men with long knives strapped to
poles of aluminum—makeshift spears. Pantolog, much
relieved, joined them at the gate.

"Here, winged one, the Fane of Saint Gerard, our

patron. Pray abase yourself." The dwarf bowed, Dyse copying him.

The fane was a *big* black cube—ten meters or so on a side—but, thought Dyse, a small basilica indeed. For small people, for trolls in a great ruin of an Island of lifeless metal and anemically yellow vegetation, a twilight world. Oh, Man, what hast thou wrought?

There were more tiny guards walking the bare metal-floored plaza of the basilica. All were clad in short white tunics, all less than a meter tall, pockmarked, wrinkly, white-haired, pink-eyed. And all were armed with knives, some very primitive as if scraped from scrap metal. The guards formed themselves into two lines between the gate of the plaza wall and the portal of the black cube of the fane. As Dyse and Pantolog walked through the outer gate, the long-handled knives of its guards crossed behind them, blocking all others out.

Pantolog, still snuffling, spoke clearly and well over the Okumura link. "Trucidate flamen, Doctor. The priesthood's determined by murder. No doubt any of these trolls'd love to murder the current Prior. He'll probably suspect us as well."

"All legend, Pantolog, all legend."

"So were the trolls, honored and erudite Doctor, so were the trolls."

"Shut up. Get out of my skull. Here we are." Two tiny white-clad creatures motioned them from the outer twilight into the cube's portal.

Dim red light, filtering through some red glassy substance in the cube's ceiling. Within was an altar, black, cubical, and over the altar a little carving, in what Dyse had been told was Plastic, of the Lagrangian sphere and tori. Before the altar knelt a white-haired dwarf identical to the rest, except that this one wore black.

The tiny troll-man rose and turned. He motioned them to stop a good distance from himself, and spoke bluntly in that archaic Lubret that seemed a trademark of this somber place:

"Welcome, winged one. You bring the Beast in all but name, or so it appears. Have you the Limestone, as was foretold in the Book?"

"I have the Limestone." The sense of the moment swept Dyse into a shiver of awe as the red light glinted in the tiny Prior's pink eyes.

"Let me see it. Place it there, winged one." The dwarf pointed at the floor three meters in front of him. "Come no closer, please."

Dyse did as he was told, leaving the dead Deepskin beside the Stone.

"How come you here, winged like an angel, from the phallus-shaped beast that sails in the Deep and speaks as a Radio?"

"Radio? Angel?"

"See." The Prior pointed to a piece of metallic furniture adorned with faintly glowing lights. A Machine? A—

Pantolog spoke: "Doctor, the Okumura bands of the electromagnetic spectrum were called Radio by the ancients. The angel was a six-limbed monster, a sort of winged man, of the European Mythos. He must mean the leaves of the Deepskins, like wings, as we came from Drought."

Even as Pantolog's words rolled into the Okumura mycelium within Dyse's head, lights glowed on the Radio and the encyclopedia's words shrieked aloud like a catfight in perfect Lubret. Dyse, Prior and Pantolog jumped as one in startlement.

"This Beast, then, speaks also as a Radio. You are indeed the ones of the Book. With your coming, I fear, my time as Prior is over. So, too, are the millennia of Lagrangia, although in what manner the end approaches, I do not know."

"We mean you no harm, honored Prior." Dyse felt the creature's fear, added, "The Limestone is a gift."

"As you are, angel, for you bear the name of Dyson. Perhaps your name is deliverance."

"Deliverance?"

"Dyson foretold the Machine that Mines from his hole on Earth. He said that one day humankind might tap the wealth of the lifeless planets, so saving itself from stagnation. Har Bates, you see, expected that a time would come when small-body resources in the Deep would become unavailable. He found the works of Dyson, Free Man, hidden away in some library, and he made known Dyson's prophecies. These offered a new freedom of cultural growth to those who might unlock the secrets of nonliving Machines. We believe that we understand something of these Machines, and thus that we may play a part in the unfolding of Har Bates's foreknowledge—if our puny knowledge be employed by someone more powerfully endowed with matter than we. And the Hand killed Har Bates. Your name—it is why we required your presence here in conjunction with the Limestone and Beast. This Beast—it is regarded as a syne, a living tool, by your people, no?"

"I am," whined the Radio. Pantolog, delighted by his

ability to speak aloud, had approached the ugly Radio and
ran a few more screeching tests:

"Skaaax. Podlo. Wheee," and then, in a terrible simula-
tion of music:

> "The Prince of the Rose had Balls of Gold
> And Women by the Hundred,
> And when he went out in Days of Old,
> The Skies of Earth, they thundered, BOOM!
> The Skies of Earth, they thundered!"

"I am glad, honored Prior," said Dyse, glaring at the
encyclopedia and the noisy Machine, "that the Radio is so
massive; I doubt that many human beings could stand the
prattle of Pantolog, here, were he able to carry it about
with him."

"There are smaller Radios," said the Prior, "such as
the Beast might wear about its neck; I would hear more of
its speech." The tiny man edged nervously toward Pantolog,
examining him minutely.

"Honored Prior," shrieked the Radio, "I would that I
had such a tiny Radio."

"You shall, Beast, if only that I may converse directly
with you."

"Perish forbid," groaned Dyse. Peace of mind, prepare
to die. The world of synes and men—the Okumura link,
the ancient harmony between humanity and its servants, all
gone if little Radios became commonplace. What a racket!

"Tell me, then," said the Prior, "how goes the diminishing of resource among the peoples of your origin?"

"Speedily," said Dyse. "Although plenty of small-
body Rocks remain, they are all guarded by retiaries and

raptores, the weapons of our princes. None are available to lesser folk.''

"Permit me, winged one, a little fable, since your coming was foretold to occur in a time of diminishing resource. Have you heard the tale of the Two By Four?"

"No, honored Prior."

"*I* have," shrieked the Radio, against which Pantolog was happily rubbing.

"Speak, then, Beast."

"The Two By Four," came the Pantolog-generated whining. "In the days of the Second Empire of the Engli, called by its people America, they killed trees to build their dwellings. The trees they cut apart with Machines into sticks, rectangular in cross section and measuring in their measure Two By Four. This was a standard throughout their vast land.

"However there came a time when trees became fewer as human numbers and dwellings filled the land. The merchant princes of the Second Engli saw this and lamented, for the people were accustomed to using the Two By Four in their building, yet the wood from which the Two By Four was cut became ever scarcer.

"Wishing not to strike panic into the hearts of their minions, for the disappearance of trees surely foretold the Closing, the princes made a decree: henceforth the Two By Four would be reduced in cross section so that more might be cut from each tree. But, also to avoid fear, it would retain its name, Two By Four, even though it was no longer such in actuality.

"Thus did the merchant princes of the Second Engli speed the dying of their Ascendancy, by creating a sense of abundance where abundance no longer existed." The Radio became silent.

"Well told, Beast," said the Prior. "So I deem it to be among your own people, winged one."

"Regrettably, the various propaganda ministries do neglect to tell our folk of the arming of the Rocks."

"Then your time, with mine, has come. But your arrival here with Beast and Limestone suggests hope, as the Book foretells. I will examine our records in the next hours, while my people riffle among the things of the ancients and endeavor to aid you in your discomfort. You will have intestinal troubles as the flora of your intestines adjust—"

"We are already having intestinal troubles, honored Prior," squawked the Radio voice of Pantolog.

"Yes. Well, you should know that your feces are much welcomed by my humble people—"

"This we know also," shrieked the Radio.

"Ah. Well, winged one, before you go to another house of healing, tell me—are all your folk as large as you?"

I've heard *that* question before, thought Dyse. "Some are larger, some smaller, though, with your forgiveness, Prior, I know of no aggregation of people as small as yours, nor colored so."

"Yes. In the days of Har Bates we were as you. However, with his martyrdom, an interdict was placed by the Fist of the Hand of Man on the environs of Earth—as you know. At that time but a thousand people inhabited these ruins. A small gene pool, too small for the diversity essential to healthy populations. Mutations occurred, mutations for lack of pigment, mutations for dwarfism. Their genes became widespread through the millennia, so that you see us as we are now, the four thousand of us that this poor ecosystem can support."

"A grim circumstance."

"Perhaps—but we are generally a contented folk, and our only act of war is that determining the succession to the position of Prior—my position."

"Then you *are*—"

"A murderer, winged one, the only one among my people. It is a ritual warfare that maintains the stability of our little world. Please do not think ill of us, or that we are of naught but barbarous habits."

Dyse thought—of the little people with their yellow gardens, their evaluation of the products of his intestines, their gentle ways, light chatter, clapping, their open countenances—however weird—their long isolation with the orb of Earth hanging without, beckoning through the centuries with a terrible beauty. And he thought of the Pups of Troy, where millions lived in barbarity for the Regent's amusement. He thought of the raptores studding the Rocks with death, he thought of the Fist of the Hand of Man, and he thought of three cooks and two synes named Moscow and Washington.

"No, honored Prior, I cannot think of yours as a barbarous kind. Mine is, or some are. Please forgive us. Our coming disturbs you."

"Disturbing the universe. Yes, prophet-named winged one, you are disturbing our universe. But perhaps for the best. Come now, and you'll be given more medicament and rest, and a Radio for communication with those on your phallus-beast that sails the Deep. I shall locate a small Radio, too, for the Beast here, that I may converse more with him."

"Oh, joy," the Radio shrieked. "Ah, no more inter-locuting steward! Ayeee!" And then again the terrible music-semblance:

> "The Prince of the Rose had a Silver Shaft
>   To ply his Lusty Maidens,
>   And while he bedded them he laughed;
>   The Earth shook with his laughter, BOOM!
>   The Earth shook with his laughter!"

Chapter 14: In which the Prior of Lagrangia reinvents the Trojan horse

"In thankful anticipation of a safe return to our homes, we dedicate this offering to the Goddess."

> —Inscription carved on the Trojan horse
> by the Greek shipwright Epeius;
> from the *Iliad* of Homer the European

ON THE CARACOR Drought, confusion reigned. It took Spider, just awakened, several minutes to establish the cause of the uproar. The physyne Swo Yeak finally signaled him aside.

" 'Twas a communication from Wirtanen, honored Major.

There has been an assassination on Summer Semerlinga. The evil Regent, Lothar IV, is dead, and one possibly more evil takes his place.''

"Homar the Misaligned," said Saker, joining them. "A fitting ruler for a misguided state." He spat, adding, "The monkeys befoul their own nest."

"Even I agree," said Spider, still rubbing the sleep from his eyes. "Homar's faction of the First Maniple is not my faction; I fear I've lost a home, and a job."

"Well lost, hairy giant," said Saker. "But you seem to have a home here, and a job as well."

"I do, although the working conditions are somewhat poor."

"Food. Yes, we'll eat shortly. Is there more news, Swo Yeak?"

"Indeed. The first edict of Homar is to have the mighty Trojan flotilla moved inward across the Rocks. This was but thirty hours ago, but we can assume that his counterpart in Aresia has followed suit. Too, Wirtanen reports that a considerable mass, much diffused, has detached itself from that flotilla and dropped off-Plate into the Hemisphere of the Hook— its trajectory would seem to be bringing it rapidly Sunward."

"And the Princess?"

"She is sequestered, Major," said Saker. "I feel that she had no great love for her father, but the Islands of Semerlinga were her friends. She fears for them."

"Her secretary?"

"She, too, is sequestered, with the Princess. She is examining the communications, and will join us at mess."

"To mess, then." And to mess they went, led by Swo Yeak.

Last to arrive at table was a haggard-looking America Berecynthia. She had spent hours with Swo Yeak, gathering word from the ailing Chancellor of the Islands of Wirtanen II. "Spider, our asses seem to be grass," said she in the Sapphonic manner.

"Yes, it does seem that way. What are our prospects?"

"Worse than we thought. You'll recall that Catuvel, whose radials were cut during our capture, was towed back to the Sisterhood associated with the leading Trojan Point for healing. Well, during that voyage she was questioned, of course."

"And?"

"And she spoke—of course. She'd been able to send one measly retiary after the caracors Drought, Hunger and Avidity, and was able to fix their trajectories before the little devil failed. Thus she extrapolated to Wirtanen, whose orbit was fixed—all, mind you, before she reached the Sisterhood."

"So Wirtanen's in their sights for the first time since her birth two millennia ago."

"Yes—but the Trojans are presently using all their resources among the Rocks, dallying with Aresia. Furthermore, Wirtanen's on a long ellipse Sunward and is far from Troy's reach at present."

"A reprieve for Wirtanen, then?" Spider, who was attempting to learn to eat with sticks in Wirtanen fashion, spilled more of his food.

"Momentary. When Wirtanen crosses the Plate, the only force near her will be the Holy Isles of the Hand."

"The Fist," said Saker.

"Yes—and Troy has already given its Hand priests the Wirtanen trajectory."

"And a flotilla, apparently, a big one." Saker shook his head.

"Possibly not, Saker. At the center of that flotilla, we're told, sails Catuvel. You'll recall that Chancellor Niagara maintained a lightlink with the branch of the Sisterhood that healed Catuvel; she seems to have prevailed upon them to tell Catuvel something of the point of view of the Islands of Wirtanen II—a sort of reeducation during the healing. She may come to aid Wirtanen in her hour of need."

"Even with such a flotilla, there's no way Wirtanen could hold out against the Fist of the Hand of Man."

"None—although the imbalance between the two is lessened, at least slightly."

"How so? The Fist is mighty, possessing raptores and soldiers beyond counting." Saker watched Merry's eyes apprehensively.

"Yes, but recall the Sisterhood, the Isle of Mothering at the Holy Isles . . ."

"Surely—they've provided the Fist with their weaponry."

"No longer. The Pollex of the Hand, Lenin XXI, demanded of them more weaponry. They refused, recognizing the threat to their own pursuit of diversity in any threat to Wirtanen. The Pollex threatened—the Isle of Mothering then destroyed herself, the first to do so since the Great Black."

"The Sisterhood is great and good," said Saker. He raised his glass. "May they live forever."

Spider, too, raised his glass, and with him the others. "May Lord Gagarin sail with them."

None spoke for a moment; then Windhover, second in command of the Whip's decade of men, said, "But the

Hand is far more powerful than Wirtanen, even with the aid of your sweep. You said so yourself.''

"I fear so.'' Merry twisted and untwisted her napkin. "You can't alter an Island's orbit—there's nothing to do even if you could, because they know where she is now. The Fist'll spread a raptorial net across a mika of space where Wirtanen is due to cross the Plate in three months. Even now, the Chancellor tells me, all at Wirtanen prepare to flee—or die. Most refuse to leave their Islands.''

"My home,'' said Saker.

"Our home,'' said Windhover and his men as one, and they began a song:

> "I'll ride me out in blackbody dark
> And slice me a piece of the Plate,
> Then home again in yellow and green
> To Wirtanen, breast of the Deep—
> To Wirtanen, breast of the Deep!''

An old pirate ditty, a love song, normally, rollicking and erotic, it came this time as a dirge. Spider and Merry listened, thinking of the old Chancellor Niagara—after centuries of Sisyphean struggle, should she die thus uselessly at the hands of her mortal enemies?

"No!'' The Sapphonic shout stopped the dirge, and Merry stood, knocking her chair to the curving floor. "No filthy priests'll get her while *I'm* here!'' ·

"Merry, where are you going?'' Spider stood too, alarmed by her ferocity.

"Swo Yeak, come with me. Monitor the lightlink. There must be something—'' Merry left the mess hall in a swishing of her short Sapphonic tunic, Swo Yeak trotting alongside.

"A redoubtable woman." Saker picked up his Wirtanen sticks, resumed eating.

"Just so," said Spider. "Trained in part by my sector of the Maniple, although I knew her not except by sight and doss before this voyage." Spider continued staring thoughtfully at the sphincter through which Merry had exited forward. "I rather enjoy her company, and she's expert with the springbolt." He, too, picked up his pair of eating sticks and set to work spilling some more food.

After the little meal, Saker had the table cleared and a çhessboard and two new goblets brought. They played slowly, Saker and Spider—the mind of each was millions of kilometers away—and spoke not at all.

The forward sphincter dilated suddenly, and Merry entered with Swo Yeak. "We've been in communication with Lagrangia! Dyse and the encyclopedia have a strange tale indeed. Go ahead, Swo Yeak."

"Hear, honored Whip. There are greetings both from Doctor Tessier and from the Prior of Lagrangia himself. We have exchanged information, Drought telling them of the doings among the Rocks." Swo Yeak then launched into a compressed account of the experience of Dyse and Pantolog, describing the somber Lagrangian ruins and their eerie inhabitants and concluding with a repetition of the Prior's message.

"The Prior feels that his time and that of his folk is at hand. He regrets the impending destruction of Wirtanen II but feels that there will yet be a chance for her. He offers his assistance, in fact."

"A diseased troll a meter tall offers his assistance?" Saker laughed mirthlessly.

"Yes, honored Whip. The troll offers his assistance, and both Doctor Tessier and the encyclopedia believe that he may indeed be of help."

"And how would that be?"

"It is not explained as yet. However, the Prior is very much interested in the Princess Linsang and her current difficulty. He desires to see her."

"I've discussed it with Linsang, Saker," Merry said. "She's willing to go to Lagrangia—she knows that Semerlinga is not long for life, and she would see the little ones with white hair and their Radio."

"Radio?"

"A Machine, a sort of Okumura link—but dead, or dead-alive, as Machines are said to have been. It gives men—those without Okumura mycelia—the gift of understanding synes without intermediaries like Dyse Tessier and Swo Yeak here. It could be useful in our circumstances."

"How interesting. I'm not sure I like it."

"Still, Linsang wishes to see Lagrangia."

"Then she may go. She is a free agent, and, if her stirps dies, a lone agent as well."

"I'd like to go also, but—"

"Not yet, Mistress Merry," said Saker. "We do not wish to lose you. Drought requires a decent muster of fighting personnel, and you may be of more use to your Lady here than lost with her in an infected ruin."

"Yes, she says the same. I'll wait, but at the first indication of trouble, I'll—"

"We'll all go, Merry." Spider grinned. "But right now

it's best we wait and hear the Prior's plan. Swo Yeak tells us that his fane is shaped like the cube of the Trickster's Sailing.''

''The Principle of Heisenberg.'' Saker grinned in turn, added, ''Where exists this cube, it seems, our luck resides. Let us wait, then, while the Princess joins her steward on Lagrangia.''

''Good—I guess. I'll see to Linsang, and you two monitor Swo Yeak and Drought. I don't want to miss anything.'' Merry strode through the forward sphincter, which contracted silently after her.

''So a pigmentless flock of tiny trolls prepares to oppose the Holy Fist of the Hand of Man. I wonder why.'' Saker stared at the chessboard.

''Why, honored Whip?'' said Swo Yeak. ''Because Lagrangia was placed under interdict by the Hand long ago, cutting the trolls off from the diversity of the rest of the Deep. The Hand, in fact, declared Lagrangia nonexistent.''

''And why was that, my foxy physyne?''

''Honored Whip, the Prior tells us that in the remotest past a long-dead Machine was activated on Lagrangia, and that it carried a human being to Earth—and back. Thence originated the curse there on Lagrangia, the infection. It was but one man, one Machine. The Earth must be quite virulent.''

''Indeed.''

''So, honored Whip, the trolls do have reason to strike at the Hand. With our help, the Prior says, with the help of Doctor Tessier, the Lady Linsang and Pantolog Five.''

''Ah.'' Saker passed his tongue over his sharp-filed teeth.

''To the trolls, then.'' He raised his water goblet.

*   *   *

The tiny white-haired escort bowed and left Dyse, Linsang and Pantolog alone in the fane's dim red light.

"Linsang. Your nose is running."

"Yes, Dyson, and my intestines also. But they stuck me with little needles—'inoculated' me, they called it—and I feel a bit better already."

"Honored Princess," whined a voice like a cat fight, "they have very effective medicines here."

"The encyclopedia! It talks!" Linsang turned to Pantolog, who wore about his neck a silvery metal collar. On that collar was fixed a small black cube, and it was from that cube that the awful whining came.

"Lady Princess, I introduce my Radio, very ancient, a gift of the Prior. He has more like it."

The Princess knelt and peered at the Radio. "It looks like this fane—like a Gagarinian shrine."

"The major's Trickster is everywhere," shrieked Pantolog. "I, for one, feel his presence comforting."

"Ah. The Prior." Dyse turned, bowed quickly in Lagrangian fashion to the dwarf. The observant Linsang followed suit.

"My respects, winged one, and to you, Lady. You also came with wings of green. Yours is a folk of marvels."

"As is yours, honored Prior. I'm privileged to be here."

"Do I understand correctly, then, that a great fleet of beasts sails from your home to engage the Hand?"

"So it seems. At this moment my secretary is endeavoring to link Drought with the flotilla's mind, the sweep Catuvel."

"Sweep?"

"A large beast, with a mind and spirit. She sails the Deep and is a lovely place to be. She commands a vast armada."

"And who commands her?"

"Formerly my father, but he is dead and she altered by the Sisterhood that healed her. She sails to the Hand's growing web—it may catch her as well as Wirtanen, in the end, but she hopes at least to divert its attention for a time. You say that there may be help for us?"

The Prior ignored that question. "Are you not of the ruling family of the allies of the Hand at the Path of Jove? And would not your sailing beast Catuvel be manned by such as inhabit that Path?"

"No longer. My brother, who dislikes me, rules there. He brings certain destruction on himself and my home. I am no longer of any ruling family—merely Linsang, sailor of the Deep. But I fight with the best, and the Hand is no friend to me. As for Catuvel, we're advised that she evacuated her body without warning, unmanning herself."

"I believe you—that you are homeless. And this one"— the Prior pointed at Dyse—"he is your servant?"

"He was, in my father's time. Now he follows his own trajectory."

"His trajectory and yours would seem to be one, for the moment—you both share our infection, permanently."

"So it seems, honored Prior."

"Then, Lady with golden hair, would you risk your life beside this Dyson Tessier and his Beast, that the Hand be crippled forever?"

"I would—if he'd have my help."

"Good. You will have noticed that your Deepskin, as you called it, died on arrival here."

"Instantly! And it began to smell of death within minutes."

"So it would be, Lady, with almost any syne that contacted the substance of this place."

"Almost?"

"Almost. The Beast here, a syne himself, has told me that the synes of great powers are so multifarious in form and chemistry that some might remain unaffected by our infection. This Beast is an example. Now, I would see the Hand destroyed before I die, every vestige of its cruelty eliminated."

"But you have no weaponry, no—"

"I have you, Lady, and Dyson Tessier, and this Beast. You will be my weaponry, a weaponry the likes of which the Deep has never seen."

"We three?"

"Hear him out, Linsang," said Dyse. "The Prior and Pantolog have become very thick together."

"Yes, Lady. The Beast's coming has long been foretold as a harbinger of the Hand's demise and the release of my people. Now, I believe, the Beast has offered us the means to that end."

"Pantolog," said Dyse, "do your worst."

"Yes, Doctor whose humility grows daily," whined Pantolog's Radio. "Lady, you know well of Lagrangia's poisonous nature—to synes. But not, I suspect, to all synes. Look at myself. The poisons of Lagrangia's substance are comparatively narrow in diversity.

"On the other hand, we know of a place whose substance is so, ah, lively with death-dealing microorganisms that a tiny portion could momentarily devour synes by the thousands. Synes, Lady, such as the Holy Isles of the Hand of Man themselves.''

''And that place is—''

''Earth,'' said the pink and white Prior. ''The Beast, seeing that he can survive Lagrangia, feels that he could also momentarily survive Earth, especially were he to wear a form of the Machine-clothing that we use on our rare forays into the Deep. Dyson Tessier concurs, although with considerably less enthusiasm.'Twould be a momentary visit—but a day or two—but that is all that would be necessary. See you this?'' The Prior pulled from within his black robe a metallic canister about ten centimeters long.

''Earth!'' Linsang collected herself, said, ''What's that you have there, another Machine?''

''Hardly, Lady, although Machine-made long ago. It is a container, of which we have thousands, in which the ancients protected certain records while maneuvering in the Deep. Records that the Deep might otherwise have destroyed. This container is airtight. Were you to fill many such containers with a random sampling of the person of Earth, and then to send them on a trajectory toward the Holy Isles—marking each, mind you, with the lupine leaves of your Trojan crest—would not the Hand, believing them to be gifts of an ally, eagerly collect them? They would appear a noble trove of matter.''

''A Trojan horse,'' squealed Pantolog, ''ridden by the Third Horseman!''

''And the things of Earth, living invisibly within, would not be noticed by the priests who opened the canisters—'' Linsang gasped at the enormity of the idea.

''And would devour the Holy Isles,'' howled Pantolog, ''committing the priests to the Deep!''

"Enough canisters," said Dyse, "enough to spread and reach all of the Holy Isles at once, would be taken in and opened—indeed, taken to the top—right to the Pollex himself, and no one would see a thing. The succubi of Earth would enter the physiologies of the Holy Isles even as the priests tried to guess what manner of gift they'd received from Stirps Semerling."

"And the mind that controls the web awaiting Wirtanen, the great spider-thing, the Hand of Man, would die—if we were quick enough." The Prior smiled his rare and lugubrious smile.

"But if all this is so," said Linsang, "why have you of Lagrangia never tried it before?"

"We have no way of sending things so far through the Deep, Lady, have not had matter to spare for millennia. We have had only hope, and the Book of Bates, to guide us. Now we have you, a vigorous and well-fed trio, and the Limestone's encouragement. My tiny people are not fit, I believe, for the rigor of an ascent from Earth, for we understand her Gravity to be most reluctant to release anything it has once gripped. It would take a mighty build like your own to survive the many masses produced in an escape from Earth. Would you do it?"

"Earth looks so beautiful from here," said Linsang, "and I have nowhere to go. I'll do it—if there's a way."

"There is," said the Prior. "You will have seen a series of projections about the equator of this Lagrangian sphere. Dyson Tessier describes them as looking like 'moths at rest.' Lady, those are Machines that were built by the ancients for one purpose: to go to Earth, the Earth of the Ascendancy, and to return here with materials for the long-ceased building of the Cities of O'Neill of which Lagrangia is the only remainder.

"Beneath this fane is an airlock to one of those Machines, a Machine that has for more than four millennia been ritually maintained by my people for this moment. Although we understand little of its workings, we know that it can be reactivated, that it eats liquid hydrogen and liquid oxygen, and that it has a brain, a Machine-mind, that will enable it both to touch Earth safely—if all goes well—and to find its way back to Lagrangia. That, after all, was its only purpose. Now its destiny may be fulfilled once more, and the Limestone's also—you will return it to its Mother, Earth."

"And how may we send all our canisters through the Deep to the Holy Isles?" Linsang looked from the Prior to Dyse, thence to Pantolog.

"Drought," whined Pantolog's Radio. "She is more than able to accelerate them—and us—near enough to release a herd of the things."

"But we can't touch Drought, nor allow her to come into contact with—"

"Your phallus-beast that you call a caracor has a set of tentacles about its body," said the Prior. "It can hold the moth-Machine, whose shell is sterilized by the Deep, while you three ride within."

"At a moment determined by Drought," added Dyse, "we release the canisters and turn away. The retiaries of the Holy Isles will be delighted to do the rest."

"And the Hand grips feared Earth at last," whined Pantolog.

*   *   *

"They're *mad!* I tell you, they've gone crackers!" Wind-hover spread his hands in disgust. "Honored Whip, Major Melliden, for all your greater experience I *still* say they're insane, and we to permit it."

"Mad they may be," said Saker, "but the Deep is full of madness now. Perhaps only more madness will stem the tide."

"But that—that *thing!* How can anything not alive pro-tect them from the Deep?" Windhover gestured toward the viewport.

"And how could a syne, any syne, penetrate the atmo-spheric membrane of Earth and live? The ancients effected the Filtration in such moth-Machines, Windhover, and our own existence is proof of it." But Spider, for all his outward confidence, still shared a bit of Windhover's unease.

Merry smiled nervously. "Linsang and Dyse—and even the encyclopedia—survived Lagrangia well enough. They'll handle the Mother as well."

"The Mother of us all." Saker peered out the viewport at the revolving view beyond, Lagrangia, the crescents of the Moon, and Earth, nightside, a black circle against the myriad stars of the Deep. "Our Chancellor reminded me before we embarked that Earth, creating life, then pro-vided four billion anni of tests that life might emerge into the lifeless Deep. She cannot be evil—or so the Chancellor said."

"Drought speaks," said the physyne Swo Yeak. "The Machine departs."

All clustered to the viewport, and Drought's rotation swung Lagrangia into view. The moth-thing that had been prepared through the millennia, that one whose cryptic European totem marks remained brightest, suddenly dropped away from Lagrangia's metal hull, falling toward Drought at the five meters per second induced by the Lagrangian rotation.

Light! Not the faint blue of the ion jets of synes, but a brilliant fusing of hydrogen and oxygen as the moth-Machine's ancient jets ignited. Glittering ice particles formed and dispersed behind the thing, and tiny attitudinal fires about its nose answered the flash of its going. In an instant the Machine was gone, passing faster than the viewport revolved.

Then they caught the Machine's light again, a fiery fleck against the nightside bulk of Earth. Beyond that black circle, Brazenface the Sun prepared to emerge; as the folk of Drought watched, the Machine's fire was overcome by a vivid arc of color—the rays of the Sun bending around the curve of Earth to smile on Her morningside air.

"S-some acceleration!" Dyse's lips pulled back from his teeth as the Machine's acceleration approached four masses. The cramped space in which he, Linsang and Pantolog lay smelled of the strange chlorinated Machine-stuff called Plastic. A thousand tiny lights covered with European symbols shone on the walls before them; above these the nose of the craft, oddly tiled in white, was visible through its rectangular viewports—and above the nose, the widening crescent of Earth.

And the four-mass acceleration ceased, as suddenly as it had begun. Freefall. The ancient Radio of the moth-Machine crackled into life. "Are you well? Speak!" The Prior's voice.

"We—we're *fine!*" Linsang felt pride, the exhilaration

of a new undertaking, a touch of strangeness, lovely strangeness. "We're *fine!*"

"I relay your words to your fellows on the phallus-beast. They wish you well."

"We're fine. We're in freefall. The Europeans must have spent much time in freefall. I'm tired—that four-mass acceleration right after the Lagrangian sickness." Linsang yawned. Pantolog was asleep.

Dyse's nervousness grew with each minute of the approach to Earth. "So this thing really lands itself?"

"So it is said, winged one," crackled the Radio, "hard to believe though it may be. It will seek a place at the edge of a sea, a great flat place called a *beach,* approximately located by the ancient Earthly measurements at twenty-nine point five north, eighty point five west. Sleep, now—your contact with the atmospheric membrane comes in but eight hours."

Sleep they did, finally, freefall cradling them while their bulky helmeted suits of armor filtered their air. Sleep, across tens of thousands of kilometers. Sleep, sleep, while the strange silicon brain of the moth-Machine guided them by its ancient memory of a place by the sea of Earth. Sleep.

And a rumbling, a shaking. In his sleep, Dyse felt a mighty Hand shaking him, shaking—he awoke, and the shaking continued, and—

"LOOK! Dyse, *look* out there!" Linsang, strapped into her weird thronelike seat, goblinlike in her armor of fabric and metal, gestured out the viewports of the Machine at the curve of Earth, subtle, dividing their view into black Deep above and cloud-flecked blue below. Pantolog, too, was awake.

"The shaking, frightened Doctor, is merely atmospheric—I think. The Machine must pierce this tough membrane with which Earth protects her living substance."

"It's said," gasped Dyse, "that after the fall of the Ascendancy the Earth was not blue for some centuries. She was as yellow as Venus."

"Yes, Honored Doctor. She was wounded, scarred. But then she healed herself, and the yellow dirt of the clouds was replaced by blue again. She had 'rubbed off humanity,' as Major Melliden might put it."

The shaking increased. The Machine, guiding itself gently downward, was moving across an ocean of deepest blue. Clouds, cotton-white, seemed painted on a pane of glass far beneath them, edged by their shadows as if outlined with a blue pen.

"Beautiful, beautiful!" Linsang reached for Dyse's arm, pointed. "Look, the colors! The horizon!"

"Look here," whispered Dyse, "the colors on the Machine's nose!" And the thing seemed to be catching fire, the white tiles glowing, first red, then yellow. "Earth resents our coming. She'll kill the Machine!"

"I think not, honored Doctor," said Pantolog. "Our passage through Earth's protective skin is swift. She believes us to be a meteorite, a falling Rock, come to strike at Her children—She would burn us. The Prior advised me that the little tiles on our Machine are designed for just such Earthly consumption, to deceive Her until we break through."

"Ah. Then you're in contact with him?"

"No longer, anxious Doctor. His Radio will not reach us here."

"And what if this thing deposits us in the middle of the ocean?"

"It won't, Dyse." Linsang grinned through the polarized globe of her helmet. "I know it won't—this is what it's been waiting for through all these centuries."

And the Machine did not fail them. Down, down it dropped, glowing like a falling star. Slower, slower, braked by Earth's tough skin of air, it came, seeking a home almost six millennia gone.

"Land!" Linsang gesticulated wildly in the roaring of the descent, pointed ahead. They touched the tops of clouds—not the smooth white and gray clouds of an Island, but spires and cliffs and shapes of—of what? The ancient gravitation-fear began to seize Dyse, and he clutched at the arms of his thronelike Machine-couch.

But Linsang pointed again through the stupendous clouds, and ahead was an expanse of sea-blue horizon—no longer curved—edged with a thin stripe of gray-green. Down, down—the place was too big for human eyes, and the enormity of it all sent Dyse's mind reeling.

The Machine banked into a long curve, turning virtually on its side to parallel the edge of the sea. "It's alive, Dyse, the Machine's alive!" Linsang knew an elation Dyse couldn't—wouldn't—share, as the thing settled ever downward across a gently undulating blue of more water than any man alive had ever seen at once, so frightfully close.

Leveling off, the craft aligned itself with a broad strip of white, white edged on one side with moving curves of white foam, on the other with a dense green of vegetation. And down farther, as the nauseating gravitation-fear washed over Dyse, claiming him for its own, and Linsang laughed a wild laugh of exultation at their rumbling fall to the flesh of their origin.

Deceleration! Sliding forward against the Machine's restraining webs, Dyse shut his eyes for what he knew was the last time as the Earth reached up to claim her own.

FWOMP—skazzzzz—FWOMP—skazzzz, ffffff, silence. Stillness.

His eyes still screwed shut, Dyse drank in the quiet. He knew what felt like the comforting caress of a one-mass rotation in his self-imposed darkness, and gradually the blood ceased its surging in his ears. He wished not to think. He was on some good Island, its rotation pressing him safely into the strange European throne on which he lay. He would not open his eyes, not until he woke out of this dream of Earth and found himself abed on Catuvel, perhaps, or on Summer Semerlinga.

Clicks and bumps, and a susurration of gentle wind against his European globe-helmet, wind underlain by a deeper roar, frightening, compelling. *Come,* the roaring seemed to say, *come, abandon yourself.* He closed his eyes tighter.

"Dyson Tessier, get *up!*" A voice of command, the voice of a Princess with ten thousand servants. "Pantolog's out on the ground—he can't get up in that armor they made for him—I'm going to help!"

More bumps, then silence but for the whispering breeze and that odd inexorable roaring, basso, something out of the very fabric of this place he refused to see.

"Gorgeous! Fantastic! Tessier, you coward, out of there!" Again, that voice of command.

All right. I'm looking *down.* He opened his eyes, slitwise, and stared at his white-gloved hands, at the bulky white fabric covering his legs, then across the metallic floor of the Machine—agh! Nausea swept him, but he stilled it and looked carefully to the side, to the threshold of the Machine's door, open, from which little steps descended to a blinding white surface. A firm surface. Good enough.

Still looking strictly downward, he lifted himself and his heavy European armor out of the seat. He made his way to the doorway, and, backward and on all fours, clambered down to the white—ah, substrate.

Looking only downward, he saw that this substrate was not truly white—it was composed of tiny grains, multi-colored, of Something—a fine sand, but not the basaltic sand of a meditation garden of the Gagarinians, or a water Island. He started backing away, still on all fours, from the shadow of the Machine—looking down all the while, he saw the way his armored knees and gloved hands left their imprint in the yielding sand. Back, back, ever backward he crawled, looking at his hands—and heard a laughing within the ancient Radio of his helmet.

"You great *ass!* You should *see* yourself! Stand like a man and look around you!"

Linsang's laughter provided Dyse with the will he'd lacked, and he shut his eyes again and gingerly stood up. So far, so good. One mass, one comfortable mass. An Island, rotating in the lovely Deep, with only a few tens of meters of bodywall between his feet and that safe Deep— right? Right. He stood straight and tall.

Dyson Teague Tessier opened his eyes and looked about him. No Island. No comforting curve of bodywall enclosing the air of his world against the Deep. None.

And Gravity seized him, pulling him crushingly down-ward against the almost thirteen thousand kilometers of rock-shelled molten steel that he knew Earth to be. And nothing above, nothing but the Deep, into whose vacuum this blue cloud-studded air must momentarily explode. Vertigo seized him, and the contents—very little, but enough—of his stomach exploded into his bulbous helmet as Gravity dragged him back against the sand like a squashed bug. His eyes shut again, Dyse suppressed the shuddering for a moment; but the stench of vomit filled his little room of European metal and glass, and he retched again. Linsang and Pantolog were there then, Linsang laughing. Dyse opened his eyes.

Pantolog wore no armor against the Pestilence of Earth.

That alone snapped Dyse into a measure of reality. "Pantolog! Where the—"

"I could not *move* in it, poor deranged Doctor. Now I *can* move, as never before, and if I die, so be it. This is the space, the open space within my cheetah's brain that I've always felt but only glimpsed once, on Summer Semerlinga! Only glimpsed, mind you, Doctor, chasing those forbidden impala! THIS is the place, and I am here, and oh, the smells!"

The creature took off, then, in a run a hundred kilometers an hour across the white sand to the edge of the sea, where waves man-high and more broke against the white flesh of Earth. Then away again, toward a forest wall of vegetal green spangled with flowers of a thousand colors; and back to the sea the cheetah ran, and off along its crashing rim, his long gold-black back flexing and unflexing in great leaps that seemed to drink the Earth's very immensity down in lusty gulps of distance.

Pantolog Five had found the Home of Life.

Chapter 15: **In which Earth sings aloud to human beings**

> And with them died their kin the Mammals,
> And Birds, that loved the air;
> And you, who live to read these Annals,
> Know well that only Death resides there!

—Versicle XXXIV of the Book of the Closing,
   from the Third Codex of the Annals of the Hand

IT TOOK DYSE more than an hour to overcome his Gravity vertigo, and it was the worst hour of his life. Linsang, meanwhile, activated the great doors that split along the Machine's metal spine; they opened on a vast aluminum-ribbed room filled with shiny little canisters, each neatly painted by the albino trolls of Lagrangia with an orange triad of lupine leaves. The canisters were light, and she heaved them out to the sand in sparkling dozens.

"They'll be opened in air on the Holy Isles remember," she called over the helmet Radios. "The Prior said to pick a variety of substrates, different soils—but fairly dry ones, if possible. We can start with sand and work through into the forest there. I've rigged a set of pannier bags from Pantolog's armor, and he can carry them back as I fill them—you toss them back into the Machine."

Dwarfed by the winged metal monstrosity, which stood on three wheeled stilts it had somehow unfolded from beneath its wings and body, Linsang clambered back to the ground. Dyse was suffering from heat, and from the vomit stench in his armor, but he set to work with as much vigor as could be expected. Linsang loaded Pantolog with a few dozen canisters at a time as she scooped Earth's substance; back and forth, back and forth ran the encyclopedia.

Starting at the edge of the pounding sea, Linsang worked her way gradually inland, leaving a strange line of scoop marks parallel to her own sandy boot tracks. If her European armor interfered, the woman said nothing about it— only squealed with delight when some new seashell, some strange flower, took her fancy.

The Sun dropped lower in the unfamiliar geometry of Earth's blue sky. Dropping, He changed colors, and the clouds around Him became a multicolored layering of light. Even Dyse had to pause to admire the display, the like of which is of course nonexistent except on Earth.

With His passing, Brazenface produced one last sky-canvas, his spectrum executing a brilliant dance with Earth's water-laden air. And before the Sun's light faded completely,

the Moon, silver and well-nigh full, rose over the sea to
touch the clouds with her own white reflection.

"Look at her, how silver—from the Deep she looked
like ash!" Linsang stood from her digging among the trees
of the forest edge to watch, and her whisper came over
Dyse's helmet Radio:

> " 'Was I deceived, or did a sable cloud
>   Turn forth her silver lining on the night?' "

"Milton of the Engli," murmured Dyse, "truly a man
of Earth." Indeed, Earth seemed determined to impress
with beauty Her trio of visitors from the Deep. The sea
bore a twinkling roadway of silver reaching to the Moon's
rising, and even Pantolog paused from his delighted running to watch.

As they stood, there came a rustling in the forest, a
pattering of sturdy feet, a thump! and Linsang, screaming,
was knocked to the ground by a brown creature almost
Pantolog's size. The encyclopedia was on her attacker in
an instant, pannier bags and all. Dewclaws and teeth
flashing, he made short work of the thing, breaking its
neck with a twist of his own.

Unhurt but shaken, Linsang joined Dyse beside the
corpse. It was a quadruped, covered in a short dense coat
of brown hair. Its ears were naked, leathery brown, and its
tail was long and scaly and almost devoid of hair.

"A *mammal*," gasped Linsang, catching her breath.
"The Annals of the Hand tell us that they ceased to exist
on Earth at Closing."

"A poorly adapted one, if it means to hunt meat."
Pantolog sniffed at the cadaver, then licked at one of the

wounds he'd inflicted. "Delicious! I shall have to pause, dear humans, and eat it. Wirtanen fare is barely edible, and the Lagrangians eat only rabbit food."

Turning the dead thing over with his foot, Dyse mused, "I wonder. This resembles certain religious sculptures on Catuvel, parts of representations of the Ascendancy. They're intertwined, forming the lintels of doors and the like. *Rats,* that was it, Rats, a sort of Earthly demon that lived beneath the great European cities and came out to devour their dead."

"I should have anticipated that, astute Doctor." Pantolog licked his lips hungrily. "But Rats were but half a meter long at most, including their naked tails. Still, they're said to have lived all over Earth, wherever the Ascendancy and its cultural offspring lived—could it be that they alone of mammals survived the Closing?"

"They're said to have been quite resourceful." Linsang, fully recovered from her shock, recalled her education. "A sort of rodent, like but unlike squirrels of Semerlinga. They burrowed, and had tails like this."

"And naked ears, like this." Pantolog snuffled eagerly. "Before I lose control, shall we examine the teeth?"

Dyse nervously reached out a gloved hand and pulled at the animal's long-whiskered cheek. The head was narrow, with a pointed nose; as he pulled, the mouth dropped open, revealing a pair of curved orange tusks ten centimeters long placed side by side at the front of the upper jaw. Parts of a lower pair were visible behind these.

"A Rat, yet so big!" Linsang stared in growing horror. "They're said to have eaten human babies alive!"

"But those were small ones, as Pantolog said. What happened?"

"Six millennia, perplexed Doctor, that's what happened." Pantolog sniffed the Rat's ear lovingly, continued, "The Rat is said to have been possessed of a great mutation rate even before it took up residence with human beings. The Closing, with its poisons, must have accented that mutation rate. Then what? Then a world from which all higher mammals had been eliminated. A period of accelerated mutation during the cloud-covered centuries of wounded Earth. Then an emergence of Rats into a world of rich, empty large-animal eco-niches.

"The Rat bred fast, and it was a generalized omnivore of primitive build. This one shows, in addition to large size, unusually long legs for a Rat as I understand them to have been. I would suggest, Doctor, that the descendants of the Ascendancy Rats are undergoing an adaptive radiation in the intensely creative environment of Earth."

"A what?"

"An adaptive radiation. Different Rats are filling the old large-animal eco-niches, taking over vacated jobs, if you will. It's said to have happened before. Some sixty-five million years ago, something killed the Dinosauria, the dominant large animals of that time. They looked something like the late Regent's toys, Moscow and Washington—or so I'm told. The only mammals existing then were much like the little insect-eating shrews of Summer Semerlinga and other large Island ecosystems, yet they repeopled the large-animal eco-niches quickly by the time standards of evolution. Those shrews produced bears, elephants—"

"Whales, horses, bats," said Linsang.

"Cheetahs—and human beings," said Dyse.

"And now that dynasty is gone from Earth and She

creates a new one to take its place. Now may I eat it?''
Pantolog leaned over his kill.

"Please do," said Linsang, looking suspiciously into
the forest. "I quit, for the nonce. I'd rather work with the
Sun alongside."

"Me, too," agreed Dyse, and the two of them started
back toward the safety of the Machine.

"By the way," shrieked Pantolog's Radio even though
the encyclopedia's mouth was already full, "I wouldn't be
surprised to find large herbivorous Rats, tree-climbing Rats,
swimming Rats and the like—all as ecologically differenti-
ated as this incipient carnivore here. That's the way adaptive radiations work."

"No doubt," Linsang called back. "If you do find
them, please eat them."

"Delicious," whined Pantolog. "I shall. As a cheetah,
I represent many millions of years' evolutionary advantage
over them; I am functionally a perfect being."

"Not quite," said Dyse. "A few million more years,
and no Radio, and you might do." With that, the two
armored humans climbed back into the Machine for a
sorely needed sleep.

Pantolog, however, had much to do. First he placed his
forepaws on the Rat's shoulders and pulled at the skin of
its neck, peeling the furry coat back to expose the muscles
of shoulder and rib. Odd, he thought, how practiced these
movements seem, how thinly my encyclopedia's genes are
laid over those of my cheetah's body. I wonder whether
my curiosity is cheetah, or syne, or both. And the taste,
the warmth of the blood, the ease and perfection with
which my teeth sever these tendons! Here is my true
purpose—the syne in me simply permitted me to get here.

Ahh, luck—the Sailing of Gagarin, that merest chance that enabled me to stumble into Wirtanen II when their prophesied "Beast of gold" was so much on their minds! Lovely it is for me that human beings are so often slaves to prophecy, to old books, to fears for their future!

The encyclopedia ate until he could eat no more, pausing occasionally to muse over some new scent carried over the breeze to his acute nose. The feline delight in the kill still surging within him, he ambled down the moonlit beach for half a kilometer, satiated yet filled with an urge to move, to seek something—anything—new.

At the water's edge he found a dead horseshoe crab of the genus *Limulus,* one identical to those that had been carried by humanity into the Deep millennia before—just as his own cheetah kind and countless other organisms had been carried out there to enrich life's foothold in the lifeless Deep. From far within his limitless syne memory came whispers of the monumental conservatism of *Limulus,* an organism that had happily persisted unchanged through hundreds of millions of anni and hundreds of millions of changes. Here I, a syne, life's newest expression, stare at *Limulus,* one of life's oldest, yet freshest, little songs. A good place to lie down, right here by this *Limulus,* listening to Ocean and watching the Moon.

A rustling in the bushes. Pantolog lifted his black and yellow head to follow the sound. From the forest's edge emerged a large female Rat, astoundingly piglike in form, yet whose leathery ears and long bare tail amply betrayed her ancestry. Her orange incisors protruded sideways from her mouth like the tusks of a boar, and piglike she grubbed with them for a moment in the soil before squealing softly. At this motherly sound, five little piglet-Rats followed her into the moonlight, clustering about her stubby feet and wrinkling their snouts in the night air, pushing for her teats. But Mama wasn't in the mood for suckling; she grunted and trotted off down the beach. Upwind from Pantolog, none of the piggy rodents had detected his scent; he, full for the moment, lay still and pondered their departure with delight. What a place, this Earth, what a paradise, what an incredible nexus of creative energy to produce such a diversity of organisms from the despised furry rodents called Rats by men. Pantolog's happy sigh was punctuated by a belch, and he flattened further onto the damp sand in perfect relaxation as the pig-Rats disappeared again into the forest.

There was an hour, perhaps two, during which Pantolog lay half asleep at Ocean's edge. Earth turned beneath Her Moon, which climbed higher across the sky in response. Ocean advanced with the Moon, held to her by gravitational links almost four hundred thousand kilometers long, and the tide crept toward Pantolog. Somewhere out with the Moon and beyond were human beings, millions of them, and synes too, but Earth seemed at peace with Herself. Having "rubbed off humanity," as the Gagarinians say, Earth was content to ignore the terrible events of the Deep; She seemed more intent on making new animals and setting them to roam about Her incomparably beautiful surface. Ah, what could not this planet do, given enough time? She could provide the best of all possible homes for the likes of Pantolog Five, that much was certain.

A sound, a twittering, a faint chirping of several high-pitched voices from the direction of his recent kill, brought the encyclopedia to full consciousness. He'd left half of the carcass behind, and something—some kind of Rat, no doubt—was making a grab for it. On his feet in an instant, Pantolog did what cheetahs do best—he sprinted back along the beach, close by the forest's edge to avoid being seen in the moonlight. No Rat, however big, would do Pantolog Five out of his dessert.

Pounding in on his kill, the cat scattered half a dozen specimens of a new sort of Rat, sideswiping one with his left dewclaw as he skidded and then rolled to a halt in the sand. Before he could regain his feet and turn again, five Rats grabbed the remains of Pantolog's kill and slipped swiftly and silently into the forest. Pantolog sprinted after them but was instantly reminded that his hunting was best done in daylight, in open country, rather than in a vast and totally unknown forest at night. Better a wound to my pride than to my person, he reflected, returning to the beach at a more prudent walk.

But all was not lost. The one Rat he'd clipped now caught Pantolog's nose, then eye; it had staggered unevenly toward the forest, then fallen, a loop of its intestine entangled in its hind leg. Now it was dead, and justly so in the encyclopedia's opinion. He trotted to the corpse, his good cheer renewed.

A new Rat it was. Lightly built, a night-gray in color, it had stood about a meter tall when on its feet; its head was blunter, rounder than the heads of either the predator-Rat or the pig-Rat, and the orange incisors, exposed in death, were short and unspecialized. This Rat's entire body was constructed for fast running, a trait Pantolog felt was vitally necessary to anything that would dare steal his dessert. Unlike the other Rats, this one and its escaped brethren moved birdlike on two elongated hind legs whose central toes were enlarged to grip the ground. The forefeet were smaller and obviously held free of the ground in life in the manner of those of a kangaroo.

Also unlike the other Rats he'd seen, this one sported a soft, wide tuft of hair at the end of its long scaly Rat-tail. The tail itself acted as a balance to the creature's body, and the tuft thus functioned as a rudder to permit it the quick twists and turns necessary to a small scavenger whose life must often depend on the ability to escape. The new Rat, in short, was a well-adapted biped, a social scavenger built light and quick perhaps after the ecologic fashion of a jackal, though with its leathery ears, scaly tail and inscrutable round black rodent's eyes (now glazing over) it was still very much a Rat to Pantolog, who decided to keep it for breakfast.

But Gagarin intervened again, and in such a manner that Pantolog broke all of his syne-encyclopedia's genetic constraints once more: he saw a thing, a thing of great importance, and refused to communicate it to his human associates. Perhaps it was his encyclopedic curiosity, a desire to "see what would happen" without his intervention; again, perhaps it was something of his Sisterhood-altered cheetah's mind. Whatever it was (and the mistresses of syne lore still ponder the act), Pantolog Five kept a secret for the first time in his life, and he kept it for some two anni after that night.

It was all a very simple thing, a single galvanic twitch of the dead Rat's hind leg that caused it to roll onto its back for an instant. The movement freed the animal's left forefoot, previously hidden beneath its chest, and for the first time Pantolog realized that the toes of both forefeet were oddly arranged: in place of a "thumb," each had a horny pad linked to the "forefinger," which in turn was separated from the remaining three foretoes by a wide gap.

In this gap on its left forefoot, the scavenger Rat clutched a small wooden bludgeon, one purposefully shaped into club form by the gnawing of rodent teeth; a last twitch relaxed the death grip, the club falling silently into the sand.

Pantolog sat down with a thump. He looked across the beach toward the silent Machine at Ocean's edge, white in the moonlight, cradling its sleeping human occupants. He looked the other way, then, into the blackness of the forest. He looked at the dead Rat again, and finally upward, toward the Deep, gazing meditatively for a time at the Moon and the stars far beyond.

Then Pantolog Five seized his dead Rat in his jaws, lifting all but the long tail clear of the ground, and minced slowly to Ocean's edge. Overcoming a latent suspicion of the waves, he advanced into the water and flipped his burden outward to the breakers, the breakers that would tell no tale. Ocean swallowed the gift, and Pantolog returned to the beach, to the forest's edge, to the carefully formed little bludgeon in the sand. This, too, he carried to Ocean, and Ocean in turn carried the bit of wood far, far away while Pantolog watched. He did not sleep that night for admiration of Earth and amusement at the humor of Her never ending artistry. And of this Earthly night the syne Pantolog spoke nothing for a long time, though its memory was with him always.

When Brazenface rises over an observer on Earth, He comes not in a gentle and even movement of reflective hoplites flicking His brilliant wind through the polarizing glass of an Island to the "valleys" below. No, Earth rotates, at almost seventeen hundred kilometers an hour at Her surface. One standing there, then, sees Brazenface in a growing blaze of light, first touching the upper reaches of Earth's incredible atmosphere, almost a thousand kilometers above. Thence downward in a gradual brightening, the colors of the solar spectrum bending through the air-skin's density as the observer speeds toward Brazenface's rising.

And finally the Sun Himself crashes above the strange flat horizon, visibly moving as the observer's point of view arcs along the vast curve of Earth, and it was this silent detonation of light that woke Dyson Tessier on his Earthly morning. The movement of the Sun above the flat eastern sea was all too apparent to him, and Dyse became aware that he was a speck on a ball whose surface was spinning at a rate of nearly thirty kilometers per minute.

Whup! He rolled out of his European throne, down the steps of the Machine, and fell on all fours, digging his gloved fingers into the sand lest he be flicked off the whirling Earthly globe and hurled into the Deep . . . .

But nothing happened, and his Lagrangian vegetable meal of last evening remained safely in his gut as he recovered his senses again. Earth, apparently, neither intended to crush him with Her Gravity nor project him shrieking into the Deep.

But She did do strange things to the light of Brazenface, scattering it generously through Her air-membrane and touching all surfaces with colors that She seemed carefully to select from the Sun's offering to enhance the contours of everything around. Earth, in fact, was making love to the Sunlight as She had done for five thousand million years, and Dyse's baffled eyes drank in texture and color as might a thirsting man drink water.

He was alone with the Machine. No Linsang, no Pantolog. A few canisters, bright in the slanting morning sun, glittered in the sand where they'd been dropped the evening before. He stood up, the weight and stink of his European armor ignored as he looked about the deserted beach. Always the roar of the sea, but no other sound.

"Linsang! Pantalog!" His voice was too loud to his bottled ears, but over the Radio in his helmet came no response. Nor over the Okumura mycelium, whose maximum range was but a hundred meters or so.

There were tracks in the sand, cat pugs and those of a human being. One wearing no shoes. And beyond the Machine's long morning shadow lay Linsang's crumpled armor, discarded beside that of the cat.

Fear took him then, fear for the young woman now unprotected from the Earthly poisons—the poisons that were to wither the mighty Hand. And then anger at her arrogance, her disregard for the project lying incomplete before him. He started following the tracks, great cat, barefoot human, along the thundering strand. He walked for almost a kilometer, and—

Ahead, a shout of laughter, distant in the breakers' roaring, and from the seething foam emerged Linsang Semerling, as naked as at the moment of her birth, her hair as yellow as the face of the Sun, her skin caressed in the weird beauty of the light of Earth. Pantolog lay up the beach on his back, belly distended, beside about a third of some new sort of mammal. The encyclopedia's legs stuck ridiculously into the air, and but for the twitching of his tail he might have been dead.

Dyse ran toward the pair, sweating in his fetid armor. "You fools! By the teeth of Pestilence's Mount, what do you think you're doing?"

"Our Doctor comes, in anger!" Linsang shouted, laughing as one deranged, to Pantolog above the percussion of the breakers.

The Okumura: "Behold, stuffy Doctor, a Princess unclothed! One would think that such a sight would defuse any human anger!" The encyclopedia staggered to his feet, his gigantic belly seeming for a moment to drag on the ground. "And look! As I predicted, a herbivorous Rat, with long central toes—incipient hoofs, I think!" The cat gestured with his tail toward the meager remains of his breakfast. "Earth creates a new world from the Rats of your ancestry, Doctor, and you sweat it out in armored fear!"

"Dyse!" Linsang's voice was muffled by his helmet, but understandable. "Get that thing off! I'm fine! Completely well—Pantolog's right! If Earth can make deer of Rats, She can make a cleaner man of you—I think." The girl laughed again, a lunatic laugh, it seemed to Dyse, and sprinted back into the sea.

"Poor Doctor, seized in a morass of fearful prudery, remove your filthy armor!" Pantolog took a few laborious steps toward Dyse and then sank back onto his bulbous abdomen. "I can hardly move—such food!" The creature began licking blood from his sandy feet. "Absurdly easy to catch," he added.

Well, they both *look* healthy enough, and Pantolog lasted the whole night—Gagarin, sail with me now!

Dyse began unscrewing the wing nuts of his headgear. He held his breath, shut his eyes, and pulled the helmet off, his lungs shouting for the air he refused them as long as he—

Exhale, and inhale, inhaling the dappled redolence of Earth, of the sea, of air that moved free about a living globe forty thousand kilometers in circumference. Wherever it went, that air recorded its mighty journey, and the flickering molecular diary of its passing exploded into Dyse's brain with all the force of four billion years' Earthly evolution.

He fell back abruptly on his rump in the sand, mind whirling with the elation of all his body's cells, and his eyes filled with tears he could neither explain nor refuse. For a full minute, Dyson Teague Tessier sat still on the beach, crying like a baby, breathing great draughts of the liveliness of this place.

Pantolog's Radio whined. "The same thing happened to me yesterday, much-refreshed Doctor. The mammalian cerebrum is derived from the smell-brain of our common ancestor, and smell still rules it. Stand again, Only Man of Earth! Remove the rest of that filthy stuff you're wearing, and join the Only Woman of Earth in that wonderful Ocean there. Myself, I must remain her and see to my excesses." Pantolog flopped languidly onto his side, ribs heaving with the pressure of his meal.

Stand Dyse did, and in a fever of ineptitude struggled with the archaic fittings of his armor. The sea called, and the golden woman therein—and, too, the forest called, echoing the sea of its origin. Quick! Quick! The armor fell away, and *Homo sapiens*, Man the Wise, stood naked in the morning sunlight of his home, sand squeezing between the toes of his spring-arched feet—feet built to run, legs rippling with sprinter's muscles.

Obeying an impulse as old as bipedality itself, Dyson Tessier's legs took him away, speeding him along the edge of the sea, touching with man's-toes the liquid fingers of the waves—and, in a great arc, he sprinted right into the face of the breakers, to be bowled over, sputtering, by a wave taller than himself.

Salt in his eyes, salt in his nose and his mouth. He stood again, the shock of the impact of Ocean bringing his mind a measure of control again—for a moment.

Then out onto the beach again, to hurl himself into the warm multicolored sand, rolling, shouting, laughing, all the way to the forest's edge. And Earth laughed with him. From the foliage exploded a riot of butterflies, dragonflies, the petals of flowers shaken loose by his passing. Above, larger fliers, white-tipped wings against the leafy canopy. They shrieked in passing, and Dyse froze where he lay in wonder.

"Bats!" The Okumura link—Pantolog had been watching his antics. "Bats, awe-struck Doctor, diurnal bats! The Closing killed Earth's birds, but bats hibernated in caves. Now Earth repeoples Her air with them, as She repeoples the ground with this superb assortment of Rats."

Dyse watched the wheeling of the day-bats, no somber brown like the bats carried long ago to the Islands of the Deep, but silvery beings with black faces and white-edged black wings half a meter in spread. The creatures settled back into the foliage, twittering among themselves and watching with bright eyes the strange hairless man-thing in the bushes below them.

A tiny pain in his ankle. He slapped instinctively at it, killing a tiny fly. Yack! He leaped up, backing away from the greenery. Another little fly, less than two millimeters long, bit him in the thigh.

Pantolog, still watching, called: " 'Insects that suck the blood of man,' Doctor. Fear not, though, we've been bitten all morning. A minor discomfort in this place, a gentle reminder from Earth that we yet live, and must tend to reality. Ahh, reality." The cat rolled over in the sand.

Dyse's legs commanded again, urging him faster, faster along the beach. Among the breakers, then, he spotted Linsang frolicking in the foam, oblivious to all but the touch of Ocean.

And those pounding legs of his, in complete control, steered him toward the fleck of wave-tossed gold that was Linsang's long hair, and he breasted the crests of water in an easy surrender of Deep-bred mind to Earth-born physiology.

There in the sparkling of Sunlight on a trillion ripples of Ocean, beneath a whirlwind of white fish-eating day-bats crying in the deep blue air, the Only Man of Earth joined the Only Woman of Earth. Even as they embraced, their Mother embraced them both in a swelling of the sea that moves in all our cells, lifting them gently from the shifting sand and caressing them with a passage of tiny silver fishes nibbling at their toes. And to a symphony of Her song, wind and wave and the reeling calls of flying beings, Earth joined Her prodigal children in the Fourfold Saraband, the Dance of the Nucleotides, most ancient and stately of all possible dances.

"I suppose we have to put the stuff back on." Pantolog snuffled disgustedly about the three stinking piles of European armor, itchy-looking fabric and metal.

"I washed my helmet, but the rest is hopeless." Dyse picked up the limp thing, goblin-shaped, sandy.

"Nothing for it but to dress." Linsang laughed. "Could you imagine our having kept them on here?"

"And my catching those wonderful Rats?" Pantolog shook himself, sand flying. "Why, I could hardly *walk!*"

Laboriously, they climbed back into their armor; then into the ancient Machine with its Trojan horse already sealed within its belly. The Machine fwumped and hissed, closing itself against the coming Deep as its makers taught it thousands of anni in the past.

For a long moment all three looked out about them. There was nothing to be said, now, but all were aware that Earth had placed an inexorable lien on them, a claim to Her own. Someday, should they survive the coming debacle, someday—

Dyse enacted the Machine's ritual, punching buttons in the order taught him by Lagrangia's little Prior. The thing awoke again, rumbling through its metal bones as oxygen and hydrogen united to add to Earth's watery bounty. Then the masses came, pressing them back into their thrones as the Machine bade its home good-by and streaked, a burning dart, into the bright sky of Earth.

Behind them on the beach glittered the transparent cube of crystalline carbon, within which floated the Limestone. The tide, rising on the link of Earth and Moon, reached for that tide-born Stone, engulfed it, took it back.

Earth smiled, adorning their passing with a white ribbon-contrail a thousand kilometers long through Her upper atmospheric membrane. The thunder-sound of their going raised clouds of multicolored fliers, day-bats with whose bright numbers She bade Her children a farewell they did not see.

But the sound of Ocean they took with them, sighing in their minds forever. *Come back,* it called, *come back to play again with me.*

Chapter 16: In which Pestilence mounts a Trojan horse

> Yea, poison, pain and sure demise,
> Convulsion, frothing, blinded eyes;
> So touch ye not that fetid place,
> Steer clear the arc of Earth's cruel mace.
>
> —Versicle CXV of the Book of the Closing,
>   from the Third Codex of the Annals of the Hand

"HAVE YOU CONSIDERED, Spider, that most of our time together has been spent in sleep?" America Berecynthia rubbed her eyes with her fists, nudged Spider Quick-to-Change Melliden in the ribs with her elbow.

"Well, Drought has taken good care of us, except for the feeding. Myself, I'd rather sleep than eat this stuff."

Spider spurned the chopped Wirtanen mess with one of the wooden sticks he'd learned to use.

"The Beast says that the fare of Earth was excellent," said Saker the Swift from across the round table.

"Without compare," whined the little black cube at the table's center. Pantolog, without in the moth-Machine with Dyson Tessier and Linsang Semerling, was yet in contact with this mess-hall Radio, gift of the Prior at Lagrangia.

"Beast, I regret this Radio," said Saker.

"As do I," said Pantolog. "Through it you intrude on my thoughts as I wake. They were far away. I was hearing Ocean."

It was but two hours before that Drought had awakened her company, both within her own body and without in the Machine she embraced with her jointed tentacles. Insulated in that Machine with Dyse and Linsang, Pantolog eyed a tube of the meager Lagrangian fare; the consumption of vegetable gels did not agree with him, and he was restless and irritable.

As was Dyse, to whom their cramped quarters were well-nigh intolerable. He itched and squirmed incessantly, his long sleep having done nothing to allay his claustrophobia. Even their short return to the great metal sphere of Lagrangia had been claustrophobic to him, and he knew within himself a new horror of Island-dwelling regardless of whether the Island be a somber Lagrangia or a vaulting forested Semerlinga.

But there was no more Semerlinga, nor Aresia Alpha, and billions of people had died in the War of Rocks so far away. Billions more, stateless, rioted on crippled Islands or sought to fend off the numberless and directionless raptores that wore out their instinct-ruled lives rampaging among the wreckages of Aresia and Troy. So Drought had reported on awakening those in her care, and the report had touched with pain their emergence from weeks of sleep.

Now, along the perimeter of the living web set by the Hand of Man beyond the curve of the Sun from Drought, raptores under the direction of Catuvel caroused about, sneaking in and striking here and there across that vast aggregation of retiaries and raptores. Hopelessly outnumbered, Catuvel's minions nonetheless diverted their adversaries' attention somewhat from the approach of Wirtanen II. Perhaps, just perhaps, they could tear enough of a hole in that net of light to—

But the Hand maintained the order of its web well enough, governing it from the safety of the Holy Isles far away, and in those Isles confidence swelled as the time for the destruction of the last nest of Batesian heretics drew near. Liturgies were sung, sonorous liturgies of joy to the Horsemen, who prepared, with the Holy Fist as their agent, to trample the Islands of Wirtanen II into the dust of which they were composed.

Ah, Holy Isles! Have you forgotten, in your liturgies, the Third Horseman, Pestilence of Earth? He resents being forgotten, you know. Even now, in the guise of a Machine embraced by one small Wirtanen caracor, he approaches your heart.

Drought spoke; with the Radio from Lagrangia, she no longer required Swo Yeak as intermediary in conversation with human beings. "Honored Whip," she said, "my retiaries report mass ahead. We must cease our approach momentarily or be discovered."

"Yes," said Saker. "Doctor Tessier?"

From the Machine, Dyse answered: "I hear Drought. When she begins the course alteration, she'll notify us at the correct moment and we'll spring the canisters. Her calculations of their trajectory are already set."

"Please couch yourselves," said Drought. "I prepare my curve, and it will be a curve of many masses."

A scramble to the couches. In the Machine, the weird European webbing held its three passengers fast. Dyse's fingers moved to the metallic toggles that operated the thing's great spinal doors.

"Linsang?"

"I'm ready and waiting. So's the baby, I feel, though it can't be but a centimeter long as yet."

"A mighty baby, Princess Linsang, an Earth baby." Pantolog's Radio was loud in the Machine's cockpit. "The baby that oversees, from your womb, the piercing of the Holy Isles."

"The Earth baby. Dyse, if they see us—"

"Look, my Princess, at that Radio of Pantolog's. What do you see?"

"Black cube. The Trickster's Sailing."

"He sails with us, to trick the Hand. Hang on."

"Doctor," Drought said, "my curve begins. Allowing for the reflex of your hand and the operation of the Machine's doors, I will signal when the moment is optimum."

The masses came, then, and the three in the Machine were pressed against their restraining webbing as Drought bent herself against the inertia of her great speed.

"Doctor—NOW!"

Click—grooooon. The Machine rumbled as its ancient engines opened the long doors along its back.

In a twinkling of light, fourteen hundred and seventy-three little airtight canisters, the entire cargo, continued on a Euclidean line toward the Holy Isles a mika and a half distant, while Drought's curve carried her back, away again toward the safety of the Earthward regions of the Deep.

"They're off!" gasped Linsang through the pressure of the curve.

Drought straightened, accelerating now at one mass, Machine and all. Within, her passengers left their couches and scrambled for the viewports.

Far away, a minute scintillation against the Deep's stars told of the long arm of Earth's reaching to grasp the Holy Isles. The Trojan horse sped on its way.

"Well done, Doctor!" Saker laughed.

"Laugh not so soon, honored Whip. We are seen." Drought's acceleration increased slightly. "I am followed by a single raptore at a distance of two hundred four thousand, three hundred twenty-seven kilometers, approximately. A fast raptore, which will already have notified its fellows. It—its path alters. It has spotted the canisters. Now it continues to match our trajectory; it will have alerted others to collect the canisters, no doubt."

"A single raptore? Surely—" Spider was interrupted.

"Major, that raptore is now joined by two others. More mass is following them, although I cannot determine its nature. Likely more raptores—the mind of the Holy Isles is suspicious. Couch yourselves—I shall accelerate to three masses."

Couched, all felt the masses grow. In the Machine, Linsang whispered through the weight, "How are embryos affected by such weight?"

"Such a spectacular baby, Princess Linsang, carried by such a formidable mother, need fear no mere masses." Pantolog's Radio spoke loudly, unaffected by weight though the encyclopedia lay as one dead in his European constraints.

"I'm glad the embrace of Drought is strong enough to hold our Machine through all this mass-shifting," whispered Dyse. One of Drought's segmented metachitinous tentacles, wrapped around the Machine's nose beyond its glassy windows, twitched in response.

"How long, Drought," gasped Merry, "will it take for the Hand's minions to carry those canisters home?"

"Less than an hour, mistress. But their effect will not be immediate. They will be thought Trojan gifts by the folk at the Holy Isles, and those folk, not understanding their contents, will carry them to their leaders. On the other hand, they may undergo a quaranty, a period of isolation. I do not know. If they are quarantied for a time, Wirtanen—and we—are lost, and the Hand becomes the sole ruler of all the Peoples of the Deep—what remains of them. We can only wait."

"Trickster, sail with us now!" Spider's three-mass whisper husked into the room from where he lay hidden by the muscles of his couch.

"H-how would the canisters affect the Hand, if they're opened?" Windhover's voice was thin, cracked by the masses.

Pantolog's Radio whined through the room. "If yon little succubi come in contact with the circulatory systems of the Isles, they will be spread throughout. They multiply quickly, and the Isles will be a delightful repast for them. Our Deepskins decayed in minutes on Lagrangia—presumably this broader assortment of succubi will invade the nervous systems of the Holy Isles, at which time their minions out here should noticeably change their behavior. But that's hours or days away.''

Drought spoke: ''Those raptores are approaching quickly. They may exceed my capabilities. They will reach us within four hours, thirty-two minutes, at present acceleration. There are twelve of them now.''

''Can they suspect our purpose?'' Merry was barely audible from her couch.

''I think not as yet, mistress. I am in blackbody, and bear no markings. They merely attempt to divert us. I have twice received lightlink impulses, but will not respond. I shall increase my acceleration to five masses. Sleep now.''

Drought flooded her air with the sweet-smelling sleep of long voyages through the Deep. On the Machine, Linsang with difficulty passed sleeping capsules to Dyse and Pantolog. Drought waited until there was no response from any of her passengers and then accelerated, the inertial web of the universe pressing her little human wards deeper, deeper into the muscles of her couches.

Awakening aboard Drought. One-mass acceleration.

''Honored Whip, I have considerably outdistanced the pursuing raptores, but they will close with us again within five hours, twenty-three minutes at present acceleration. I fear keeping the Lady Linsang's developing offspring under continuous five-mass acceleration. The sleeping capsules of those on the Machine will cease functioning shortly.''

''Good,'' said Saker. ''Spider, are you with us?''

''Barely,'' said Spider as he clambered from his couch. ''I'm glad, Drought, that your jetting is so excellent.''

"Myself, thank you, Major. However our flight has aroused the wrath of the Hand, and more than a hundred raptores now pursue us. Food for my jets cannot last at these accelerations. We have passed the interference of the Sun, though, and I have been in lightlink with Catuvel for some time. She is indeed a changed being since our encounter among the Rocks. When Doctor Tessier awakens, she would speak with him."

"Changed?" Spider recalled the luxury of the sweep, her food.

"She, ah, was educated. Physically she remains the same, but her military capabilities were enhanced by the Sisterhood that healed her—ostensibly to serve the Regent in his war, but she evacuated, as you'll recall, the minions of Homar into the Deep."

"The Sisterhood has a long reach."

"Major, the Chancellor Niagara of Wirtanen has a long reach."

Pantolog's Radio snarled a greeting. "Do I understand my friend Catuvel to be in reach?"

"She engages the Hand's web some one hundred and thirty mikas away; she speaks, but there is a seven-minute light-lag between us. You must allow her to have her say, and when she pauses you will have yours."

Dyse, now awake also, spoke from the Machine: "Drought! Can Catuvel speak to us?"

"Indeed. One moment, while I convert her lightlink to Okumura and Radio. Patience, Doctor."

Then the melodiously familiar voice of Catuvel, both in Dyse's Okumura mycelium and aloud on Pantolog's Radio, filled the Machine.

"Doctor, it's been more than an annus! Drought has told

me something of your exploits. Princess Linsang, your home is dead, but I understand that you miss her not; also that you carry a child, and that you and Doctor Tessier have launched a small Trojan horse, one ridden by the Third Horseman, to the Holy Isles. Let him ride swiftly and well—I am sorely tried by the Hand's minions out here, and the Islands of Wirtanen II approach swiftly. All of our lives ride with Wirtanen, and with your Trojan horse. I—my sensory perimeter is being blinded. Now.''

The voice of Catuvel, as always, seemed too calm. And seven minutes away by light—a maddening distance.

She spoke again, still calm, words of death. ''My raptorial perimeter is breached. I am approached by a flotilla of raptores, big ones; I shall have to hurl my own body into—I am—''

''Catuvel!'' From both Drought and the Machine, the shout went out across the millions of kilometers of Deep.

Then Drought: ''Honored Whip, regrettably our pursuers are increasing their acceleration. They have also increased their numbers, with several curving away from the line of our trajectory. They may anticipate evasive curves on my part, although I see no aid in such curves. They are fast enough without—''

''Without what?'' Saker drummed his foot against the bulkhead.

''Honored Whip, those raptores are increasing their acceleration, but they are also dispersing.''

''Dispersing where?''

''All over. Their formation is breaking.''

''But what—''

''Perhaps they've been called to the web awaiting

Wirtanen?'' Merry peered out the port, but of course nothing was to be seen but the star-flecked Deep.

The Radio whined with the voice of Pantolog: "Honored Whip, assembled humans, might I venture a presumptuously optimistic—"

"Speak, Beast, and have done with it!" Saker's fear edged his voice—the imperturbable Whip was cracking at last.

"If, indeed, the pursuers are dispersing, we might guess that the Trojan horse has found a stable—honored Whip.''

"Honored Whip, we are certainly no longer pursued.'' Drought paused, then: "Catuvel speaks."

Catuvel's motherly voice, crossing a string of light seven minutes long, again filled Drought and the Machine.

"Doctor, Princess, a thing most odd has happened. The raptorial minions of the Hand pierced my perimeter on a leeward trajectory straight toward me—I could not have defended myself against them, dispersed as my own minions are. But the flotilla of Hand raptores came to me and then *passed right by*. And now the entire web is dispersing in what appears to be random movement. I will continue advising you, but know that my own safety appears assured for the moment.''

"Honored Whip,'' Pantolog's Radio screeched and cackled, "would you wager with a mere Beast? I think that I would like to bet with you that the Trojan horse—''

But the voice of Pantolog was drowned out in a burst of cheering as his human companions in both Drought and Machine abandoned themselves to triumph. Pantolog turned to Dyse and Linsang, but these were silently locked in an embrace as deep as the Deep itself.

"Ridiculous,'' muttered the encyclopedia. "I lost a good crack at that Whip, too.''

Chapter 17: **In which again we dance the Fourfold Saraband, wherein all ends and beginnings are one**

All things are changing: and you yourself are in continuous mutation, and, in a manner, in continuous destruction; and the universe too.

—*Meditations,* IX: Marcus Aurelius of the First European Empire

IN THAT TIME strange beings indeed sailed the Earth-Moon System. Retiaries, hundreds of thousands of the little creatures, spread their numbers about the System, and raptores in neatly peaceable clusters, tentacles intertwined, rolled among them. Six silly forty-kilometer drivers, abdomens curled in resting spirals, spread their leaves to graze on the Sunsea as well.

But the strangest sight of all in that Earth-centered space was the sweep Catuvel of Wirtanen II, her glittering crescent-shell revolving in long two-minute circles about her many-eyed center of mass. She sang to herself, did Catuvel, and crooned to her six grazing drivers. She danced her reflective hoplites in twenty-kilometer minuets of shifting heraldic forms—the Nucleotides Intertwined of Wirtanen II, her new home, alternating across the hours with that newest crest of all, three lupine leaves arrayed about a boar's head, plant and animal, the crest of Earth, Home of Life.

Catuvel rode a geosynchronous orbit about Earth, seated comfortably above Her equator. From the windows of her Great Hall she offered a view of Earth, now a black nightside circle blocking the Sun's brilliance with Her body. Folk of Wirtanen moved to and fro in the Hall, carrying great trays of food to those seated about Catuvel's new round table with its inlaid map of the Plate that bisects the Systemic Sphere.

The Whip Saker the Swift grinned a point-toothed grin. "I shall miss that Beast, although I would never want it to know."

"Likewise," said another Whip, a new one, Spider Quick-to-Change Melliden. "Pantolog would've loved this meal."

"He spoke incessantly of the meals in his future home, though—best he'd ever had, he said." America Berecynthia laughed. "I'll miss him too. A greater storehouse of trivia we'll never see."

"You'll find trivia enough in the Mind of the Libraries

of Wirtanen II," said the Chancellor Niagara from her couch at the place of honor. "Study them well, Sister, and you may approach that Beast in learning."

"It'd take many lifetimes, Lady Chancellor, and I have but one."

"Indeed. No escape from the Sisyphean boulder, though, young Sister, for you. Your labors have just begun. Still, your Sapphonic origins, your recent trajectory through history, all your life so far militates in your favor. The future diversity of the Peoples of the Deep rides with you, America." The Chancellor raised her glass. "I would drink the safe and fruitful trajectory of the first non-Chimaeric Chancellor of the Islands of Wirtanen II."

All raised glasses—no water this, nor tea, but red Palivan wine from the great cellars of Catuvel. Indeed, Saker, unused to the stuff, was becoming unsteadier and more mirthful than might befit his rank—his slanted eyes were bright, and his sawtooth smile grew with each of the many toasts offered over that long meal.

"And what, Mistress Merry," said he, "will be the first direction of this trajectory of yours?"

"Ah, so much to think about. But first will be the collection of enough oxygen and hydrogen for the reactivation of the rest of the moth-Machines. I would have the old Prior see his people's new home before he dies."

"His new place, from what I hear, will be bounteous indeed compared to Lagrangia—I hope the little Lagrangians handle themselves with their bounty better than do I with this excellent wine." Saker settled lower in his seat, crossed his short legs beneath the table. "But they're a folk accustomed to frugality, and revere the virginity of Earth. I believe they'll do well there. So, no doubt, will the two priests who share their trajectory.''

"This collection of hydrogen and oxygen will take but a few months," said Albemarle, Lord Durrell, late of the Tetravalency, whose outposts had been destroyed in the War of Rocks. "Through the centuries we lofted stores, frozen megaliters of the stuff, into orbits off-Plate; those that approach the Path of Earth we'll divert to Lagrangia. Do I understand Catuvel still to have the voice of command for non-raptorial synes remaining from the Regency's destruction?''

From the black Deep-sterile Lagrangian Radio at the table's center came the melodious voice of Catuvel. "I have; I have many drivers and other servants at my disposal, and have already ordered some to drop off-Plate and skirt the Rocks. Some have been gathering matter throughout the destruction, as befits their function. They bring it here.''

"I'll never get used to this—this Radio." Durrell peered at the cube suspiciously.

"Nor I," said the wobbly Saker. "However, if I regard it as a representation of the Principle of Heisenberg, it becomes tolerable.''

"The Trickster's Sailing," said Spider. "A fine and mighty Sailing it's been to me.''

"Mistress Merry," said Saker, "once you see the Lagrangians released on Earth, what will you do?''

"Most of the garden-Islands of both Troy and Aresia were not damaged in the fighting—no military consequence." Merry looked to the Chancellor, who spoke:

"Yes; and we are told that the large-animal eco-niches on Earth remain unoccupied, despite the efforts of Rats to invade them. Those garden-Islands support elephants, giraffes, lions, tigers—cheetahs—thousands of species of mammals and birds that Earth would likely welcome as warmly as She welcomed Her recent visitors.''

"Linsang and Dyson," said Spider. "Ah, the Deep's emptier without them.''

"But their place in the Deep is no longer. Let's hope that their place on Earth is managed better by their descendants than it was by our ancestors.'' Saker turned his ruddy drink in his hands, lifted it again to his lips.

"It will be—at least we can hope so. The Nucleotides dance diversity, after all, and diversity is conflict. Still, the future Earthly generations will have all the learning and experience of the Deep at their disposal via the Radio of Lagrangia—and the Lagrangians, as you point out, are a frugal folk. I think that their way will prevent another Ascendancy—for a time.'' Merry looked to the ancient Chancellor she would soon succeed.

"Yes, there is that,'' said Niagara. "The Prior has said that Earth should remain a place of human peace; he does not intend that his folk and the two priests should remain long in that place where the Machines go. They hope to learn to build boats and sail southward to a place of congenial islands called by the ancients Caribbea. There they will remain, so as not to trouble the ecosystems of the continents.''

"Humanity is a race of Island-dwellers. It's a fitting decision.'' Merry sighed. "Then there are the Islands remaining alive out along the Paths of Mars and Jove. We estimate that some three billion folk still survive—they'll want release from the Black of noncommunication. We'll be attempting to reach them in the coming years, to offer them means of defense against the raptores in the Rocks. And we'll have to work on those raptores, too—clean 'em out. It'll take centuries, and fighting men, and raptores of our own—matter.''

"Ah, matter." Spider smiled. "And what, Chancellor Niagara, does the Sisterhood of Wirtanen say of the Lagrangian records—the Machine-drivers that lay on the Moon?''

"They tell me that drivers can be grown that will survive the Gravity of sterile moon surfaces; they'd be permanently located there, of course—a Seed would be dropped, much as on an ordinary Rock. Then it'll spread leaves and grow a driver whose abdomen length will be commensurate with the Gravity of the body on which it's planted. The driver will chew matter from its substrate, and the abdomen will accelerate that matter into the Deep. Catuvel's retiaries in low orbit about the Moon here have found the ruins of the European Machine-drivers that provided much of Lagrangia's matter; the Sisterhood will examine those ruins with hopes of growing synes like them. It shouldn't be too difficult.''

"Dyson of the Machines—Dyson of Earth. *Both* men of Earth, these Dysons, with almost six millennia between 'em. My old commander Busork Tek had the right idea. Dyse didn't believe a word of it at first." Spider chuckled. "Now he says he intends to walk north along that 'seacoast' of his, where he says the Second Engli branch of the Ascendancy had many great cities. He'll become an antiquarian, I guess—Linsang's main interest also. Maybe they'll find more of use to us in the Deep." Spider picked up his knife, carved himself a piece of pork.

"I wonder about that Earth baby," said Merry. "I

would like to have a child before I die, and would like to raise it to join the Earth baby someday. No Earth-born creature could return to us here for company, and 'twould be a lonely baby indeed without some companion of its own generation to walk that seacoast. Such a huge place. I would that my offspring could see it.''

''As would I,'' said Saker. ''My Chancellor has granted me a Writ of Generation, as you all know—my wife will be Sandpiper Flautist of Wirtanen. She, too, would like our youngster to see Earth—though our own place remains in the Deep.'' He raised his glass. ''To all the children of Earth!''

They drank again, and the Chancellor's bright black eyes fastened on Merry. ''What, Sister, would you do for a mate? You'll be the first of the Chancellors not to be a sterile Chimaera, yet you won't have the Sapphonic opportunity to select from vials of dossed seminal fluid. Have you a suitable father in mind for your Earth child?''

''Ah. A problem indeed.'' Merry reddened a bit. ''It was the custom of Sappho to choose the genes of fighting men of a size commensurate with our own. Many of those genes were selected from the officer sept of the First Security Maniple.''

''There is no longer a First Maniple,'' interrupted Spider.

''A sad thing,'' said Merry. ''Then I must select from among the free folk of the Deep in all their diversity. But my Sapphonic prejudices remain—I prefer the idea of a mate of training and genetics similar to those of the late First Maniple.''

''One large, no doubt, and with great appetite,'' said Saker.

"And perhaps hairier than the men of Wirtanen," said Durrell, grinning.

"And, Sister America," said Niagara, "one on whom the Trickster Gagarin shows a tendency to smile—an Earth child will require luck in its parentage."

"Alas, that none of this type remain who are of general grade," said Spider. "Only those of general grade in my sept are offered Writs of Generation."

"I," said Saker, "am a Whip—by definition of general grade in Wirtanen II. I am spoken for already, though. I wonder what manner of Whips remain who would suit the rising of our new Chancellor? Surely not a little pirate Whip with pointed teeth—"

From the floor nearby came the soft voice of one Swo Yeak, physyne. "I am aware of one who might suit the requirements of Mistress America. One large, with a most extraordinary physiology, one well favored by the Principle of Heisenberg, one admirably preadapted by genes and education to aiding the new Chancellor in her coming labors—"

"Ah, uh, we'll *all* be aiding the new Chancellor, Swo Yeak," said Spider. He licked his lips, which had suddenly become dry, added, "Myself, I shall be sailing among the remaining—"

"I have perhaps neglected to add to word of your promotion to Whip, Quick-to-Change, the fact that the mind of the Islands of Wirtanen II has recommended for you a Writ of Generation of your own." Niagara's eyes flicked to Spider, looked him up and down. "I believe that this Writ, if fulfilled, would well serve the diversity that we all seek—if, of course, you were to choose a mate suited to your own unique qualities of resourcefulness . . .

for which, I must guess, you received this name, Quick-to-Change?''

"Indeed an honor, Chancellor—though sometimes I fear I don't live up to my name so well." Spider gulped a large draught of wine. "Sometimes I feel that my 'resourcefulness,' as you call it, is but the whim of Gagarin, who surrounds me with tiny pirates—"

"And great ferocious Sapphonic amazons," snickered Saker.

"You are intoxicated, honored Saker," said Swo Yeak from his place on the floor. "Indeed, I fear both of our honored Whips are intoxicated. The Whip Spider shows a singular resistance to the inevitability of Change, that Change for which he was named. This is no doubt due to the action of wine on his nervous system, however, and will soon wear off." The physyne licked the glossy red fur of his forelegs, but his yellow eyes remained fixed on Spider.

"My own experience with this new Whip of ours is brief," said Durrell, "but I know him to be a fighting man; indeed, he is fighting at this moment."

Niagara winked at her old friend the carbon-broker. "He fights opponents that he may not defeat this time, Durrell. He fights, I think, the Nucleotides." She turned again to Spider. "I am still Chancellor, my giant Whip, and you are mine to command—in certain matters. The mind of my Islands will require of you much information concerning the nature of the raptores patrolling the Rocks, that we may set about eradicating them. I would, therefore, that you remain at Wirtanen during the transition of Chancellors, visiting the Libraries and speaking of those raptores. You will be, ah, working closely with my successor in these matters. And henceforth there will be better food there, food such as Catuvel offers. I think you will find your, um, tasks pleasant enough.''

"Yes, fellow Whip," said Saker, "and I and my wife will sail the edges of the Rocks in your stead. She is a candidate for the lay Sisterhood at the Islands of Wirtanen, you know, and will make good use of the experience. We'll both have need of your interaction with the Libraries and your new Chancellor. You once told me that you, ah, 'rather enjoy her company.' ''

"Well, yes," said Spider. He refilled his glass. "Yes, I, ah, well. I've never been worth much in scholarly pursuits.''

"But you do know those raptores, honored Whip," said Swo Yeak.

"And I, your Chancellor, require that you share that knowledge with the Libraries—and with the new Chancellor." Niagara turned to Merry. "And you, Sister, will learn a good deal from this Whip Quick-to-Change—I'm certain of it.''

"He's most astute," said Saker. "He may even advise you on the whereabouts of a suitable father for your Earth child.''

"I'm no good at such advice," growled Spider. "I know only that advice in such matters is rarely well taken.''

"Yes," said Niagara, "I imagine that your future Chancellor will tend to form her own opinions in that area— already has, perhaps.''

"Ah. Good." Spider poured his wine down his throat, refilled his glass. "Then she can command this prospective mate to—''

"No one can command marriage," said Durrell. "Did not our friend Linsang demonstrate that some time ago?''

"Her father commanded. A Chancellor could command."

"A Chancellor only commands administrative matters. No Chancellor has ever married or had offspring. No Chancellor capable of marriage would dare command in such a matter." Niagara laughed her rare whispery laugh.

"Good." Spider looked apprehensively about the table. "Well then, to the father of our future Chancellor's Earth child, whoever the lucky devil may be. May he and his bride and their Earth child sail with Gagarin." He raised his glass, the others following suit.

The Chancellor-to-be then raised her own glass. Her face was suffused with color due not only, perhaps, to the effect of the old Palivan wine of Catuvel. "To our new Whip, Spider Quick-to-Change. May his Lord Gagarin sail with him."

"Gagarin the Trickster," said Swo Yeak. "Gagarin the Conspirator."

"Trickster," said Spider, "sail with me now!"

The black cube-Radio at the table's center spoke, then, with Catuvel's motherly voice: "The Trickster sails with others, you know. The time for the Machine's entry into Earth's air-membrane approaches. I am oriented for a viewing from my leeward galleries, and Chancellor Niagara has arranged for the Symphony of the Hemispheres to play as we watch. My retiaries will provide an augmented view of the sailing to complement that from my gallery windows. Let us do our sailors honor."

All rose as one, Durrell taking Niagara's arm and helping her from her couch, the sharp-toothed warrior-servants of the Hall following. Others appeared, cooks, warriors, domestics, and the throng filed through Catuvel's carved halls hung with old Trojan and new Wirtanen portraits and statuary, past a pair of splashing fountains, down a curving stairway on which they all felt the slight increase of mass that signaled their approach to the low-level leeward galleries.

And then into those galleries, actually a great long room, curving, fifteen meters high, where the sound of an orchestra's tuning filled the air. The members of the Symphony of the Hemispheres, all in green-piped black, were seated in rows of chairs at the Sunward wall, chairs arrayed within a great wooden sculpture of a seashell thirty-five meters wide from which, in centuries past, the Symphonia Troia had entertained generations of Semerlings and their guests.

"And what music, Niagara, do you offer us tonight?" Durrell seated the old woman in her couch, carried from the Great Hall by two green-clad warriors.

"A song of Earth," said the Chancellor, "written by a man of Earth. Beethoven the European was his name, and he wrote this work as a love song to his planet. It was his Sixth Symphony; I believe it to be singularly appropriate right now. It's the closest, I think, that music has ever come to portraying the Fourfold Saraband—even though this Beethoven died long before the time of discovery of the Dance of the Nucleotides. His was one of those minds that spans the centuries."

"The millennia, beloved Chancellor," said Durrell.

The tuning swelled and receded as the Symphony of the Hemispheres prepared to begin. People seated themselves, the gallery's immensity filling with the sounds of creaking leather and the woody scraping of chair feet on inlaid floor. All the human beings of Catuvel were here now, some four hundred, wearing the various liveries of their stations. Closest to the central windows sat the little party attending the Chancellor—her successor-to-be, her two Whips, an ex-carbon-broker, a foxlike physyne, all brought together in a momentary backstep of the Dance that all life dances.

From the inevitable black-cube Radio, Catuvel spoke again: "You see Earth's nightside now. In seven minutes Brazenface will appear beyond Her curve; I will select from His light that your eyes will not be discomfited. See the large black object between the central windows; this is a sensory-interface screen over which my retiaries will provide a closer look at the point of entry. The Machine will touch Earth's membrane at a place between nightside and rising of Brazenface, and will move toward that rising."

Whispering, the folk of Catuvel looked out the vast windows at the gently whirling Deep, the black of infinity spangled with billions of diamond-bright multicolored stars. Against this backdrop the Earth was a black circle, one edge of which was already touched with the faintest of violet.

"Well then," said the old Chancellor. "We are indeed lucky to be here. Let us now salute with Earth song the homegoing of Her three children, Linsang, Dyson and Pantolog. May their descendants treat Her with the respect due the Mother of Life; and may our own descendants, recalling what has gone before, seek to emulate the Mother in creating diversity, never again narrowing the options of living things."

The conductor of the Symphony of the Hemispheres saluted his Chancellor with a click of heels and, turning to his orchestra, tapped an ivory baton against the inlaid ivory podium before him. Catuvel dimmed her photophores, and her wheeling windows seemed brighter in contrast to the new darkness within.

Then across a space of nearly six thousand anni the mind of Ludwig van Beethoven spoke in song of Earth, the strains of his love filling the gallery and riding across the electromagnetic fabric of the Deep to Lagrangia far away, where four thousand tiny folk—and two priests of the dead Hand—listened over a Radio to the doings at Catuvel. With Beethoven's voice, the tiny Lagrangians felt the nearness of deliverance from their long imprisonment, and even the two priestly newcomers were touched by that song of the Earth they'd so long dreaded.

As He had for five billion anni and more, Brazenface the Sun hurled His gift of light into the Deep; across a hundred and fifty megakilometers of space that solar wind soared, eight and a half light-minutes, to caress the airy skin of Earth, His queen. She took the light, then, parting it, scattering it in color, an arc of color whose arms spread in a growing embrace about the curve of Her person. Selective as ever, Earth flicked some of that light back into the Deep and into the eyes, watching, of human beings and other creatures born and borne in the Deep forever.

But most of that color she kept; it was the gift-jewelry of Her Husband, token of His everlasting affection. She played with the color, reveling in it, adorning Herself with it as fancy dictated.

To the sensory-interface screen, then, Catuvel's Earth-ward retiaries passed a vision—first a moonlit dot against Earth's night, silvery-white moth-shape, white reddening with the heat of falling, the Machine of Earthflesh carrying Her offspring.

Earth, seeing their return, seeing the many watchers from the Deep, and, perhaps, hearing again in Her own way the swelling of the ancient music of Her son Beethoven, took red light from the treasure of Brazenface and painted the Machine's path with crimson, a crimson ribbon contrail turning to orange, to yellow—and on into the Sun's rising, across a glowing sheet of shifting wavelengths of light, at last to disappear, a multicolored spermatozoon, into the ovum of the world from which all spermatozoa, ever, have risen.

From the Deep, the European Beethoven's immortal mind poured out his undying passion, his own Fourfold Saraband. With the Lord Gagarin, though before him, Beethoven sang and sailed as must all living beings:

"Out of the Earth I sing!" he cried,
  And out of the Earth sailed he.

Glossary

LANGUAGE, like any living thing, evolves and adapts to new eco-niches—or becomes extinct. Therefore, to those who neither sail the kindly Deep nor share their lives with synes, explanations of many terms in this tale will be useful in bridging gaps of form and function.

Abarricama Blee: The official name of the Island Icarus VII of the Aresian Isles on the orbit of Mars: location of one of Aresia's major universities and many other scholarly institutions of the Imperium, home also of Stirps Carraghan, the exiled Stirps-ci-devant of the Trojan Regency.

Allegories, Bharrighari: See Bharrighari.

anlace: A light throwing-dagger often fashioned with a groove or hollow tip containing poison. The weapon is favored by ladies, and its use by men is considered effeminate.

annus, anni *pl.*: The measure of time it takes for an object on-the-Radius about 150 mikas (the orbit of Earth) to circle the Sun once; this measure is derived from the Earthly year, to which so many living beings are yet attuned and is the standard year among almost all of the Peoples of the Deep.

Apollo: Namesake of a class (Apollo Objects) of asteroids whose orbits crossed that of Earth during the European Ascendancy.

Apollonia: The earliest great civilization of the Deep, so named because its origin was based on matter collected from Apollo Objects *(see above)* and grown into the old Apollonic Islands whose capital was located in the Islands of Old Wirtanen *(q.v.)*.

Apollonic League: The military-economic alliance linking the ancient civilization of Apollonia; established in PC 3276, the League remained a major force in the affairs of the Peoples of the Deep until its destruction by the Holy Fist of the Hand of Man in PC 3519.

Aresia, Imperium of: The civilization that grew from matter collected from the inner belts of asteroids (those nearest the orbit of Mars, hence the name Aresia, taken from an ancient European name for the red planet). Traditionally held to have been founded in PC 782 by the Brothers Newgard of Wirtanen, Aresia quickly grew into a mighty state that dominated affairs of inner-asteroidal economics for millennia. Aresia Alpha, I Aresia and the other Islands of the capital archipelago of Aresia are located on the orbit of Mars at about 227 mikas on-the-Radius.

Ascendancy, European: *See* European Ascendancy.

Assegai: A sort of long-handled knife or short javelin

much favored as a weapon against knife- or sword
wielding opponents. The School of Assegai is a Trojan
institute whose students learn the weapon's use and
religious symbolism; their skill is rated on the Dodecade
of Assegai, a twelve-point system of grading based on
the shape of the weapon itself; thus a student with a
rating of five will bear on his assegai a colored band
five twelfths of the way from its butt to its blade or Tip.
Depending upon the size of its user, an assegai is between one and two meters long.

- **Aten, Isles of:** An archipelago of old Apollonia whose
matter was acquired from Aten Objects (asteroids whose
orbits were largely within that of Earth). Aten supported
many Apollonic institutions of music and higher learning,
and was destroyed during the Chimaeric Wars in PC
2129.

Axis: On an Island, its center of rotation, a zone of
freefall extending from end to end and much used for
rapid transit from one end to the other.

badan: A jetted weapon-syne, unmanned and usually less
than two meters in length (although some are much
larger). Badans are multifarious in form and highly
specialized; some, for instance, are capable of chewing
their way through the integuments of Vessels, others of
launching multitudes of smaller badans to destroy retiaries
(q.v.). Most badans are about as intelligent as socially
predatory whales like orcas ("killer whales"), from
whose genes their minds are grown. Badans are the
equivalent among the folk of the Hemispheres of the
raptores *(q.v.)* of Plater states, and resemble these in
form.

banj: A stringed instrument much used in chamber music,

consisting of four played strings and a drone string sounding over a tambourine-like body across which a parchment membrane is tightly stretched. It is said that the craftsmen of the Hemispheres construct the best specimens; it is also said that in so doing they use the skins of human beings, tattooed skins being especially favored.

Bates, Har (PC 1098–1221): The heretic philosopher who founded the Batesian Heresy ("Batesianism"); disemboweled for his beliefs at Point-of-Earth. Bates was a native of Wirtanen.

Batesian Heresy: The belief, promulgated by Har Bates and his followers, that it might be possible to defy Gravity *(q.v.)* and approach large-body matter resources safely; its corollary, that Earth was not an evil being, earned this heresy's followers unending persecution by the Hand of Man.

Bharrighari: A fabulist of Old Wirtanen (PC 3312–3401), comparable in impact to the European Aesop. His moralistic Allegories are universally read to and by children.

blackbody: Completely nonreflective (absolutely black) garb or "coloring" used as camouflage in the Deep. It is extremely difficult to locate an object in blackbody; the condition is therefore generally associated with piratic and military behavior.

bolt: A springbolt projectile; *see* springbolt.

caracor: A manned jetted syne of the Hemisphere folk; roughly equivalent to a Plater galliot *(q.v.)*.

castellan: A household trooper in the service of a powerful stirps.

chebek: A jetted syne of between thirty and forty meters, manned by between one and five warriors and commanded by a Knife (platoon leader) of the pirate tribes of the Hemispheres. Chebeks are equipped with projectile-launchers and are usually closely symbiotic with large numbers of badans *(q.v.)*.

Chimaeric Wars: An eleven-year period during which the Apollonic Islands and Aresia grew humanoid synes with which they attacked one another (PC 2120–2131). So horrible were these monsters (Chimaeras) that their impact has survived the millennia in the form of demonic legendry. The Anti-Chimaeric Bulla of Pollex Darwin Shibuya III (of the Hand of Man) ended the war by establishing religious prohibition of use of any human gene sequences in syne growth.

Christ, *or* **Jesus,** or both: A prophet, the legendary Initiator of the European Ascendancy whose end two millennia after his death he is said by the Annals of the Hand to have predicted. Along with Saint Marx and Saint Darwin, Christ is part of the European Trinity of the Annals of the Hand. Like so many other prophets, he attracted the attention of the ruling powers of his time and was brutally lynched.

chung: Tuned bells used in certain traditional music.

Clarke, the Blessed Arthur: A philosopher-priest of the First Engli branch of the European Ascendancy and one of the principal prophets of the Filtration *(q.v.)*. He was something of a fabulist, a few of his writings remaining central to the education of students of Ascendancy history and thought.

Closing: The time of the extinction of higher animals on Earth, closing forever the links of transport and communication between that terrible planet and the Peoples of the Deep. Because the time of those Peoples began at that point, historians set their time reckoning from the Closing, thus: AC = Ante-Closing, PC = Post-Closing (*see* Chronology at beginning of book).

crystallization: The process in which order arises from disorder, the opposite of entropy. Life itself is a form of crystallization in which the crystal pattern alters itself as it unfolds; hence the Order of Crystallization is central to the religion of the Sisterhood of the Nucleotides; it is enacted in the growth of synes, by what means only the Sisterhood knows.

Darwin, Saint Charles the Deliverer: A prophet and philosopher of the height of the European Ascendancy, the legendary initiator of the Awareness (*see* Chronology); Along with Christ and Marx *(q.v.)*, Darwin is part of the European Trinity of the Hand of Man; he was, like the others of that Trinity, martyred.

Deep, the: The home of humankind, called by the ancients ''Space.'' Because of its beauty and benignity, the Deep represents in popular speech pretty much all that is good in life (''Deep, deep food, thank you, ma'am''), and in allegorical art is represented as a cornucopia.

Deepskin: A syne designed to allow a human being free movement in the Deep. A Deepskin is a sort of integument with leaves to catch the energy of the Sun, thus permitting a person to live for weeks, if necessary, within a completely closed ecosystem utilizing the waste products of his own body.

doss: A syne that seeks and retains information. Most dosses are small animals resembling tiny monkeys and can speak through either vocal cords or Okumura links, or both. ''To doss,'' in its original meaning, was to acquire information by setting dosses on (a person or thing); the verb has since come to connote a sort of curse.

driver: A syne used in transportation of large objects across the Deep and deriving its motion from the mass of lumps of iron-rich rock accelerated down a long straight peristaltic magnetic field in the driver's abdomen and off into the Deep; such pellets of rock may then be retrieved by retiaries and reused, and thus matter is not wasted as it would be in the use of jets. Drivers range in length from a few centimeters to many kilometers in length, most of which consists of the abdomen. The creatures hold onto a payload with jointed legs, a pair of which also holds the reaction mass (iron pellets) with whose repeated launching the payload is accelerated before being released into a prearranged trajectory to drift across the Deep. Drivers curl their abdomens into spiral coils when not accelerating a payload; in this compact form they sail wherever they are needed, often in vast flocks herded by jetted shepherd-synes with the intelligence and general behavior of sheepdogs.

Earth: The third major planet from the Sun, on-the-Radius about 150 mikas, on which life originated and from which it sprang at the end of the European Ascendancy. Because of Her central role in evolution's beginnings, Earth plays a major part in all mythos of the Peoples of the Deep. She somehow became uninhabitable during the Closing, during which all of Her billions of people were killed; luckily, of course, the Filtration had already taken place so that human beings and many other living forms might continue their existence in the safety of the Deep. The Annals of the Hand of Man maintain that

Earth is an evil goddess, a blood-bespattered being with the face of a corpse; adherents to the religion of the Hand of Man therefore regard Her with fear and loathing as a place of "worms that live within the eyes of men, and insects that suck their blood." She is a place of banishment and eternal punishment to which the spirits of the evil dead are sent by the Forces of Selection. The heretic Har Bates of Wirtanen, on the other hand, suggested that Earth was a virgin who was raped by humankind, hence the rift that has separated Hand and heresy for millennia. After the Closing, Earth remained wrapped in a yellow cloud cover like that of Venus for several centuries, then spontaneously cleared off to reveal Herself as a forest planet. No one approaches Earth, of course, Her vicinity having been placed under interdict by the Hand of Man in PC 1221.

Earth, Mouth of: *See* Gravity.

Earth, Point-of-: The location of the Holy Isles, at which is centered the ruling apparatus of the Apostolic Vicarage of the Hand of Man, located at 150 mikas on-the-Radius and 180 degrees opposite the Sun from Earth Herself.

Ecology: The study of the distribution of Matter, Energy, Space and Time by living beings. Ecology is the central discipline in many traditions of scholarship, meditation and monasticism, and is held by some to be the only proper religion; the Sisterhood of the Nucleotides, for example, calls Matter, Energy, Space and Time "The Faces of the Living Tetrahedron," which tetrahedral form is their symbol of the Order of Crystallization.

Engli, First and Second: The Engli were the westernmost Europeans *(q.v.)*; so fierce were they that they established two successive Earthly empires, the First Engli (called the "British Empire" by its people) and the Second Engli ("America"). Engli thought and language dominated much of the latter end of the European Ascendancy *(q.v.)*, and the Second Engli in particular are held by some to have helped pioneer the Filtration *(q.v.)*, although for some reason they abandoned Filtration in its early stages and left the process to the Rose *(q.v.)*, which empire built the first Islands, the Cities of O'Neill *(q.v.)*.

Europe: A region on Earth at the western end of the Palearctic Biome (the land mass called by the ancients "Eurasia").

European Ascendancy: A historical period of about two millennia in length usually begun by scholars with the birth of Christ *(q.v.)* and ending with the Filtration and Closing. The period of the Ascendancy embraces the historically sudden rise of the peoples of the European region; most records surviving from the time date from its latter half millennium during which the Europeans perfected chemically powered projectile-launchers (the *firearms* of the Annals of the Hand) and the use of fossil organic fuels from the crust of Earth. These accomplishments permitted Europeans to splash their culture and genetic stamp across the entire face of Earth in no time (historically speaking) at all; the resulting carnage ended only with the Closing. Figures from the European Ascendancy figure prominently in the various traditions of the Human mythos.

Evolution: In the Apostolic Vicarage of the Hand of Man, the process of Unfolding in which the Tree of Life is pruned by the Forces of Selection. The Gagarinians call Evolution the Trickster's Sailing; the Sisterhood of the Nucleotides call it the Fourfold Saraband, the Dance of the Nucleotides.

Felan: Rich, dry sherrylike wine from the vineyards of certain semi-arid Islands owned by Stirps Semerling of Troy.

Filtration, the: The short period of time (less than a century) at the end of the European Ascendancy during which life invaded the formerly lifeless Deep. The Filtration is so called because those organisms leaving Earth were carefully selected—filtered—in order that the ecology of the Deep might be untainted by the disease parasites and other more horrible creatures of Earth.

Filtration began when the nations of Earth, most notably the Empire of the Rose *(q.v.)*, foreseeing the coming of the Closing, sent fertile eggs of human beings and many other organisms to the Islands of O'Neill *(q.v.)*. With these eggs and spores and the like were sent records of their Earthly ecologic requirements and, in the case of human beings, national origins, histories and ancestral mythologies.

Those making the Filtration move into the Deep included such delicate beings as great whales, elephants, higher carnivora, birds of all sorts and many useful insects, fishes, bacteria, protozoa, etc., whose genetic diversity provided the bases for all future ecosystems and, indeed, founded the Synthesis that ensued. The Filtration rid humanity of all the competitors, inquilines, communicable infections and other demons which had plagued the doomed peoples of Earth; in essence, therefore, the Filtration is held to have been a process of

cleansing, of purification of the bloodlines that would
forever thence people the Deep.

Forces of Selection: See Horsemen.

Free Deep: That volume of the Systemic Sphere compris-
ing the Hemispheres *(q.v.),* so called by its inhabitants

Gagarin: In folklore and religion, the First Man in the
Deep. Gagarin is a Trickster figure who, among the
military especially, is said to be forever outwitting the
Forces of Selection. He represents the principles of
uncertainty and surprise, the uncountable and unknow-
able aspects of life in general and warfare in particular

galliot: A jetted syne of about thirty meters in length,
favored troop transport of Plater states.

Generation, Writ of: Permission to reproduce, given by
an authority such as a ruling stirps. Because of the
limited capacities of ecosystems in the Deep, Writs of
Generation are generally issued only to persons somehow distinguishing themselves in the service of authority

Gravity (always cap.): The force of attraction around
aggregations of matter, consisting of a bending of the
Deep itself and as such distorting and killing living
beings when present in any quantity. Gravity is sometimes personified as a witch-woman or as the Mouth of
Earth, the All-Devourer. Because of their warping effect
on the Deep, such objects as planets and their large
satellites that possess large forces of Gravity are regarded as intensely evil by the Peoples of the Deep and
are hence scrupulously avoided; such objects are the
very embodiment of starvation and entropy. *(See also*
mass.)

Great Black, the: A period of cultural disarray, isolation
and stagnation spanning the millennium between (approx.

PC 3000 to PC 4000 and originating with the greatest of anti-Batesian pogroms.

Hamtsan, the: A syndicate of matter-brokers specializing in the transport and selling of oxygen. Founded sometime around PC 1400, the Hamtsan Brokerage is one of the oldest of brotherhoods. Hamtsan dwellings and ports of call are scattered among the Rocks; oxygen is transported frozen and sold in megaliters or fractions thereof.

Hand, Annals of the: The Annals of the Hand of Man comprise the Holy Writ of the Systemic religion. The Annals are divided into three great Codices: the First Books (the Koran, Bhagavad-Gita, Bible, Eddas and other texts); the Ascendancy Tracts from the height of European power (the Books of Darwin, Marx, Lenin and others); and the Wanderings in the Deep of Post-Closing times. Each Codex is both a record of its times and a series of moral and religious strictures.

Hand of Man, Apostolic Vicarage of the: The Systemic Religion, for millennia the dominant thought structure of the Peoples of the Deep. The Hand, as it is more usually known, is an oligarchy ruled by the Pollex of the Forces of Selection and ten Phalanges, each of which is in itself an administrative hierarchy of cardinals, archbishops, bishops and the like. Tracing its history back through the Ascendancy Tracts of Marx, Darwin and others all the way to the time of Christ the Initiator, the Hand rules from the Holy Isles at Point-of-Earth; agents of the Hand are primarily responsible for maintaining the Rites of Quaranty (*q.v.*) and for shrouding dreaded Earth in secrecy and legend.

Harvest: A gathering of matter, especially matter in the form of periodic micrometeoric dust clouds like those that caused the ''meteor showers'' of Earthly legend. Harvests are traditionally conducted by rich and powerful men, these being the only ones who can muster the immense numbers of jetted synes necessary to locate and capture their immensely valuable rocky prey. A Harvest is a time of partying and competition between nobles, and, as most such ''showers'' of stone move obliquely to the Plate, often a time of danger—for pirates inhabit the Hemispheric reaches into which the Harvest celebrants must pursue the speeding particles of wealth.

Hemispheres, the: The volume of the Systemic Sphere above and below the Plate. Because of the scarcity of matter in the Hemispheres, its human inhabitants are few and generally descended from fugitives of various sorts (most notably Batesians and pirates); such persons must prey on matter concentrated in the Plate in order to maintain their diversity.

hoplite: A jetted syne functioning as part of a mirror or shield or leaf. Hoplites are swift and maneuverable and are especially valuable in the collection of the Sun's energy.

Horsemen, the Four: The Forces of Selection, Pruners of the Tree of Life, personified as four mounted men. Their names are ritually enumerated in the Horsemen's Counting, thus:

> First is Famine, Hunger's Waste;
> Second War, his thrall;
> Third is Pestilence, of Earth,
> And Fourth is Death for all!

Island (or **Isle**): The largest of living beings, an immense syne fixed in orbit about the Sun. Islands are gigantic ecosystems of usually cylindrical shape, set in rotation to keep the civilizations of their inner walls in mass *(q.v.)*; they range from about one to thirty kilometers in diameter and up to several hundreds of kilometers in length. Islands grow from Seeds implanted on Rocks of suitable size, and in the pattern of their development are said to be physalian, or echoing the development of the physalian Siphonophora or colonial zooids like the Portuguese man-o'-war of oceanic habitat. A single Island of interior dimensions ten kilometers in diameter and 100 kilometers in length sports an inner surface almost thirty-three hundred kilometers in area; such a creature can support many millions of human beings within its body walls, although many Islands are given over to habitats that are oceanic or supportive of birds and wild mammals instead of human beings. Islands are grown in pairs with opposite directions of rotation such that their Sunward ends remain Sunward with a minimum of energy used in orientation.

Islands That Fled from the Sun: In legend, a few Islands that were grown from Rocks in motion away from the Sun; their inhabitants were for various reasons desirous of locating themselves an energy source other than the Sun Himself. Once beyond the Cloud of Oort, however, such Islands are said never to have communicated again with the Peoples of the Deep; certainly, no one has ever heard from such an Island in the lonely interstellar Deep. Theirs is a mythic image of loneliness, therefore, and cold.

Isles of Mothering: The Islands in which live the Sisterhood of the Nucleotides *(q.v.)*.

jetted: Equipped with jets; capable of precise and rapid maneuvering through the Deep by means of reaction organs other than drivers. Because jets, using gases squirted irretrievably into the Deep, waste valuable matter, peaceful trade and transit are usually accomplished across precisely precalculated drift trajectories with drivers (whose reaction-mass is retrievable) as accelerators. Thus jets for locomotion imply that their user intends some foul play involving rapid dodging and feinting. In colloquial usage, "jetted" is a pejorative adjective impugning the trustworthiness of its object (as in "jetted politician").

Jove: The planet Jupiter.

Jove, Eye of: The Great Red Spot of the planet Jupiter's atmosphere.

Jove, Path of: The orbit of Jupiter, in which lie His two Trojan Points and, hence, most of the civilization of Troy; hence, Troy itself.

Lagrangia: A civilization, legendary, founded by the European Ascendancy during the Filtration *(q.v.)* and composed of Island-like Machines *(q.v.)*. So named because it was located in Earth's Lagrangian Points, areas of gravitational stability created by the interaction of Earth and Her Moon.

leaf: A Sun-net, a foil on which energy from the Sun is trapped and converted into forms directly usable by living beings. Some leaves, such as those of plants, create carbohydrate molecules or other energetic compounds to trap the Sun's energy, while many leaves of synes simply convert the Sunsea to electricity; both such processes are called photosynthesis, the building from light. Leaves, then, are the primary interface between Sunlight and living systems, and through them the life of the Peoples of the Deep is maintained. Their shapes thus play important parts in both heraldry and religious symbology *(see also* mirror).

leeward: Away from the Sun; on the shadow, or cool, side of an object in the Deep, opposite of Sunward.

lightlink: Communion over threads or rods of coherent light (the *laser* of the ancients). Not only may messages and visual information be transmitted across lightlink, but precise distance and velocity data may be obtained through analysis of its bounce. Lightlink in use as communication is impossible to eavesdrop on, in that anything attempting to eavesdrop must in so doing interrupt the very signal it intends to bug, thus ending the communication. Being invisible in the vacuum of the Deep, lightlinks are pretty much impossible to find and interrupt anyway.

looper: A syne-Vessel for sailing the Deep under mass and having a radial muscle of less than half a kilometer in length *(see also* sweep).

Lubret: The Systemic language, that spoken and written by the educated classes and diplomatic corps of all civilized folk. The structural continuity of Lubret is maintained through the centuries by the Hand of Man, which claims that the language derives from Cyrillo-Niponic roots dating back nearly to the time of the European Ascendancy. Despite the Hand's efforts, however, many mutually unintelligible dialects of Lubret have evolved over the millennia.

Marx, the Blessed Karl: In the Annals of the Hand, one of the European Trinity from which the Hand of

Man derives much of its writ. Marx was the chief deity of the Empire of the Rose, and his name is taken by many rulers and other officials throughout the Systemic Sphere.

mass: The sense of weight produced by rotation or acceleration in order that human beings and other animals may walk about unaided; hence, also, such rotation or acceleration itself. Because living things originated on Earth, the standard mass for human-inhabited environments duplicates the force of Earth's Gravity *(q.v.)* at Her surface. Thus one mass creates in a person the sense of weight that he would experience if standing on Earth (perish forbid!). Nonetheless, of course, the sense of mass is very different from Gravity in that mass is a localized artificial imitation of the universal and unalterable (and therefore terrible) force of Gravity.

matter: Physical substance, first Face of the Living Tetrahedron *(see* Ecology) and that Face which, in the Deep, is in least abundance. As the limiting factor affecting life in the Deep, matter is of paramount importance in the unfolding of the history of the Peoples of the Deep.

metachitin, metakeratin: Proteins incorporating heavy-metal compounds; these proteins are often the most important constituents of the integuments, jaws and other hard organs of synes. Metaproteins in general tend to control the flow of cosmic rays and even projectiles because of their immense hardness, and are characteristic of all manner of shielding and armor.

mika: One million kilometers, a megakilometer; the standard unit of measure of the Radius *(q.v.)* and long journeys.

mirror: A Sun-steerer, converse and complement of a leaf (q.v.). Leaves net the Sun, mirrors reflect it (in order to concentrate it, to redirect it to leaves, etc.). Mirrors also direct light for lightlink messages, gather faint signals as in mirrored telescopes, and figure prominently in art and heraldry, where their forms often duplicate the forms of leaves used as crests. Large mirrors (100+ meters in diameter) tend to be composed of many physically separate jetted reflective hoplites in multiple lightlink with one another and acting in concert through a centrally directed nervous system. During the Synthetic Wars, some peoples are said to have attempted the use of mirrors as weapons in hopes of fricasseeing their opponents; however the slow and stately movements of large mirrors renders them ineffective trackers of any jetted being.

muscle, radial: On a sweep, looper or other non-jetted Vessel carrying human beings, the muscles connecting the living quarters with the center of mass and keeping said quarters under proper mass in rotation. By contraction and relaxation of the radial muscles, such Vessels adjust the mass-sense of those aboard and synchronize their rotatory speed with that of their ports of call.

Mythos, Human: The body (considered as one) of origin-myths of the Peoples of the Deep.

no-Rhône: A red wine and its place of origin, one of the Holy Isles; the prefix no- in conjunction with a place name indicates that the name was used for another place in the past, perhaps some dead Island of Apollonia, or even on Earth.

Nucleic Acid, the: Deoxyribonucleic acid, the seed of the living crystal in all its multifarious incarnations.

Nucleotides, the: Four simple organic compounds derived
from sugars and, when arranged in the double helix
of the Nucleic Acid, forming the code dictating the
form and function of living beings. The order in which
Nucleotides occur in the Nucleic Acid determines the
nature of the organism that will grow from it, much as
the order of the letters in this book determine its content
and distinguish it from an analysis of feminism as a
social force during the late European Ascendancy or a
tract on the growing of hallucinogenic fungi in freefall
environments. In allegorical art, the Nucleotides are
represented as four beautiful sisters whose dancing about
with one another provides an occasional mutation or
distraction of the Four Horsemen *(q.v.)*; these foursomes
are also said occasionally to bed with one another,
especially at important junctures in historical evolution.

Nucleotides, Sisterhood of the: The order of syne
growers, all female, about which very little is actually
known. They are said to have descended from a group
of women who, alone, preserved the technique of ordering of Nucleotides during the widespread destruction
resulting from the Synthetic Wars *(q.v.)*. In return for
matter and certain political favors, one may purchase
synes from the Sisterhood; otherwise, the order does not
contact anyone outside itself, nor do the Sisters show
themselves. Indeed, approach to their residences (the
Isles of Mothering) results in the destruction of those
Isles and all within, in order that the secret of syne
growth may remain secret. Thus the Sisterhood has
remained intact through nearly six millennia of the historical ebb and flow of the Peoples of the Deep, and a

good thing, too; the entire existence of life in the Deep depends on the ministrations of that Sisterhood.

Okumura link: A mycelium (syne-fungus) modified so as to be sensitive to the radio spectrum or parts thereof, and grown into the brains of humans and synes that are intended to be able to communicate silently across species boundaries.

O'Neill, the Blessed Gerard: A European, associated in legend with the Second Engli *(q.v.)*, said to have been one of the first prophets of the Closing and a great advocate to the Europeans of Filtration. In legend, the civilization at Lagrangia *(q.v.)* is called the Islands or Cities of O'Neill; those Islands were, it is said, made of glass and aluminum rather than being living Islands, but nonetheless served as the incubating places for all of the resultant Peoples of the Deep and their associated living systems. As a link between life and its Earthly origin, O'Neill is important to both the Human Mythos and the liturgy of the Hand of Man; even the heretic Batesians acknowledge his importance to the unfolding of life.

Oort, Riders of: A matter-brokerage specializing in the collection of nitrogen and other cometary volatiles, whose members live beyond dead Pluto in the Cloud of Oort, a diffuse nebula of cometary matter surrounding the Systemic Sphere. The Riders of Oort do not communicate or trade in person, and little is known about them save that theirs is one of the most ancient of matter-brokerages.

Passing, Rite of: The ritual enacted over a dying person, in which his material form is bequeathed to the Nucleotides to further the Tide of Life.

physyne: A syne specialized to medical functions and combining diagnostic and treatment (including surgical) capabilities in one funny-looking package.

Plate, the: That disc-shaped volume, approximately fifteen kilomikas (billions of kilometers) in diameter, containing most of the naturally distributed matter in orbit about the Sun. The Plate precisely bisects the Systemic Sphere, and, containing as it does most of the wealth of humanity, is the location of most of the life of the Systemic Sphere.

Pollex: In the hierarchy of the Hand of Man, the man sitting at the top—the Hand's fearless leader.

Priam: One of a number of Islands grown from the ancient asteroid of the same name in the trailing Trojan Point of Jove; location of the Academy of Stewards for the training of house servants to ruling stirpes of the Path of Jove.

Pups of Troy: A dozen Islands associated in vertical orbit about the person of Jove with the archipelago of Troy Prime, capital of the Trojan Regency. The Pups are bondsman Isles on which the human population is not, for reasons known only to the Regency, regulated by Writs of Generation. Thus these Pups are chronically overpopulated and their densely clustered masses of human wretchedness have for centuries amused the voyeuristic folk who own them.

Quaranty, Rites of: Any of numerous rites of admission, originally intended to prevent the contamination by one Island ecosystem of another, now petrified in ritual and lavishly swathed in panoply. The Changing of Garments, in which honored guests are presented with exact replicas of their native clothing, is a familiar Rite of Quaranty.

Radius, the: The standard territorial measure for Peoples of the Deep; the position of Islands and other permanently located objects in the Deep is measured in mikas *(q.v.)* on-the-Radius, an imaginary line extending infinitely outward from the Sun. Territorial holdings are thus shaped like flat tori (doughnuts) with inner and outer diameters delimited by two points on-the-Radius.

raptore: A war-syne, any of thousands of specialized sorts used by the inhabitants of the Plate. An unmanned, moderately intelligent creature whose purpose is to destroy.

Regency, the: Of Troy (the Path of Jove), the ruling stirps and its apparatus of state. The Regency was originally founded by the Trucidate Stirps Carraghan, which at first claimed that it would presently relinquish power to a body representative of the peoples of the Path of Jove; Stirps Carraghan took power in PC 2471, and, while retaining the appellation "Regency," never left the seat of power until forcibly dislodged in PC 5211 by Margrave the Disturbed, first of the Trucidate Stirps Semerling.

retiary: Any jetted syne functioning as a sensor of mass, light, etc., and symbiotic with others of its kind as a sort of nervous system for larger (usu. manned) Vessels.

Rheda: An extinct Isle of old Apollonia known for its poets and musicians.

Rock: Any of billions upon billions of asteroids, planetoids, meteoroids and other debris left over from the condensation of the Solar System. In religious practice, a Rock is the uncrystallized matter from which life grows by the addition of a Seed *(q.v.)*; hence, in the communion of the Hand of Man, the bread is offered "that you may, by the Seed within yourself, convert this Rock to life, in so doing once more extending the Hand of Man."

Rocks, the: The vast belts of asteroids and dust between about 227 and 777 mikas on-the-Radius, the largest collection of Gravity-safe (and therefore accessible to human beings)' matter in the Systemic Sphere. Because of their easy maneuverability, the Rocks are the prime source of life's expansion and thus play a central part in the economics of the Peoples of the Deep.

Rose, Empire of the: During the latter years of the European Ascendancy, one of the two major powers of that civilization. Located on the Eurasian land mass, the Empire of the Rose is said to have been the home of the Trickster Gagarin and to have been a prime mover in the Filtration into the Deep. The chief deity of the Rose was Marx (the Blessed Karl), and to the Rose we owe the Blessed Karl's presence in the pantheon of the Hand of Man.

sailing: Any path, as in a lifetime, a trajectory, a process, a series of sequential events.

Sappho: An Island largely occupied by a large oceanic ecosystem and inhabited only by female human beings, located at the leading Trojan Point of Jove. From Sappho are recruited the female servants of the ruling Trojan stirps; in return, Sappho requires active semen from certain distinguished Regency soldiers with which to impregnate its child-bearers. On Sappho, there are no male children; spermatozoa are screened to eliminate those carrying the Y chromosome that produces males.

scan: A syne specialized to the recording and transmission of images and other visual data, often holographically.

Seed: A nucleic acid *(q.v.)* and associated structures necessary for its encrystallization to a living form, especially a syne. Capitalized, the word signifies the immensely complex biological structures that, when applied to a suitable Rock and exposed to the Sun, unite matter and energy to grow an Island or other syne.

Semerling, Stirps: At the time of this tale, the ruling house of the Path of Jove. Founded in PC 5211 by Margrave the Disturbed, a general in the security apparatus of the Trojan Stirps-ci-devant (House Carraghan) who assassinated his master Yersokin (VII) Carraghan, Stirps Semerling has ruled the Path of Jove with an iron hand for more than half a millennium.

Semerlinga, Winter and Summer: Twin Islands, one sporting a subtropical ecosystem, the other a wintry ecosystem, linked in vertical orbit about the person of Jove within the archipelago of Troy Prime, the home of the ruling Stirps Semerling. Each Island is about a hundred kilometers long and twenty kilometers in diameter.

seneschal: A high official of a ruling house, one who coordinates social, security and other functions to permit his masters to live a life untroubled by worldly concerns.

sept: A genetically linked group of human beings; a hereditary caste of functionaries, as soldiers, seneschals, etc., whose continuity is determined by Writs of Generation issued to outstanding members of the caste.

spinder: A syne, derived in part from the genetic sequences of higher Arachnida (spiders), which is capable of extruding immensely strong metaproteinaceous cables of various specialized sorts. Some spinders also create clothing.

springbolt: The typical hand-carried projectile-launcher of the Peoples of the Deep, and the most complex nonliving apparatus known. A sort of mini-crossbow, the springbolt launches a bolt or dart whose kinetic energy is insufficient to break the body wall of a Vessel. Many sorts of such bolts (broadhead for killing, hypodermic for stunning, etc.) fit into each springbolt.

Stewards, Academy of: On Priam *(q.v.),* the ancient school of the "Hospitable Arts," those of mood-manipulation through the offering of pleasure and contentment. Graduates of the Academy are in great demand by stirpes of power, and because of their specialized training are often further groomed for sensitive positions in affairs of state.

stirps, stirpes *pl.:* A mighty family; a stirps-ci-devant is the former ruling house of an Island or state.

summit: A word retained unchanged from the time of the European Ascendancy and referring to a meeting of heads of state for the working out of sticky differences. As a reference to the end of the Ascendancy, which was preceded by many summits, the word often implies ultimatum and embodies considerable foreboding.

Sun the: The Systemic Star, giver of life. In folklore, Old Brazenface, the bringer of gifts to children at the celebration of orbital cyclings, etc.

Sunsea: The solar flux, the *sum toto* of matter and energy emanating from the Sun. The Sunsea is the supporting energetic medium for dwellers in the Deep, the nutriment of all living things; hence sometimes used to refer to the Systemic Sphere as a whole.

Sunward: Toward the Sun—the lighted side of an object, the side on which energy is gathered.

sweep: A syne-Vessel for traveling in mass *(q.v.)* without jets, and possessing a radial muscle of greater than a half kilometer in length *(see* looper). Sweeps are generally self-sufficient (discounting the drivers that accelerate them into proper trajectory), possessing their own mirrors and leaves, and are intelligent commensurate with the complexity of their facilities. Because of their large size, delicacy and inability to alter their directions once accelerated on trajectory, sweeps are usually lightlinked to a protective escort of symbiotic retiaries and raptores extending thousands of kilometers into the Deep in all directions.

The size of a sweep is measured by her period of rotation, itself a function of the length of her radial muscle; a two-minute sweep such as Catuvel of this tale sports a radial muscle about 3.25 kilometers long when carrying her passengers in mass.

Sword-and-Helix: The symbol of the Hand of Man, consisting of a few loops of the Nucleic Acid circumventing the blade of a sword.

syne (pron. "sine"): Any organism grown directly from nucleotides artificially prearranged to serve a specific purpose, as for a conveyance or physician. While alive, self-healing and, where required, intelligent, synes are all "mules"; they are nonreproductive. In order to duplicate a syne, one must "work up" from nucleic acids in a process monopolized for millennia by the Sisterhood of the Nucleotides *(q.v.).* Hence each syne,

while destined to be a slave-specialist, retraces metaphori
cally the evolution of living systems and is for som
folk a hallowed icon in itself.

Synthesis: In religious practice, the impregnation o
matter by energy to produce life; historically, Synthesi
was the linking by the earliest Peoples of the Deep o
the infant sciences of cybernetics (computer science
information theory) and biochemistry. Synthesis occurre
at the point in the cultural evolution of humanity where
computers capable of rapidly analyzing large numbers o
possibilities were set to dissecting and recording se
quences of nucleotides in the DNA of various organism
in order to probe the significance of their nucleotide
arrangement in the final forms and functions of organisms.
Once direct relationships between nucleotide sequence
and genetic code had been established, the way lay open
for direct synthesis of living beings for specific purposes
(synes, *q.v.*), hence the name. At the point of First
Synthesis, the Hand of God and the Hand of Man are
said to have become one; this occurred less than two
centuries after Closing.

Synthetic Wars: The series of social upheavals resulting from the achievement of Synthesis *(q.v.)* by the
early Peoples of the Deep; these wars are believed to
have occurred between one and two centuries after the
Closing *(q.v.)* and mark the piercing and evacuation of
the Islands of O'Neill *(q.v.)* and the loss of many records pertaining to Earth. From the ruin left by the
Synthetic Wars arose the Hand of Man as it is now
known, along with the Sisterhood of the Nucleotides,
which alone preserved the secrets of Synthesis itself.

Systemic Sphere: The imaginary sphere of approximate diameter fifteen kilomikas, bisected by the Plate *(q.v.)* and centered on the Sun. Beyond the Systemic Sphere both matter and energy become increasingly scarce; although some peoples (the Islands That Fled from the Sun) have ventured out in hopes of finding Something Else, any others save perhaps the Riders of Oort *(q.v.)* would merely shake their heads at the idea.

Tetravalency, the: The syndicate of carbon-brokers, who derive their name from carbon's unique four-sided chemical bonding and consequent centrality to the formation of the giant molecules characteristic of living matter. The Tetravalency is ruled by a Directorate of four hereditary syndics known as the Bonds of the Tetravalency; these live with their associates somewhere among the Rocks, although the precise location of their bases has remained a Tetravalency secret for more than three millennia. The Tetravalency is the only significant polity of the Plate that adheres to the Batesian Heresy.

toxor: A syne derived from the augmented smell apparatus of higher mammals such as dogs and designed to locate molecules of poisons in food or drink.

Trickster: *See* Gagarin.

Trojan Point: In the Path of Jove, either of two areas of gravitational equilibrium that have, through the eons, collected asteroidal matter that served as the foundation for the civilization of Troy named after them. The Trojan Points of Jove are located 60° ahead and behind His Person in His Path.

Troy: The civilization of the Path of Jove and the Outer Rocks.

Troy Prime: An archipelago (aggregation of Islands) in vertical orbit about the Person of Jove and embracing the ruling apparatus of the civilization of the Path of Jove.

trucidate: Succeeding to power by murder; said of ruling stirpes, etc.

velite: An elite hand-to-hand skirmisher; the best of soldiers.

venator: A syne-robber-fly, venomous; a sort of weapon for close quarters.

Vertical and Horizontal: Respectively, the human central nervous system (brain and spinal column) and the human abdominal and chest viscera. These terms are used in training novices to use assegais, swords, knives and other piercing weapons.

Vessel: Any syne, from Deepskin *(q.v.)* to the largest Island, carrying human beings and by whose integument and metabolic processes human life is sustained in the Deep. Because they are basic to the existence of life in the Deep, Vessels and their ways play an important part in all religions and folkways of the Peoples of the Deep.

An early and important result of their symbiosis with Vessels was the abandonment by human beings of explosive projectile-launchers in any intra-Vessel settling of blood disputes. The discharge, for example, of devices such as the *firearms* of the ancient Europeans within any Vessel would surely have wounded the Vessel herself and thus destroyed the operator of the *firearm* along with his intended human victim; thus such weapons long ago ceased to exist. Within the sanctity of Vessels, human beings settle such arguments as require the spilling of blood with the traditional fangs of their kind—the sword, the knife, the assegai—thus achieving in mortal combat a measure of intimacy undreamed of by the ancients with their long-range *firearms*. It must be noted in passing, however, that persons and synes attacking from without cheerfully abandon their hereditary good taste and employ all manner of explosive projectiles to pierce and destroy both enemy Vessels and those within; but, as someone of the European Ascendancy is said to have remarked, *Sic pilum iactum est* ("That's the way the spear is tossed").

Whip: A chieftain of the Hemispheric pirates, often the leader of an extended clan as well.